DAVID ARMSTRONG

Accidental Coincidence

THE RESURRECTION OF MARY

LONG STORY
SHORTER

First edition

Editing by Terri Leigh

This book was professionally typeset on Reedsy.
Find out more at reedsy.com

Everyone has a moment in their life that defines the before and the after. My first was in 5th grade when Mr. Vendetti told me 'it was OK to be creative', holding my arm, spoken directly and clearly, he stated again; David, it's OK to be creative. Thank you Mr. Vendetti, it has made all the difference.

But if any man hate his neighbour, and lie in wait for him, and rise up against him, and smite him mortally that he die, and fleeth into one of these cities; then the elders of his city shall send and fetch him thence, and deliver him into the hand of the avenger of blood, that he my die.

- Deuteronomy 19: 11-12

1

Evil shall slay the wicked; and they that hate the righteous shall be desolate.
  - Psalms 34:21

I t was the first time Lori felt normal, and the first time she used her new name. Her apartment felt normal, although in a city she'd never been to. She was no longer in the spotlight, not here, Denver was new to her, her life was new too. She wouldn't want anyone to see it anyway. Her collection of decorative knick-knacks, which at the time seemed so hip and smart to purchase, now looked unimportant, versus her experiences over the last year. She had been barely sleeping for the past year neither in a hotel or the secret, secluded rental house in Virginia. This bed felt good, the temperature was right. She recalled the celebration dinner from last night, although that is not what Ralph and Jack called it. It would have been a bit morbid to say it out loud, *celebration*, which created an unforced, but unnatural smile in the soon-to-be sunlit darkness of her apartment. The apartment she didn't have a year ago. Things had changed. She didn't have a single modern appliance and if someone didn't know better, you'd think it was the fifties, except for the alarm clock with its modern digital display plugged in across the room. She strained to see it but gave up quickly. She had lost her ability to sleep from the never-ending angles her unprecedented murder prosecution case had taken and now she was examining the previous year in the same way. She needed the sleep.

Last night, when she was still called Mary, she even had the rare drink or was it drinks, she couldn't recall, at dinner to initiate the process of healing. Ralph had been there, Jack was there and she had laughed more than she had in a while, about a year to be exact. She knew Jack had planned this as the beginning of the healing process for her. He thought he was sly, but she knew better, she paid attention to the details, all of them. Jack was settling the past and beginning his own future too. The last year was a busy one for him too, and his years to come, joining Joe Callahan's campaign and then being appointed as the new President's Attorney General wouldn't be a walk in the park, even for the famous Jack Rucker. The campaign was run on judicial reform, and she had contributed in a very odd way. She smiled again and her thoughts of the details caused her to doze off into much-needed sleep, in her new life as Lori Philbus. She was adjusting her pillow haphazardly and attempting to get a few more minutes. She knew for the first time in a long time, she didn't have anywhere to be, no details to discover, and nothing to worry about.

She closed her eyes and remembered it now. Thinking back to just a few days ago, she was then Mary and was surprised how been strong; she had been part of the first trial and a careful observer of the second trial. She was also in the observation room for the execution. It was a team effort, but the catalyst was Mary. She was obviously motivated and was meticulous with the facts. Jack sat impressed as Ralph was sharing details of the case. Mary, becoming Lori, had two drinks so far, something Jack always kept track of while at dinner. Ralph was still focused on his lifelong passion of establishing new case law, which was the work he had done for the last forty years. Jack let the rehashing of what everyone already knew about the case go for a while and would interrupt with future-looking comments, instead of the past which is where Ralph was, and where he always seemed to go after a big case was closed.

Jack Rucker had lived a life of precision, always curtailed his emotions from getting the best of his judgment. Others would disagree, but Jack knew his actions, even those actions that others thought were emotions, were calculated, exact, purposeful responses to move the situation forward. "Maximize the future value," as he would say often during critical, problematic events. The situation always changed, but the planning, options review, and actions never were missed, *never* he thought to himself again. His purpose this night was to comfort this soon-to-be lawyer for her efforts towards the truth over the last year. The execution of another human being would get to her and Jack knew the healing process started tonight. That is why he set up this celebration, not celebrating the killing of another human, but the prevention of the killing of others. Jack didn't think of the dinner, Angela did. As Jack's assistant, Angela knew Jack better than he knew himself. She was one of the only people that he really respected, as Angela was always one step ahead, and Mary was similar. Both women were impressive and a little mysterious as they were both difficult to predict, even for the newly appointed Attorney General of the United States.

3

Behold, I am sending you out as sheep in the midst of
wolves, so be wise as serpents and innocent as doves.
  – Matthew 10:16

The air was thinner at altitude in Denver, as Lori took in needed deeper breaths of her new life. Lori tried to get a peek at the time, but she couldn't focus on the little red glowing numbers from her modern, out of place, alarm clock across the room. She always wanted to get one with bigger numbers, as she had this problem every day, normally from getting up too early and doing a self snooze button in her head. She accepted that the first day of her new life couldn't start too much differently than the previous year. The time to wake was her habit and she had long ago put the alarm clock across the room, as the electronic version of the snooze button, actually pressing it, seemed to make her late for everything. She rolled over again, not worrying about the time, what did it matter, she had no plans today, Jack made sure of that.

She had turned off her phone last night at Jack's suggestion, as the national newspapers and every online blog would surely have her picture. The two trials of Mark Solier had overwhelming press coverage, yet his execution had only one, standing alone outside the gate of the prison. She realized that everyone knew who she was from the trial, the second trial that is, the first trial was a disaster she remembered, a devastating blow to have a suspect acquitted when the facts were clear. She groaned once again and thought how long it would take to rid herself of the last year, even though the second trial found its justice. The "Mind Killer", which she never called him, Mr. Solier as she had called him, was now dead and the seemingly unrelated murders, accidents to everyone, would now stop. This gave Lori a feeling of peace for at least another round of snooze.

She couldn't snooze for long and kept thinking again about last night, Ralph had been asking questions of Mary as the salad was being delivered, somewhat to compliment her to make her proud of her work, but Ralph saw the sometimes puzzled look she would get as he had somehow intrigued her interests once again. He also thought he may be patronizing her, as her intelligence impressed him over time. Ralph hoped it wasn't the case here; his questions were designed to have her be proud of what she had done. Jack had to remind him more than he was comfortable about her name change, from Mary to Lori and the need to make it a quick transition. Ralph knew and suspected Jack thought it too, a name change and a new life on paper wouldn't allow her to escape her past and move towards a deserved future. Jack reminded Ralph a little sternly, even for friends of forty years, and Ralph hadn't made the mistake the rest of the night.

Lori was again recalling details from the dinner the night before in Virginia and while awakening even further remembered the questions that Ralph had asked her the night before. One had stuck in her mind as she sat up, the sun was directly in her half-open eyes, with nothing on her mind but Ralph's statement, really a rhetorical question that Ralph had asked wondering, curious almost, to know what other murders were out there, that they didn't uncover. She was a bit angry; the proof was there, documented evidence of multiple murders for the first trial, DNA evidence for the second and why did there need to be more murders to uncover. She was glad that Ralph wouldn't be part of her future.

"Beyond a reasonable doubt," she said aloud. She repeated it a few times as it went from a verbal statement, one that fell on the deaf ears of her cheap apartment and fifties style furniture, to one that fell heavy on her mind. "What murders?" She remembered asking, as Ralph reminded her of her success. "It was a question of rhetorical proportions, not one you need to solve, now or ever. The suspect was convicted, sentenced and executed, as justice was served."

She cleared her head of the thought that morning and cleared her head of the annoyance of Ralph. It would take longer to clear the rest, she sighed and put her head back on her pillow and dozed off for the third time, a normal thing for the previous Mary even before she became a public figure, seemingly important, more correctly, infamous.

She half dreamed and half-remembered that Jack interrupted their conversation by telling Ralph to stick the rhetorical questions up his ass and take a drink. It caused the laughter that Jack wanted and he smoothly, without notice, changed the subject to the menu and to the history of this Virginia restaurant. An establishment that was visited by the founding fathers, Jack always knew more than others, facts about things everyone else had forgotten or didn't care enough to remember.

Lori woke up suddenly, eyes open and her brain was slowly catching up. She couldn't remember the rest of last night as she continued to get accustomed to the new mile-high air she heard so much about before moving to Denver and her new life. Although she remembered listening to Jack intently, just the facts of the restaurant weren't sorted and stored in her head for her to recall right now. 9:23 am was the time, she finally cleared her vision enough to catch a glimpse as she laid her head back down. She remembered the ride to Denver, sleeping a bit on the brand new government jet plane, being awakened by Jack, still in his suit, tie still perfect. It was a gentle ride from the private airfield to her downtown apartment. She recalled the time was 1:40 am locally in the mountain time zone, 3:40 am where she just came from, when she turned down the covers and turned out the light. She remembered that she had been purposeful in reminding herself that she had nowhere to go tomorrow, that had turned into today and on this day, for once, time didn't matter. Her tenacious efforts had worked, when everyone, except Jack, gave her reasons to quit. Justice was served and she was on her way, no longer the former shadow of herself. She had big plans to restart her life and today, although slow in the start, was the first day, for Lori. It had all worked, her efforts, Ralph, Jack, and

Thomas too. She slept well last night, compared to the last year, with help from the alcohol, and she reminded herself she was in love. She turned on her phone and sent Thomas a text message to meet her for brunch.

Lori got out of bed, determined to get something done before meeting Thomas for brunch. She thought she would spend the day getting her life back in order. The change of her name was new for her and she needed to transform her old life into her new life. Jack had made her new life possible by leveraging his many connections. He gave her a new start and a promise to let her follow her dream. The first step in her plan was to get cleaned up, get some brunch downtown with Thomas, and "file away" the last year of her life. She intended to keep the facts straight.

4

And the LORD thy God will put all these curses upon thine enemies, and on them that hate thee, which persecuted thee.
  – Deuteronomy 30:7

The party was complicated to plan, different in 1968 with invites done by phone and the mail. No one without a small child on the anniversary of their birth knows the pleasure of the first birthday party. It was a great day outside. The first year of life was impossible for the Soliers, or what was left of the family. Alice who gave birth to baby Mark just a year before was now worried about the day ahead. She wanted to make it something special. Mark couldn't care less. The house was full of people, decorated beyond what was needed. Alice Solier had survived the year as a sudden, young widow, and she felt she was on the upside of a very deep downside. This day was a major milestone in her life with her young son, without her husband, his father. The day was to be perfect.

Jessica, as older sister's often do, judged her sister Alice as a strong woman, but was constantly confronted with the reality of her sister's love for baby Mark. She went overboard with him, and not in a positive way, all the time. This baby got whatever he wanted before he even knew that he wanted it. Jessica, trying to, but not yet able to have a child of her own, always thought that Mark had basic needs, he was a baby, for Christ's sake. Now frustrated with her own temper, with building frustration, Jessica pulled the air into her lungs through her now gritted teeth. This damn baby, not yet a real child, and her sister was pathetic the way she went overboard on everything, especially this stupid, over-decorated party. She knew not to come but had to. She thought Alice obviously was sick, so-called sick from her supposed mental trauma, and was compensating, going overboard again, from the sudden death of her husband. No one was helping her, it seemed others were truly happy for her. Jessica would have seen it differently if she knew it would be the last party of its kind for her, Mark and Alice would have more.

The spirit of Mark uplifted Alice. She was in a difficult situation, but you'd never know it. Not that she hides anything, she doesn't. Alice is the type of person that what you see is what you get, and what everyone gets is that Alice cares for all. For a while, people thought she was showing only the good side, covering her suspected depression from the last year in a facade of outward appearance. So many have told Alice to seek counseling even though she didn't seem to need it. How could she not? Losing your husband overnight, to a mysterious, undiagnosed illness within weeks after the birth of your only child that you waited so long, worked so hard, and prayed so strong to have. Alice never talked about Jim, nor did anyone else. Everyone just focused on Mark.

Jessica found herself feeling very jealous of Mark but couldn't really understand why she felt this way. When she was with him, he was a wonderful baby. He seemed to know the way to show love for someone but knew not of the steps an adult might use to manipulate that feeling. Around the baby, she felt complete, but the environment was too overwhelming for her this time. Her feelings overwhelmed her but she did not take action towards Mark, it only boiled inside her. The feeling of hate had risen in her, not all at once, as in rage, but more of a progression since the day he was born. It was nothing specific, but she knew it was hate, she had felt it before, towards her own husband, who was still alive but unable to help create their own child. She knew she had to leave the party soon, as she couldn't get away from the noise while in the house. She knew logically it was supposed to be about Mark, which only frustrated her even more. She needed to get away now and lower her stress, she needed to leave.

Jessica left abruptly. She said her goodbyes and Alice tried to get her to stay longer, but it wasn't working. As Jessica pulled out from the driveway, she had to force herself to wave as Alice had Mark, embraced in her arms, and she had his arm up high, she was flopping his hand up and down to wave "bye-bye." Jessica waved, but openly cursed her sister for not being smarter about life. This time she was alone, so no need to only think it, she said it out loud, talking to herself, knowing no one could hear her and not caring if anyone was watching her silent, hateful rant.

Her feelings only worsened as she pulled out onto the main road on her way to the interstate and then to the city. If she was just mad, she knew it would pass, but she wasn't, this was beyond being just mad. She had a hard time controlling her feelings this time, not that she tried. She knew what it wasn't, she was confident in her life. She was exactly where she wanted to be. She was ignoring her real angst about not being able to conceive with her own rotten husband, so she knew it wasn't about her. She realized that it was about her frustration with her sister, focusing so much on that damn, near-perfect baby that she didn't realize her own life was going bad. After Jim died, Alice didn't reach out for help, at least not to Jessica. She didn't get counseling, didn't cry, nor talk about Jim. She rarely and barely showed any signs of mourning. Jessica attempted to talk with her, but Alice would change the subject, often to something about baby Mark. Jessica knew this was not natural or even close to normal behavior, and she assumed that Mark was clouding her adult, yet younger sister's feelings. This baby sure did get in the way. Jessica thought to herself it was a little weird for her to have such negative feelings towards a one-year old, but she knew she was right, just nobody else saw it, or probably no one had the guts to do anything about it.

An hour had passed since the cake and candle presentation and Alice barely even heard the phone continuously ringing with so much going on. Mark was opening his presents and her regularly conservative, organized life was upside down, and she loved it. She normally didn't have callers; as she grabbed the phone and said hello, she was shocked into reality. The operator told her that her sister was brought into the hospital from the rest stop on the interstate. Alice was initially controlled but growing ever frantic as there was no information. The only thing the operator knew was that it wasn't a car accident, she'd been attacked.

The interstate system was relatively new and wide open in the late sixties. Massive concrete roads poured through what used to be pristine farmland. The new massive roads created a connected country, in the beginning, it still was and felt like open farmland, with a permanent concrete scar in the Earth. The man had to make a choice; he had a family of his own, only ten feet from where he stood, and only twenty feet from where the bear was attacking this middle-aged woman. His decision was instant, he checked his own family with a glance, where he saw his wife and six-year-old staring at the attack, and they were safe, although horrified at the blood. He started to yell at the bear as it randomly and repeatedly struck the now nearly indistinguishable lifeless body on the ground. The bear didn't even notice his presence. He quickly identified his only option was to physically attempt to attack the bear. He struck the bear with his fists, with absolutely no reaction. He was more surprised by the sudden striking of the bear with a worn baseball bat. As things were happening fast, the man realized a few others had come to this poor woman's aid. The bear paid no notice to the now five men attempting to save this now bloody woman. The bear's last act was to step on the bloody chest of the body, once a woman and now almost unrecognizable, making a horrible cracking noise. It then almost casually walked towards the woods for twenty or so feet and then picked up the pace. It acted as if the men screaming, yelling, and hitting it didn't even exist. As he

20

turned to check on his family, there was an instant of fear as his wife was not in the car. He visually located her almost immediately at the call box phone, she was crying and had a look of fear. The previous four men now were massed to about eight, and they had set up a perimeter of protection. A group of them, clearly ex-military in their appearance, or looked like it, had rifles they had quickly retrieved from their trucks, a common practice in rural Virginia. They had them up to their shoulders and carefully pointed hopelessly towards the woods, no shots were fired, but they had the situation under control. It was impossible to understand even what the situation was, as the mangled body of a woman, lay bloody and motionless, as one of the men was caring for her, with a seemingly high skill and efficiency. He was calm and working to stop the bleeding. He now only had one thought, to try and save her life. He saw the attack, it was not just a one-time swipe of the bear's paw, but an outright attack. It was an aggressive repetitive attempt of the bear to kill her. She was nearly dead now, a fading pulse and injuries he couldn't fix. She would die, he was sure of it. An ambulance pulled up, and the EMTs took over the now futile life-saving process. As the sirens whaled and the ambulance sped off to the hospital more than twenty miles away, the man, who attempted to save her, sat down. He would be asked by a local reporter to share his first-person testimony of what he saw. He was unable to understand what happened, what had he just witnessed?

ACCIDENTAL COINCIDENCE

5

Therefore, since we are surrounded by so great a cloud of witnesses, let us also lay aside every weight, and sin which clings so closely, and let us run with endurance the race that is set before us.
  – Hebrews 12:1

L ori's head was beginning to clear, clouded both by the events of a late night on the other side of the country and the low oxygen air of her new location, higher altitude, and new life in Denver. The hot shower helped her with both. She didn't really recall the trip from the bed to the shower, even less than she recalled the overnight private government jet flight from Richmond to Denver. She only remembered getting out of bed, feeling the chill, and cautiously navigating her naked body to the bathroom. As she had lost track of time, Lori consciously moved her thoughts towards the future and her to-do's for that morning. She realized that none were critical, as much as the past had been, but Jack told her to keep busy. She had decided even before her multiple snooze morning that she would get her life organized. Her new life, she reminded herself with another forced, unnatural smile. Her mail was being checked and forwarded to a safe box within her new post office. Jack had the service for his mail for years and it was an easy setup. Jack wasn't a fan of what he still called electronic mail, known to normal people as email, but Mary realized that he had services that were similar to a "rules box" within a modern email system; however, he had real people, rather than computers doing it all for him. She never realized during the last year that the service was a safety measure, one that was effective in keeping Jack alive. People can have long memories he once told her and set up the service for her that day, way before things got too public. She was feeling thankful now. She did get most of her mail over the last year, those items that anyone would expect; it was all scanned and x-rayed. Since 9/11, it was even chemically tested. She hadn't sorted the non-designated address mail for a while, it was all junk anyway, but thought today would be a good day to get things cleaned up. As time passing continued to be purposely neglected, the shower temperature started to wane a bit from warm to cold. She organized her thoughts that would take the rest of the morning, shut off the water, and quickly warmed herself with a towel. The apartment seemed cold, she shivered as she forced away yesterday's memory of her first witness to death, a calculated, legal execution, one an outsider could say, she caused.

6

But mine enemies are lively, and they are strong; and
they that hate me wrongfully are multiplied.
  – Psalms 38:19

Mark as a boy lived a great life, he was happy and the complexity of the adult world was outside his awareness. He was born and raised in the seventies as anyone could want, except he was raised without a father; his dad died when he was only a few weeks old. His mother was close to remarrying a few times, but her life was full of unrecognized, and untreated depression, as the few close ones either disappeared, got apparent cold feet, or as in the case of Greg, died. Greg wanted Mark to call him Dad, and Mark remembered him to be a bit hot-tempered and condescending for no reason. Greg grabbed his mother a few times which Mark, even as a young boy would make clear that was not ok. Mark would take the slaps and pushes to the ground from Greg. Mark knew what was right and wrong, Greg, seemingly, did not. Greg was killed in a car accident by an elderly man who passed out while behind the wheel from an epileptic seizure, on his way to church, nonetheless. The elderly man didn't have a scratch and didn't even need to go to the hospital. It didn't really affect Mark, nor did it seem to swing Alice either way, towards being more happy, or away from her depressive demons. Mark was a normal child as they come, emotions were created and controlled as maturity took over. He seemed to be a typical kid, indifferent teenager, and a productive adult. Things happened to Mark over his life, no different than others. Independent of each other, they were merely daily events in the course of life. These events created a half-completed puzzle that no one could see the full picture, not even Mark when by coincidence, the puzzle was completed by a stranger. It was completed years later by a smart, determined young woman wanting to be a lawyer.

Jim Solier died in his sleep. Mark didn't have memories of his father, how could he as a baby, just memories created from seeing pictures and he knew the story from others and even retold it a few times himself. It was a Saturday and Alice had already been up, fixed breakfast, fed the baby, and started hanging out the wash. She expected to see Jim by now, he was no early riser as the Friday shift at the shipyard was used to complete the week's work, it never was easy and always was a double, in at 7 am and home at 11 pm. She knew not to disturb him, he never said anything, it was just her instinct.

Mark had let out a cry, more of a loud cackle, as he never cried, but she heard him and went inside to be sure he was taken care of. She noticed Jim's breakfast was untouched. He had always been specific about his breakfast and she was always on time and exact with his requirements, so untouched was something she never had seen and didn't even know how to deal with it. It seems simple, a breakfast routine, but Jim was more than routine, he was uncompromising about it, so she was sure to get it right. As she was in her confused state, her baby let out another noise, temporarily distracting her from the unusual breakfast scene.

That morning, after taking care of Mark, Alice called the newly implemented Veterans Affairs 800 line. As the phone rang, she was fixing Mark's lunch and simultaneously doing his laundry. The phone was answered after being on hold for a few minutes.

"Thank you for calling the Veterans Affairs Medical Appointment Line. How can I help you?" said the operator.

Alice told the operator that her husband was still asleep, he was probably sick. She didn't give any other details or symptoms even after multiple questions from the operator, who answered her call and was reading from some type of script. What Alice didn't know, was her inability to provide any details or answers to the questions was why her husband was so low on the list when the on-duty nurse prioritized the printout of needed appointments for today's sick call.

The VA doctor arrived as soon as possible, that's what he kept saying. Four hours after being called, I guess the delay was expected with so many military in the area, the veterans were supposed to come first, but often felt last. When the doctor arrived, he didn't know Jim Solier, but he brought the normal assortment of patient treatment items. He met Alice at the door, mentally remarking that she seemed to be a typical military wife, a young baby, in the kitchen and mostly unaware of the world outside of her home.

The doctor started to look at the baby, but Alice interrupted him and said the sickness was with her husband, not with the baby. The doctor was even more confused now without the patient or a list of symptoms. He asked the obvious question to him, but seemingly lost on Alice, of where was the patient? Alice told him the story about the breakfast routine; the double shifts on Friday and said that Jim had been asleep all day. The doctor noted it was now just after three o'clock pm. Alice led the doctor up the stairs and to the bedroom and then she abruptly turned on her heels, somewhat rudely disappeared from the room and returned to the baby in the kitchen, a remarkably quiet baby thought the doctor, checking his watch, going on now for more than seven hours of his daily duty of dealing with the often cranky children of military families.

A few opening, unresponded to pleasantries, and the doctor only had to see the face of his new patient to know he was dead. Rigor mortis had already started to set in and the color of his skin was a pale blue. As an overworked VA doctor, he had been in such a routine that at first he was annoyed at the visit and now almost shocked at the initial result. You didn't really show up on house calls and find people that were already dead, without the knowledge of at least one of the family members.

Alice only felt relieved that she would no longer be under the scrutiny of Jim. His way was uncompromising. She was overwhelmed with the relief that his abuse of her was now over. She could leave Norfolk now, no longer a Veteran's wife, no longer restricted by Jim from doing what she wanted, giving Baby Mark everything he wanted. She started planning their move back home to Ackerford.

7

Thou shall not hate thy brother in thine heart: thou
shalt in any wise rebuke thy neighbour, and not suffer
sin upon him.
  – Leviticus 19:17

As Chief Waterson sat at his desk preparing to review the case documentation in front of him, he remembered his past and his friend Jack. No longer was Jack Rucker a boy from a small town. He had persevered over too many obstacles to give anyone else credit. Jack was a boy who had a temperament that couldn't be changed. His own mother, who used to reinforce his ideals, even became weary that his methods and approach would get him in trouble or even killed. His graduation from Yale Law school, and now an eternal secret alumni of Skull and Bones, was only the beginning and everyone that knew Jack, knew he had yet to begin his quest. This quest of his was not something on paper, but a life to date of lessons learned about injustice. Injustice to him, his family, animals, strangers, elderly; the list would go on if you asked Jack. He shared the details too, he remembered them all, as often it is with someone's passion. It wasn't work to him, although it seemed like work to everyone else.

He played hard as a kid. It was play, but it always took a serious tone. His best friend growing up was Danny. You wouldn't know they were friends at times due to the daily arguments, sometimes with fists over who was right, or as Jack would often proclaim that he was "most right" for the ten plus years of their childhood friendship. But people knew, regardless of the adult-like intensity they often saw between them, if you could find one, you would find the other. They developed an adult-like approach to life, way too early was always their parent's concern. Often questions of deep thought would be brought up around the dinner table, most of the time the adults didn't know or have an opinion on the subjects. Danny's parents were always worried about the influence this young Jack Rucker had on their son's behaviors and values. They did know that Jack was the only boy Danny trusted, he looked up to Jack even though they were the same age, most of which came from Jack's willingness to stand beside Danny during the toughest times, all of which started when someone started the constant teasing of Mikey, Danny's older brother by five years. Mikey was born with a severe case of Down syndrome, a misunderstood genetic disease before people even knew the word genetic. Jack made this type of altruistic stand his entire life. Later, as a young lawyer, he personally handled all the legal work to be sure the Waterson's and Mikey had their rights protected instead of the state deciding what was best for Mikey. He did this up until the day Mikey died. Jack made a name for himself by accident as he did what was right, not what was popular. He was always that way and could be trusted to pursue justice regardless of the law.

Jack got started the same day he graduated. He did two things, the first was to register to take the bar exam, a technicality to Jack where it was seen as the golden pass to everyone else. The second was to subscribe to every newspaper in Virginia. The method to register for both the bar and newspapers was as cumbersome as could be if seen by a casual observer of the computer age, but a necessity in the early seventies to fill out the forms. The bar exam was graded by a human, by manual effort, no machine grading, and no need for a number 2 pencil. Jack would later lead the effort to clean up the bar exam grading methods, removing the human influence, introducing automation, as the injustice of cheating was beyond what he could tolerate. Jack's inspiration was to redo what was wrong and prevent it through the introduction of the law, whether new or amended legislation. From an early part of his efforts, he realized that precedent, the act of using the past to support and justify the present situation, was like legal rationalization. Case law assumed the past judgments, written down as a judges ruling which were just human interpretations of a written law, were right. Specifically, the law itself was often at the root of injustice and Jack set out to fix them. All of them if he could.

As youths, in the late fifties and early sixties, driven by endless energy and no barriers to their efforts, Jack and Danny both aligned and pushed each other towards the right thing naturally. As adults, Jack and Danny learned that people often do what is best for them, disguised as the right thing. Especially those elected, wanting to be reelected. Politicians wanted to be around the right people more than they wanted to be righteous themselves. It was a simple fact of life, that righteous people often blended into the scenery and never received credit for their deeds. The ironic part is what often drove their righteous behavior is the lack of need to be recognized, it was always, or almost always an internal drive. Jack was being recognized, not by the lawyer community but by the political community. He opened his practice the same day he passed the bar.

Danny (now Daniel), more than forty years later, sat at his desk, looking over the growing stack of documents related to the Backson case, the police report from Billy, the stack of images now back from the crime scene photographer, and the autopsy from the state medical examiner. He was now the Chief of Police in Ackerford, the town they thought they owned in their youth, wondering how Jack would handle this case. He knew one thing, he could be sure the now famous Jack Rucker would pursue justice, regardless of the popular or expected opinion. Danny learned to accept the expected, as the alternative always turned out worse. He wondered how it would go this time, he and Jack were seasoned adults thrust together again not by choice but by coincidence.

8

I hate and abhor lying; but thy law do I love.
   - Psalms 119:163

C hannel 5 news always had the best stories first, even though the other local channels serving the metro Richmond area claimed it, everyone knew it wasn't true. After a half-day of classes and another half day of doing bullshit admin stuff he already forgot, John didn't really register much this time of night, but you never knew when his interest would be peeked, as opposed to the sleeping drivel everywhere else on the TV. He was always on the edge anyway, not the edge of adventure, but more the edge of procrastination, and tonight was no different. His class was expecting an assignment tomorrow for mid-term and he was pressed for something that would challenge them. He was under pressure from the school to pep up the law program. The school was now in a marketing mode, creating what they called "value add" programs, as he physically did air quotes alone in his living room while he waited for the commercials to end, as opposed to classes, what a joke. So, John had to come up with something, and as always, last minute and eleventh hour was his norm. He also had a knack for creating something from nothing, so his slow style worked well with his creative touch. Maybe he should be in marketing, and then he laughed to himself.

As the commercials ended, they previewed a story for tomorrow by this interesting reporter, Stephen C. Canner. This guy was so into his self-promotion he didn't even know it. He wasn't tabloid, because Channel 5 was a serious station, but he always seemed pretty close to the edge. His stories were always secret and always previewed for tomorrow. The norm was that the preview was done when he made a breakthrough or discovery on one of his stories.

The next story was about a sad accident on highway 29, on the outskirts of the town of Ackerford, a far suburb of Richmond. Slow news night, thought John as he got up to take a piss. Over the sound of his own piss, he only caught a few facts, but each was pretty sad; a man, a car accident, no real cause, widow, and now two fatherless children. What a shame, as he finished his duty. He wondered what his students could do with this? Not the piss, but the accident, as he smirked. What a great challenge for them, and it meant he was done and needn't worry about the "value" added class tomorrow. Another five minutes of news and it looked like they were making stuff up, must have been a slow news day. John sure looked forward to the story by Stephen C. Canner.

9

What then shall we say? That the law is sin? By no means! Yet if it had not been for the law, I would not have known sin.
  - Romans 7:7

John often took the simple way, most people saw it as lazy. He was seen as, and actually was, the type of adjunct wanna-be professor that made it easy for the students, but also fulfilled the requirements, the bare minimum, but fulfilled nonetheless. John's class started the same way, everyone was late and John was last, if nothing, he was consistent. He always attempted to energize the class with classic quotes he had memorized from Perry Mason, but they hit their mark less than half the time, his students thought even less.

This class, like most at this close to the city, but near suburbia junior college, was full of diversity. Every possible background was in the class, every possible scenario was represented, John couldn't help but think they represented what every jury should, diversity without pre-selection. They were all pre-selected in a way, without any real logic, as these kids were all lawyer wanna-be's but none could afford the path to become a real lawyer, regardless of talent. John didn't really pay that much attention to his students, why should he, talent or not, these losers weren't going anywhere. It almost felt like an elective course, one for fun to boost your GPA. The sad part is that most of these students still had the energy he no longer had, albeit not every day.

Mary seemed to be annoyed constantly. She took the lawyer wanna-be to its max, every day. Some days John almost felt motivated, as at least she was consistent, not wanting the power or money these other pre-selected kids did. Although she often tested John's patience with her out-of-the-box thinking, that is what she called it, John just called it wrong. He thought about making a poster for her that stated, the law was based on facts and precedents, not ideas or theories. In a little bit of sarcastic tone, he told, "You should be a reporter like Stephen Canner, they use ideas to make a story, a lawyer uses facts to present the truth, something that can be proven, not something that could happen, but something that did happen, beyond a reasonable doubt."

Was he the only one that watched the news? This supposed "diverse" group had not even heard of the accident, nor even the town of Ackerford, a little more than a mere forty minutes from the classroom they were currently seated in. He didn't know Mary knew the town well. She grew up there, went to Sunday school there for years. She was desperately trying to escape her hometown. Shaking off his attitude towards these losers, John presented the assignment. He gave specific instruction, while looking at Mary, that they were to base their briefs on facts and precedents. He continued to explain case law, for those not paying attention the last two years.

"Case law is the collection of past legal decisions written by courts and similar tribunals in the course of deciding cases, in which the law was analyzed using these cases to resolve ambiguities for deciding current cases." John looked up and sighed.

Mary, bored and now irritated, recognized he was reading it from somewhere, she searched from her antiquated laptop and using the slowest internet the school could get, found it, clicked the top link and the recently launched Wikipedia website provided her the answer, he was reading it, word for word. She wished she could afford a better school.

The assignment was to find a legal method to provide the survivors of Charlie Backson some relief. There were lots of questions, these kids always wanted specific instruction, as most have made it this far in the copy/paste world of paper writing. He only responded by telling them to think, use facts and precedents with the goal of providing relief to the survivors. It was time for the end of class and John was done. He noticed Mary efficiently left the classroom, John couldn't even remember if she even unloaded any books out of her backpack. He used to care about details because he had to, now it didn't really matter. The more confusion he created, the less work he had to do, he laughed at the lack of "value" and his attitude he brought to the table. Mary was about to bring her own attitude to this assignment. If John knew her better and the consequences about to come, he would have put more work into picking a different assignment. Laziness rarely works, John was about to learn this.

10

The bloodthirsty hate the upright; but the just seek his soul.
  - Proverbs 29:10

The police station was built when things were more practical, made of brick, wood, and glass. It could have been in any small town. There was a knock at the Chief's door. Seeing through the blinds, it was both the CSI-bound college student 911 dispatcher and Sandra, the department's long-term, only ever admin. Being around for the past twenty years as the Police Chief and the previous twenty as a town constable pulling triple duty; deputy, fireman and as the town's handyman, Chief knew everyone, so he was taken aback to see standing behind them was a man the Chief didn't know; And this man had a badge.

Chief said what he always said to strangers, "What can I do for you?" as the reality was that everyone but your true friends wanted something. Stephen C. Canner introduced himself as such with just a slight annunciation on the "C" middle initial. Details were the Chief's ultimate nagging fear, so he paid attention. The badge was a press badge from a television network from the city, Channel 5 it said, with a little logo of a building it seemed pretty serious looking, bar code and numbers, details, more details, the Chief sighed.

Chief got so caught up in the reason for the visit that he thought something interesting might have happened, but then he realized that the police Chief was the first to hear everything, so no doubt there would be no surprise today. Mr. Canner was instantly surprised and took offense via his abnormal body language at the Chief not knowing him. The Chief knew what these city slickers thought of small-town law enforcement, and he used their arrogance to his advantage. Canner was assuming exactly what the Chief already was thinking, "Who's this asshole?" Canner knew he wasn't the best friend of the police in Richmond. Canner thought the word of his 'assholeness' would get around, even to small towns, the word was supposed to travel fast in small towns, right?

Stephen C. Canner cut right to the chase, talking a little fast for the Chief to follow, that it was almost offensive, maybe even on purpose. His business here in Ackerford was to detail the process by which small-town local "yokels," his exact words, investigate a case. As the Chief was already annoyed, he started to ask a question, but this reporter just kept going. Saying, really demanding that there were two ways this could go, a story about the needs of a small-town police force to serve their community, or the "Barney Fife" way, again his actual words, to show the incompetence of the small-town police force, showing it to be inept and downright wrong on some issues, essentially wasting taxpayer money. The Chief interrupted him, not a normal thing for the Chief as he liked the critical details he got from listening, but the Chief suspected this guy could go on for a while. The interruption was simple, "What are you talking about? Investigation? We don't have anything going on right now, just traffic tickets and such," which couldn't be interesting enough for a trip of over forty miles for such an important guy like this. "The death of Charlie Backson," as he was framing it in lights with his hands came out of Stephen C. Canners mouth. The Chief was so surprised, he had to ask who he was again, missing a detail, but caught off guard by a stranger on a Friday wasn't the norm either. Stephen C. Canner took some notes on that one.

The Chief immediately responded, "I know who Charlie is, who are *you* again?"

Ignoring the question, probably because he didn't hear it thought the Chief, Stephen C. Canner asked the Chief, "So which way is it going to be? Either way, I will have some fun." Chief called in Billy and essentially both were silent after the Chief made the request of Stephen C. Canner to leave us to our own business, attempting and awfully convinced that this would be the end of it. It was actually the beginning of something that no one, not even Stephen C. Canner could imagine, even on his forty-mile lonely drive back to the city. He was tired of chasing small stories and was determined to create something for himself.

11

But he that sinneth against me wrongeth his own soul;
all they that hate me love death.
  – Proverbs 8:36

T he news was getting it all wrong, a car accident in modern times wasn't that hard to get right, not that it surprised Chief Waterson. He had seen everything this town had to offer over the last two decades. Surprisingly, he wasn't worn down the way people might think. He loved his job, not the task really, but what it stood for in the community. People looked not to him directly, but to the police, the team, his team that he selected and trained personally over the last twenty years, to keep order and keep it safe. The Chief knew this wasn't a daily thought of the citizens of Ackerford, but more of a non-discussed expectation and Danny liked it that way. So, since there was little action, then the Chief must be doing a good job was the general consensus, again, not like it ever came up though. No one even ran against him during election years, but in order to make it fair, there was always another candidate. One year the local priest was put on the ballot, and even got some votes, three to be exact.

But now, this Backson situation was a joke, a bad one, with the local college creating such a ruckus about the terrible accident to that city man who lived in the country. Nobody really even knew the victim, Charles Backson. His family was in service each Sunday, but he, the devoted husband and dedicated father, now dead, never attended. He was thought of as a good man because he had such a wonderful family. Susan, his wife, was someone who people instantly trusted, and his kids, you would think they took some secret potion to make them so polite. But his death on highway 29, just outside of town, was devastating. Ackerford isn't big enough or even active enough to have a full-time ambulance crew or even fire crew, so when you hear the sirens, you know something unusual was happening. Good people stopped their activities to volunteer, prioritizing their small town natural civic duty, and came to the rescue of a fellow member of their community. In this case, it was Charles Backson.

When the sirens went off, they echoed through the town, physically off the turn of the century brick buildings and emotionally, as everyone knew everyone. The long-time volunteers, dropping their current activity, running towards the sound, not yet knowing the details, yet knowing they were there to help. The switchboard got hot. Not that the town still had a switchboard, but more of a figure of speech, thought Sandra, who had seen everything as the only lead dispatcher Ackerford even knew. As everyone was calling their loved ones, making sure it wasn't someone they knew and a relief each time it wasn't. As the ambulance and fire truck accelerated through town everyone came out to watch, at least those that weren't on the phone. The Chief sent a car out there too.

44

Deputy Billy Jackson was already going that way anyway, no doubt he was also caught up in the excitement. He likely forgot to radio into the station of his change in plans from his normal town patrol.

The 911 call came in from a woman that was passing through on her way to Richmond, from her cell phone. She had said she saw a car go off the road and over the embankment.

"I didn't see what happened after that, but I called 911 anyway," she said with a bit of pride.

The Chief listened to most of the call as it happened, the only 911 dispatcher the town had was only two rooms away, in the corner of the small police station, with the door open, the sound was turned up and it echoed. He heard the sirens start outside, limiting his ability to hear the rest of the now droned-out 911 call. He witnessed through the window the rescue crews sprinting towards their responsibilities. As now multiple sirens now started, those of fire trucks and ambulance pierced the quiet morning, his deputy was also headed out to the accident. His estimated arrival was about five minutes. Chief looked away from his office window and made his way over to talk to the 911 dispatcher. The sirens faded as they left the town towards the country. The call had ended by the time the Chief got to the corner office. He asked to have the call played again, he wanted to catch details he may have missed. When the dispatcher replayed the call again, as it progressed, each of them in the room, a group had now gathered, had the same thought, that the caller, seemed to be a little too relaxed. She identified herself as Lynn Henderson and giving her phone number twice, so maybe the accident wasn't that bad based on her relaxed tone. She didn't stop at the scene to help though, the Chief always wondered why people never stopped, too busy he figured, knowing good Samaritans were a thing of the past, accepting it but still not understanding why. The Chief thought again, hoped really, that the accident was not bad but knew he'd have something else to do. He did have all the details as the 911 dispatcher was excellent, a local college student studying to be a CSI detective. This gave the Chief some hope for the future, some people still did good work.

The ambulance and the police cruiser arrived at almost the same time. The ambulance crew started to unload the regular assortment of items they used, or rather practiced with, as it was almost never for real, but this time it was. The deputy, Billy Jackson, reached the mangled car first. He was yelling for Mr. Backson. Billy was pretty smart for a small-town deputy. The 911 dispatcher radioed him the exact location and car description while he was still en route. He knew the caller had identified the car as a four-door white sedan, real shiny. Billy was considered by others to be a car guy and he had admired this man's car from afar since he got it a year ago, so he knew it was Backson's Mercedes S 550 SMG Sport, even though he had never met the man. Billy prided himself on the details. The man was slumped over the steering wheel, but his head was tilted back, too far back, was Billy's immediate assessment. The first of the ambulance crew arrived next, a mere five seconds behind Billy. "Holy Shit!" were his first words, as filled out on Billy's report later. The training never prepares you for the real thing. The rescue crew went through the process, even though everyone knew the outcome. Charlie Backson was pronounced dead on the scene, although no one there really had the authority to do it. His neck was broken, not just a little, but a lot. These weren't the exact words from the county coroner, but the interpretation of the rescue team counted for more, as Billy put it in his police report, 'his neck seemed to be broken a lot'.

The Chief didn't like doing the next part, but he knew he was the best suited for the job. Taking the drive to the Backson house was long; he hadn't come out here much. Once when there were some wild animals near the Backson house, and Charlie called in for help, sheepishly admitting he didn't have a gun and wasn't sure what was making the noise. So the first time to help Charlie chase away a single raccoon, and this time to help his wife cope with his death. Little did the Chief know, it would get bigger, as he would have to help her cope with her husband's murder.

The lady that called in the accident finally returned the Chief's call. He didn't like doing it, but dropping a little legal language on a voicemail the previous evening after reading Billy's initial report, almost always prompted a callback. She was a nice lady, over the phone anyway. Her name was Lynn Henderson, she shared she was a drug rep, which she felt it was needed to explain to the Chief was not related to illegal drugs, but was a real profession nowadays. Lynn shared she was passing through on her normal sales route, although she did say this was a slight detour versus just going up the freeway.

She quickly over-explained the detour had forced her this way and after figuring out where she was, "I thought it easier to just go through town instead of turning around and wasting more time."

So now the Chief had more detail than he wanted, but that was part of the job. You never really knew which piece of detail would complete the puzzle, so you had to get plenty.

The accident occurred about 5:45 pm, which was the time stamp on the 911 call record, on a Wednesday. Ms. Henderson had said the white Volvo, which the Chief corrected her as a Mercedes, which Billy had already clarified, and Lynn paused, stating, oh that's right in agreement. She said it passed her at a regular rate of speed, it was in its own lane, and she was in hers, she was careful to recount the details of the traffic laws thought the Chief but was lost on the type of car. Anyway, with a mental sigh, the Chief clarified that she was coming westbound, into town and Charlie was going out of town, back towards the city of Richmond. She confirmed he was going east, away from Ackerford, towards Richmond, and he reconfirmed it was eastbound. She seemed annoyed, but annoyance or not, the Chief wanted the details.

Billy did all the necessary detail work that had to be done, he seemed to enjoy it and overdid it compared to what was expected, but the Chief appreciated it and Billy was good at it. He measured about every possible thing to measure. The distance of the skid marks, the distance from the road, the angle of the embankment, on and on his report went for twelve pages, no doubt a sign that things don't happen much around here. The Chief did stop abruptly at a piece

48

of detail covered in the personal contents of the vehicle, a gun, specifically a Glock 17 gen 4 with a seventeen-round factory magazine. Chief thought, a serious gun for raccoon problems, and the Chief was thankful again for Billy's details. The Chief personally ran a check in the NCI system to make sure it was registered; proper registration was something that law-abiding gun owners did, except for maybe Charlie. But the gun came back registered to Charles Backson, who had a concealed handgun permit, commonly called a CHP, and no reported problems. The gun's safety was on, and it was properly stored in the car, all according to Virginia open carry law. This is probably why Billy didn't mention it when he hand-delivered the multi-page report to the Chief directly, no big deal, everyone had a gun and everyone had it registered, never a problem.

The Chief remembered talking with Charlie about his willingness to help him select a gun and train him if he wanted. He felt bad for Charlie at the time, scared of a raccoon and not even a pellet gun to scare it off. He didn't know how lucky he was it was the Chief on duty that night. If it was Billy, he would have done fine, but the fella's sure would've heard about the raccoon scare and they would have laughed it up for sure. Chief Waterson never did hear from Charlie nor did he follow up to ask him again. A gun is a man's choice, not one to be discussed more than once. Chief again reviewed the details, a Glock Gen4 with an extended magazine seemed excessive, Chief imagined the size of raccoons Charles must have imagined and the overzealous salesperson advising Charles on the gun he needed to own. Chief let it go for now.

During his obligatory visit after his death, Chief had asked Susan, Charlie's wife, about the gun. He was recalling the story of the raccoon, making it sound more like small talk versus a line of questioning, that was probably the last thing she needed. It wasn't nagging at him, but more of a piece of detail he wanted to know. She told him nothing surprising, that Charlie had bought the gun, and been trained near the city on its proper use, safety and practiced a few times on the range. She didn't know this for sure she said, but just recalling what Charlie had told her. She did say that he normally kept it in the garage, as he felt that was the place he would most likely need it. She didn't know that he had moved it to the car or why he had it in the car. She just knew she didn't want to touch it and asked the Chief to keep it, give it to someone else. The Chief agreed, saying he would have Billy bring out the paperwork to transfer ownership to the police department. Not a trick question, as you see on some TV shows, the Chief thought, but he did have another question, just a piece of detail that he didn't know.

"Mrs. Backson, why was Charlie going back to the city at 5:45 pm on a Wednesday?" Chief asked.

"I am not sure, Chief," said Susan.

"Please call me Danny."

"Ok Danny, I'm sorry I just don't know, Charles was often too busy to share where, when and what was going on," said Susan.

"He didn't always tell me everything, as his schedule was so busy all the time, even weekends."

"Thank you for your time, I'm sorry and please contact me any time." Chief shared as he handed Mrs. Backson his card, with contact information in bold.

Walking down the steps and the footpath of their near immaculate lawn, he was frustrated and knew he would be haunted by missing details. He never was short of clues, and always had more than needed, but he constantly worried about not having the complete puzzle in place before closing the case. Mrs. Backson was nice, but not helpful towards the case. She only knew what Charlie had told her, which wasn't much and that wasn't helpful either.

12

They that hate me without a cause are more than the hairs of mine head; they that would destroy me, being mine enemies wrongfully, are mighty: then I restored that which I took not away.
  - Psalms 69:4

Lori walked down the street, Denver looked and felt safe. The past year of trials and death was behind her. It was in her memory but one she was doing everything she could to forget. She needed more air and the exercise too. The post office address Jack gave her was close by, convenient on purpose, set up by Jack (Angela more likely) no doubt to keep her out of sight and focused on her recovery. She had to wait as the mail clerk verified that two names, her previous name of Mary Morgan and her new name of Lori Philbus were attached to the one PO box. She confirmed it with the postal clerk. She even had to remind herself. Getting her mail took longer than she liked. It seemed to take an eternity for the postal clerk to reappear from the rear area of the post office. Her patience was anew now that she had little that she actually had to accomplish that day. She was a little annoyed when she saw him return with nothing and as she got ready to speak, he spoke first and asked if "she would like some help out with it" and in the same sentence "if her car was parked close?" She obviously looked confused as he answered a question she didn't even ask. The mail had backed up to an amount that far exceeded either of their capacities to get it out of the post office and it caused both the clerk and Lori to be at a loss for a solution. Her old car was still in Richmond and she likely wouldn't keep it. She had taken a walk from her apartment, walked the three blocks, past the Araaj courthouse, walking off her anxiety, past the Abraham Lincoln park to where she now stood, Denver's downtown post office. The clerk said there were four postal bins full, sorted by what looked like letters, junk, and other items. There was also a selected forward on certain mail to the office of Jack Rucker. Lori acknowledged and asked for the letters only, for now, she said she would be back to pick up the rest, really without any intention as she cleaned up her life going forward. It was her first day in Denver and the first time in months she had received her own mail. Angela had been doing it for her to eliminate any distractions. Lori thought that probably, some important personal letters got sorted to the bins and now would be a good time as any to get caught up and cleaned up. As the postal clerk brought the bin of letters to the front, eventually that is, she was shocked at the real backup of mail, there must have been a hundred or more letters, over four hundred when she was done. She concluded that her afternoon was now full. She attempted to take the mail bin however noted the firm grip the over-ambitious clerk had on the bin. She reached her arms around the stack of mail, bundled in a few groups with thick rubber bands, and started out the door.

To her annoyance, the clerk inquired about the other mail and she said she would pick it up later; he looked annoyed more than she felt and loudly stated "next" as he moved on with his job to the now growing line of customers. Lori picked up her pace as she exited the post office, paying close attention to her grip on the bundles of letters, now getting heavy, and remembering she did have one planned event today, brunch, with the man she was falling for, the only bright spot over the last year.

13

Do not be surprised, brothers, that the world hates you.
    – 1 John 3:13

C oming back from the Denver post office, Lori took her time, more as a requirement, not a choice. Her arms were full and she still couldn't get enough air in her new city. As her arms were more tired than expected she climbed the stairs slower than normal. She liked her new apartment, she liked the view from the upstairs window. The first time she climbed them last night, she had been oblivious to the narrow stairs to reach her entry door but this time, when her hands were full, carrying the previous several month's worth of mail Angela didn't sort, the stairs suddenly became a chore, nearly hazardous. She was careful not to drop anything as she was probably too lazy to stop and pick anything up. Even though she knew she didn't drop anything, she glanced down from the top of the narrow staircase to be sure. As she fumbled with an arm full of mail from the previous months and as she fumbled for her apartment key, she found guilt and humor in her attention to details in all things but the organization of her personal life, the mail being the glaring and now heavy in her arms example. She was looking for her keys out of habit, realizing her new apartment had a keypad. Living a new life, trying to remember her door entry code, she never saw it coming, in her hands, buried in the unimportant letters of the last few months, a letter, from a stranger. Something never expected, not even by the great Jack Rucker, the man who plans for everything.

14

So whoever knows the right thing to do and fails to do it, for him it is sin.
- James 4:17

Rarely did big-city television stations from Richmond cover news from a small town like Ackerford. Big things happened in small towns every day, the interest level was usually low in the city but could be the talk of that small town for some time, often years as it marked time for people who had little else. The big city television station Channel 5 highlighted the story from Ackerford about a single-car accident, the death of a near nobody to others outside of Ackerford, and caught the entire town off guard. Even John Stacker, who had used it just that day to challenge his diverse group of college students and a last-minute attempt to create "value" add programs in a minimalistic kind of way.

The town of Ackerford was on TV and this was an occasion. It was such an occasion that the "switchboard" got hot again, this time fifteen minutes into the Channel 5 news. There were even discussions in the streets. The problem was that there was video coverage of the town, the Chief, and the Backson's. Not like a tabloid but close. People were pretty mad as the Chief was involved and he involved no one, didn't even tell anyone. Ironically, Billy had the day off and was watching Channel 5, the Chief's phone rang at 10:15 pm disturbing the Chief, not from sleep, but from his pipe, and his needed quiet from the noise of the day.

After calming down Billy who called sometimes when he was nervous about something that impacted his beloved hometown, the Chief hung up his phone. Chief didn't get mad, didn't get even, just stayed focused on the details and the solution. This time he was surprised, things were moving too fast, and although he wasn't worried about himself as his reputation was a true one of honest, hard fact police work and town service over the last forty years. Outside of the previously closed cases, Rucker reopened when he came back to town, things were run by the book, by the law. Chief did respect Jack's persistence for justice aligned with the law, even on the simple cases. They were reopened, then closed again properly. Chief appreciated Jack's help, he always had from when they were young. It also helped Billy get his Miranda Rights memorized. The police department was very well respected, within the town and in surrounding areas. It had even won some awards, but Chief couldn't remember what they were. Surprising even himself at his memory loss. He was worried about the town as the town was one that was old, in buildings, its people, and its values. Last thing it needed was a label that was undeserved.

John was watching as he had thought about the Stephen C.

Canner teaser most of the day and was finished with his nightly routine by the time the news started. He was surprised to see the story was about the accident, the one he assigned his class. This was sure to be "value" add to the school. That was more a thought that was risky, as it could make it seem cheap, but John found it interesting anyway.

Most days, John liked working at the local college. It was fun enough, but what he liked most was that people left him alone. He could assign anything he wanted and nobody had to approve them or ever questioned them. Similar to any junior college, it was full of part-time students, those trying to find a new career usually because they had to, and a few students who had potential, but just not the opportunity. John knew they were poor. John thought of them sometimes as losers but felt guilty for thinking that. The students in John's class were fairly judged by most to be lazy, easy way out students. It was hard not to expect this as they grew up in an age of excess, advances in technology that widened the gap between what we could do and what we needed to do as humans. Almost reverse evolution, filling the gap with technology and therefore making things easy. This was true for their approach to their studies, not that they chose this method over hard work, as most didn't even know another method besides "easy way" existed. Some of his students were losers, they actually thought the easy way was hard; reality check was non-existent at times.

From his own experience, John knew there were possibilities in the insurance area of this case as the opportunities for precedent were almost endless, and the facts were hard to disprove. No one liked insurance companies, except maybe lawyers. What John didn't know or even suspect was that Mary Morgan started her research in the insurance area and mentally mapped out her entire brief. It was something she thought was real law. She abruptly stopped when she saw others doing the same. She hated being normal, being part of a group. She didn't want to be seen as lazy nor taking the easy way. She didn't want to be seen as a loser.

She couldn't help making herself a little (a lot) nervous with the changing of her legal strategy in the middle of due process, a big no-no in any legal proceeding as it is interpreted as guilty, regardless of facts. She could only identify one other path to the case, and that was murder, if not an accident, it must have been foul play. More foul than she could imagine.

John was excited; the school didn't have class tomorrow and he had the day off and as usual, had procrastinated planning anything. He decided to go see Stephen C. Canner.

What John Stacker, Mary Morgan, Chief Waterson, or Deputy Billy Jackson didn't know, others more important than the city news were paying close attention as well. Jack Rucker was briefed on the subject, for the second time in as many days. His staff was good and paid attention to everything, especially televised happenings of Jack's hometown.

15

But if we walk in the light, as he is in the light, we have
fellowship with one another, and the blood of Jesus his
Son cleanses us from all sin.
   – 1 John 1:7

T he city news in addition to the reporting on the
local Ackerford accident was populated with the
current president's approval rating, the campaign to
be reelected, and the constant, unknown facts of the slander
efforts from the other party. The current president couldn't
win; doing the right thing caused more controversy and
fighting with fire, made it worse. At the center of the argument
was the slow economy, being blamed on lack of production
and innovation. It took a million avenues as everyone had
an opinion from the decline in math and science scores of
America's youth, to the trade agreements creating more free
trade. An issue that would normally be buried, but had
multiple high-profile hits was that of judicial reform. Starting
with Jack's involvement a few years ago in the case related
to the death of Chief's brother, Mikey Waterson. Judicial
reform, and the often wrongful case law rulings of lazy judges,

were now getting more attention. Judicial reform got even more attention as cases emerged of sexual predators getting released, and then committing crimes that could have been prevented. The momentum grew as more current cases being ruled on the loose and biased judgments of previous cases were highlighted, where the "technicality" list was getting longer and longer. It was causing the perception and reality of problematic rulings with real criminals, with good lawyers, where they were not proven innocent, but couldn't be proven guilty. The country was getting cynical on all these subjects and the political process picked up on it and started to exploit it. It seemed an easier win than the other rooted issues.

As Jack and his team spent their day in the details, their night's building relationships within the community, and the time in between keeping the campaign up to date, it left little time for error, which by working for Jack, you knew was unacceptable. Jack liked facts, not opinions, and was driving the recently nominated Republican presidential candidate to do the same. Jack had the campaign rallied towards going slow with facts, instead of going fast with opinions. Jack didn't like the taste of crow and wouldn't be involved if he had to eat it, even once, and Joe Callahan knew it. They had history together.

For once, a presidential candidate deserved all of the accolades he received. Joseph Callahan was a man that Jack knew from years ago. Jack closely watched the role of this long-time friend, former sheriff, turned councilman, then a United States Senator, elected for three consecutive terms. Jack paying close attention to the changes in New Mexico via his legal work more than fifteen years ago. A then young Jack and an equally young sheriff from New Mexico crossed paths via a telephone conversation, Jack could recall the details like it was yesterday.

"Sheriff, this is Jack Rucker a prosecuting attorney from Virginia," said Jack upon the Sheriff getting on the phone. Joe knew the name and knew the man too. Jack was a friend from nearly twenty years ago as a young Joe Callahan, was transformed from a returning, often disrespected warfighter in Vietnam, to an important and mission-focused Bonesman.

"Well, Jack Rucker," said with a little Bonesman sarcasm, "I'm sorry to have made you wait so long, but having to wait that long, and being an attorney, I figured you have something important to say," was the now more serious response from Sheriff Joe Callahan.

"Without taking too much of your time, I wanted to say, from afar, I've watched your actions, your results, and your recent problems about your interpretation of the law in New Mexico." They had not spoken in years, yet instantly connected as if it was yesterday.

Jack didn't want to be confrontational but also didn't want to waste anyone's time with the usual political pleasantries. If Joe Callahan was still the real deal, as he was many years ago, Jack knew Joe's response to his inquiry would tell him.

Joe stiffened up in his chair and responded the way he was raised, the way he was trained, in a straightforward, no excuses way with only the facts. Fellow Bonesman or not, he didn't know or care how the no doubt high-priced lawyer from Virginia would react. "Jack, I appreciate your call, as I also am concerned about the troubles, but doing the right thing and being supported by the people who elected me, is more important than any news story or political agenda of my own or anyone else."

Jack was pleased, nearly forty years had passed between now and the Skulls meetings at Yale, not that they actually existed or were ever documented. The distance of the telephone was hiding his rare smile from his soon-to-be old but new again partner in the faraway land of New Mexico.

"Joe, I support what you are doing, I too have found myself to be isolated at times in the dark adult years, ruled by self-interests and agendas that have short-term results and long-term pain. I've called to help, provide unsolicited legal advice, which I think can help you continue your much-needed example in this country, away from precedent decisions, and more towards the true spirit of the law."

Joe remembered like it was yesterday the meetings at the citadel at Yale, often called by others a tomb, the meeting place for Yale's Skull and Bones. Joe's memory flashed quickly and in perfect detail, the first entry was memorable, a massive door with an intricate array of locks, more memorable was the room of red velvet with screaming skeletons. People don't forget things like that. Joe vividly recalled the intense emotional feeling of being a part of the inner workings of privilege when 'tap night' happens to fifteen newly-tapped members, who go through an ordeal that others can't fathom.

Joe was part of that fifteen, Jack Rucker was also there, as his sponsor, soon to be his fellow Bonesman. He remembered Jack then and knew his voice now. Every Bonesman knew that the experience was the education for life, and relationships once established, were lifelong as well, unbreakable.

Joe was in the moment, mentally processing his member responsibilities and responding as only Bonesman would.

"Well Robin Hood, sounds good to me, what are your thoughts?" Joe calling Jack by his peer-selected Bonesman name.

"We should talk in person, I'll come see you very soon, Titanic," Jack said.

Joe knew this was the Jack he met many years back, outside at Yale, sharing their dual interest in 1969 of the then just-released book *Slaughterhouse-Five.* Jack now calling him by the name given to him that night of entry into the tomb with skeletons screaming. This name was given to him by his fellow Skull and Bones members, Titanic. He didn't like it then, didn't like it now, but it wasn't a choice. The name was given sarcastically, on the edge of cynical, for being unsinkable in his mission for application of the law.

"Looking forward to it," Joe said, hanging up slowly, without saying anything more.

That day, an important American relationship rekindled, one that would not make the history books, but one that changed the country. Jack and Joe linked their history together, their personal passion, values, and willingness to turn them into action and bonded again that day for a lifetime. For the next two years, they worked behind the scenes not on any political campaign, but more on an American campaign. Joe kept his values, Jack kept his passion, and together, in a true Bonesman way, without a leak to the press, made an example of the way to do business that overcame the negative and became a local and national legend for doing it the hard way, the right way, and the way that was expected by the voting public, the majority, not the minority with the often louder voice.

Joe rose to be a national hero among sheriffs, was elected to local office more for his personal values than his notoriety, and began a steady change from small town to regional law enforcement. Then, when prompted behind the noise of all the public accolades by Jack, and in public by prominent others, to include his dying mother, to run for the New Mexico seat within the US Senate. He won by a landslide with limited campaign spending and a focused agenda, he campaigned for New Mexico to lead the way on judicial reform, others called it getting justice. With two complete terms and a third more than halfway through, the public had asked him to bring his agenda, his leadership, and his results to the national level. His Republican nomination and unblemished approach have made him the media darling. Years ago he was not much more than a media whipping boy, but that was the past.

16

How long will you lie there, O sluggard? When will you
arise from your sleep?
  – Proverbs 6:9

John Stacker was lazy about most things, and Stephen C.
Canner had a large gray area for the facts he reported.
The day was perfect, but unnoticed by John as he arrived,
easily parked on a Tuesday afternoon and entered the building
where the news was collected, edited, and shared with the
hungry for dirt public viewing audience. John found the
newsroom on the building directory, pushed the elevator
buttons, and rode in silence with others to the fourth floor.
When John finally met Stephen C. Canner, he wasn't that
impressed. Maybe it was the hour-plus wait in the vinyl
chairs from a decade (or two) ago, maybe the rude admin
assistant as she did nothing for the hour, and probably the
hours before, thought John, or the lousy waiting area with
magazines nobody reads; on top of that, they were outdated
too.

The meeting lasted no more than fifteen minutes with an

excuse to leave that John couldn't even remember. John wrote more things down than this pompous reporter, and John only wrote down one thing, the name of the school where Stephen C. Canner went to college. It was over as John was told thanks for his time by the admin, almost as a closing script she uses for every visitor. Click, it was like a switch was pulled after fifteen minutes and the exit process started, the preplanned excuse, the closing script, and then he was gone.

John caught the 6 pm news sitting at the bar. He didn't go often, and they didn't even know him at the bar, even though it was a block away from his apartment, and he had lived there for twelve years. He needed to come by more often was his thought, but he knew the ole procrastinator in him wouldn't be back for months. As John sat eating what he had ordered, the Channel 5 news said there would be a special edition of Stephen C. Canner tonight. With the disinterest he showed the Backson story, John was hopeful there was something a little more exciting brewing on the newswire.

17

And let none of you imagine evil in your hearts against his neighbour; and love no false oath: for all these are things that I hate, saith the LORD.
  - Zechariah 8:17

Mary felt desperate, she wanted to separate herself from her peers, avoid the follow-syndrome and stay within her strong beliefs about the spirit of the law. This was an equation she couldn't win, but she was determined, really because she had no choice, she had only seven days left until the assignment was due.

Mary, on the same day she decided to switch to the murder path, albeit a week into a two-week assignment, visited Baxter Enterprises. Baxter Enterprises and Charles Backson had some history, twelve years of history, where Charles started a paid internship after graduating from college with his bachelor's degree in biology. Baxter Enterprises paid and supported him when he went to medical school and received his D.O., a Doctor of Osteopathic Medicine. He was, without a doubt, successful within the company and respected.

Baxter Enterprises was an American success story, a company that adjusted during the good times to weather or excel during the bad times. They relocated from a small office in downtown Richmond to a sprawling state-of-the-art facility in a suburb of Richmond, in the Virginia countryside. Baxter Enterprises is a provider of drug research utilizing clinical human trials and nontraditional, experimental, genetic human treatments. Sitting in the parking lot in her old, out-of-place car, she was connected to the Baxter guest WiFi network. Mary continued to read the Baxter Enterprises online brochure done well on their corporate state of the art website. The company's origins were in drug development and they have had remarkable success. They've been involved in financing and benefiting from gene research for the last forty years. The majority of their success has been through leading-edge innovation, exploring areas where no one was leading, except Baxter themselves. Without a doubt, a good company, both in the financial and moral communities. Mary in her preliminary research could not find a single negative action or opinion towards Baxter, and it was the sole purpose of her efforts that day.

She closed her aging laptop carefully, got out of her car, and walked towards the main entrance of the Baxter Enterprises building. She found so much, she had to parse through it, this time, even when searching for negative, she found only positive. She figured they either had a great PR group or maybe they were really that wholesome. Her thoughts disappeared quickly as she started to get slightly nervous. She approached the building, it was nice, clean, and almost unremarkable for such a successful company.

Mary entered the lobby and noted the multiple dark-colored camera balls hanging from the ceiling, often seen in high-dollar department stores. She noticed numerous wall hangings showing the different countries Baxter was in, and a trophy case full of awards. She saw nothing that she didn't expect from her research. As she approached the desk, the receptionist almost leaped at her. Louise, the first person Mary met at Baxter, wanted to talk and obviously needed to talk. She was the receptionist and the classic corporate lobby face, bored most of the time, and bothering everybody that was in the lobby, she even joked herself. She had been with Baxter before it was Baxter.

"It was a family company back then. Charlie started when the company was still in their downtown office. It then became a public company with a very successful IPO and became Baxter Enterprises."

Mary was doing everything she could to listen to the information she already knew.

"It was in growth mode." Louise demonstrated a little sarcastically with two non-verbal quotations in the thin air. Mary figured Louise didn't have any stock options.

Through research done prior to her visit, Mary found out that Charles (Charlie) Backson, D.O., was an Executive Doctor on the Baxter Enterprises review board. The review board duties were a little vague, but she gleaned that they provided next step direction and detailed review of current progress on their leading-edge products and initiatives. She also read, just that morning, the previous year's stockholder 8K filings with the SEC, those that are required to announce major events that shareholders should know about.

Mary tried to hurry the stories Louise was telling along a little faster, as she felt again overwhelmed by her decision to change mid-course to the now seemingly impossible to prove, the legal definition of first-degree murder. Mary knew the definition well, the killing of a human being by a sane person, with intent, malice aforethought (prior intention to kill the particular victim or anyone who gets in the way) and with no legal excuse or authority. Her anxiety grew with every word out of Louise's mouth.

Louise wanted to talk and didn't want to hurry anything, especially the only visitor she's had in a while. Mary took a lot of notes, she was normally as detailed as she needed to be as she saw events pretty fast, reached accurate conclusions as fast, and used her instinct, something she wasn't worried about. The only interesting fact was the gossip related to the token Christian in the office, her words that Mary wrote down, Charlie calling Mark an asshole, and Mark calling Charlie Judas Iscariot over a copy room dispute of all things; Louise was going on and on, saying she didn't know the biblical Judas had a last name.

This was a new name to Mary. She interrupted the endless talk from Louise.

"Who is Mark?"

Louise looking exasperated with Mary from the rude interruption, shared the short answer. "He is the lead on the ethics board."

Mary, ignoring Louise's anecdotal drivel, now remembered his unique last name and picture on the website, Mark Solier. She also recalled looking for his name in her research of the companies public financial documents. She hadn't seen Mark Solier was a stockholder, yet Charles Backson recently was given ownership with his new role. Charles Backson was made a board member, and Mark Solier too was listed as a board member. With Mark Solier having an important role for a drug company, yet not having any ownership in its future was odd. She'd be sure to check her memory, but she was sure she was right. She didn't know of any time a board member didn't have stock in the company.

Mary was relieved, as another person needing the attention of Louise came through the door headed towards her desk. Louise said aloud in a voice loud enough to scare Mary awake, "Well, speak of the Devil." The man was instantly offended, and immediately Mary was uncomfortable in the company of strangers, although at this point, she was pretty sure she knew every story Louise had in her memory. He immediately spoke, but it was a tone that was instantly soothing and comforting, joking with Louise as if he actually liked all her stories. He did say something profound, almost prepared as if Louise had called him the "devil" before. Mark easily quoted the scripture, "And no wonder, for even Satan disguises himself as an angel of light. That is from Second Corinthians, Chapter 11, Verse 14." Louise laughed uncomfortably. Mary remembered it, because she wrote it down, looking humble and studious as a way to gain additional comfort with these strangers.

This was the first time she met Mark Solier. Louise was still talking about something when Mary introduced herself to Mark. Louise then caught on and only repeated the introduction and without allowing a single moment of silence, she told Mark, and loud enough for anyone, if there had been anyone in the lobby to hear, that "Mary is here from the college investigating Charlie's accident." Mary immediately started to protest, she never used the word investigate; study, review, fact-finding maybe, but not investigate. Even though the volume of Louise was at a level to inform the world, only Louise, Mark, and Mary were in the lobby. Mary assumed that probably the rest of the Baxter employees, nearly a thousand at this location per the website, have heard the endless stories from Louise, and chose to actually work the day in their offices. Mary wished she hadn't come. Then Mark said something way out of the ordinary that snapped her attention back to the lobby, he said, that he was saddened that he didn't get a chance to tell Charlie that "he still loved him." Mary didn't need to write that down, as she wouldn't forget that one. Mark informed Louise of an important visitor coming from Ackerford today and then told Mary that it was nice to meet her. He walked away with a purpose in his gait. He went through the door which he entered the lobby only a few minutes ago and at the click of the security device on the door, it closed, leaving Mary alone with Louise. Louise said something strange too, although not so surprising as Mary had her pegged as someone who says all kinds of things without thinking first. Louise professed as if the fact was

74

written down and tried by the Supreme Court, "Did you know that Mark has never had a girlfriend? You'd think he was a priest or something." Louise looked away now as if she had suddenly become self-aware of her need to share too much, or that she had been rejected by him more than once.

As Mary desperately wanted to frame her case with at least some facts, she asked Louise for some company literature. She also wanted desperately to get away from Louise. Mary had more questions she wanted to ask but just couldn't bear another minute finding the answers. Mary knew from her own legal research that corporate doctors (Backson) and Ethics Boards (Solier) were always in combat? Were there any open issues at this time? Was it enough for motive?

Louise gave Mary a stack of glossy pamphlets and a few professionally bound reports. Mary would have normally been surprised that the receptionist would give away the corporate phone directory, even without the request, but she was glad to have it. Mary stepped outside, took a few extended deep breaths, committing what just happened to her memory. Making the same loud, now ominous clicking to lock people out, the door to the lobby closed behind her.

18

And as for you, brothers and sisters, never tire of doing
what is right.
  – 2 Thessalonians 3:13

Mary put her phone in her purse and took a deep breath. She had parked far away as the parking lot was full and she was realizing now, it was large. She started to walk in the general direction but barely recalled where she parked her car. She filed away everything that had just happened and carefully let herself calm down. It didn't work. With every step towards the direction, she thought her car was parked, was just another step in doubting what she was doing, why she was doing it, and really not knowing how she was going to do it. She questioned herself more and more as she was closing into where she thought her car was parked. By the time she found it, her old car among all the shiny cars of the Baxter employees, she was about to give up. She just wanted to feel normal.

She put her purse on the passenger seat, put on her seat belt, and put her keys in the ignition. She didn't start it, she let go of the keys and put her hands to her face. She cursed herself for being different. She didn't want to be different but was always the outcast from the norm. Always alone and she was tired. Physically tired and mentally tired from fighting for what she thought was right. Now she was getting emotional.

"Why am I so different?!?" she whispered aloud as she screamed it in her mind.

She took a breath, trying to calm down. She went through what she knew and what she wanted. She could feel something here. Something was different, not just her. She knew this was not an accident. She also hated that she couldn't prove it. Even to herself, she could barely solidify her beliefs around what she felt to be true. She reached for her keys and again hesitated to start her car.

She grabbed her purse, found her phone, and called someone she knew would listen. It was his job to listen.

"Hello, Mary," as he had recognized her number.

"I'm sorry to call you."

"Are you in trouble?" he quickly needed to know.

"No, I'm safe, thanks for asking." She always appreciated how he put others first.

"Good to know, what's on your mind?" again, always listening.

She knew she couldn't give him the details, as it would sound crazy in short bursts, over the phone, so she went hypothetical, allowing him to help her without needing to ask questions she likely didn't have the answer for.

"I'm struggling knowing what is right, what is the right thing?" She knew his history of building the church in Ackerford with his bare hands, literally cutting the boards and assembling them, a little each day. Everyone knew the story, yet few were there when he did it in what she recalled was the late sixties or early seventies. The church still looked perfect. He disrupted her brain's need to see the details. His voice was commanding.

"Mary, doing the right thing is not the hard part, the hard part is deciding what is the right thing. Good people of any religion, even the atheist are compelled to do the right thing, once they know what it is."

Mary's attention was full.

"Everyone can feel what they think is right, some react to that and often get it wrong. They take wrong actions as if they are right because they think they are right, as they have not given the time to know what is right."

Mary was feeling better, his words were aligning her feelings and her thoughts.

"We are wired to feel, and we have a responsibility to think. To think about what is right, to determine the perspective of others, not who is right, but what is right."

She wanted to know more, and he continued to inspire her.

"If you reference your Bible, you will see more about righ-teousness than you can ever remember, even you Mary with that perfect memory you have."

She was always amazed how he remembered details about her she either took for granted or forgot herself. Her memory was often a curse.

"Forget the Bible, and process how you feel, into how you think."

Rarely do you hear preachers tell you to forget the Bible.

"Know your history of those that came before you, doing what was right. Dr. King, MLK," using the common abbreviation like he knew him, "said 'on some positions, Cowardice asks the question, Is it Safe? Expediency asks the question, "Is it politic?" And Vanity comes along and asks the question, "Is it popular?" but Conscience asks the question, "Is it right?"

Mary was flooded with emotion, she had lost track of time and only recognized this as the sun was setting behind Baxter Enterprise's large, corporate building she just left. The glare went out of her eyes and she felt she could now see what was right.

"Thank you." She knew what was right. Her determination

was now taking over.

"You're welcome. I compel you to follow your conscience."

And as if scripted, he lightened up the conversations and predictably asked what every great pastor asks, "We miss you, we haven't seen you in service enough. When can I expect to see you?"

Mary's attempt to do the same, asked a question she thought he'd know, "Did Judas have a last name?"

"He did, it was Iscariot, but you already knew that which is why you asked."

"I did, it always gets my attention when I learn things I didn't know, it makes me think what else I don't know."

"Do you have a few minutes?" he asked to get her permission to share what was on his mind.

"I do." As she sat in her car, the sun now set and darkness overcoming her car.

"Judas is assumed to be a bad guy. I can't talk this way on Sunday, but I'll share something with you, hopefully, to make you think. Are you ready?"

"I am," she replied with confidence and wonder.

"Judas is responsible for the salvation of the world. Think this way, if he didn't take the step to call Jesus "rabbi" exposing him to others for what he was, he would not have ignited the true faith from which the crucifixion was the start. Judas gets blamed, but should he get credit? Was he trying to do the right thing? More critical, was he trying to do what he thought was the right thing. In the Gospel of Mark, it gives no motive for Judas to betray Jesus. He was paid, yet he used the money to buy a plot of land to bury strangers."

Mary sat in silence. Her pastor continued.

"The Gnostic Gospel of Judas, not readily accepted nor read by many, tells a different story, one that is more righteous than any story since."

Mary knew her life was about to change.

"Judas was asked by Jesus to betray him, and he alone was the one that knew the true teachings. He did the right thing, overcoming the powers of cowardice, expediency, and vanity."

He stopped, as he said what needed to be said. Somehow he knew what she needed to hear. She could sense her feelings and her thinking was uniting.

"Thank you."

The electronic click of the phone echoed in her car. She reached for her keys, this time she started it, knowing what she had to do next. She knew what was right.

19

Mary was reading every word of the article she found. The article was old, from 1968, and it detailed the killing of a young woman by a bear, at one of the then-new interstate rest areas. She squinted, her headache increasing as she struggled to read the small print on the old and small computer screens at the library. The article having been only captured on aged, 1968 microfiche. She learned from the article of Mark's Aunt Jessica, being killed by a bear, and about the bravery shown by a group of men, some military. Mary was alone in the library, now dark as the sun had set hours ago. The library was about an hour from closing. She looked up and felt nervous, she felt alone. She also felt scared. What would have scared her even more, what she could never have known, were the strong, negative, near rage level feelings of Aunt Jessica. Baby Mark's only aunt, and Alice's only sister, was full of rage that day, with moments of anger and hate towards Mark. The power of the baby was beyond her scope of reasoning, for now at least. Mary wrote furiously the details on her now full legal pad, she had more questions than answers. She realized she didn't have any real answers as she searched for a new pen, her notes had run her pen dry and she had thoughts racing. She couldn't connect them, but later she would, bringing facts to conclusion.

Mary sometimes forced herself to re-read the details to keep anything from being missed. She was looking over her notes and wanting to look again, maybe she missed something. The newspaper showed significant interest in the death by bear accident that occurred at the rest stop. It made the front page for a few reasons, Mary surmised, one it was a story of chance and a story of bravery. The accident was reported in the newspaper on the day after, making the main page headline, it had occurred on November 22nd, 1968, in a suburb of Norfolk, Virginia. Mary had only found it on the fourth or fifth page of her internet search, a more legit source Mary thought often overlooked by many as people rarely went past the first page of a search engine's results, and she knew most of those results were buzzworthy only. This buried story had told the known and assumed facts, sorted by Mary herself as she read. The woman's name was released the same day of the accident, Jessica Bonley, noting that her car had overheated and she was making a call from the recently installed call box at the rest stop. Mary, not wanting to be overly critical, but priding herself in the facts, noted that no reference about the car overheating or her intentions was noted, only the testimony of the men trying to fend off the bear attack. It must have been assumed by the local writer. Mary filed the information, both mentally, electronically and a soon-to-be hard copy as the library's printer came to life, the printer's front panel icon lights turned on and it started to warm up. She had now found another uniquely defined accidental death connected to Mark Solier. This assumed that her case about the Backson accident was going to be proven as murder. She knew she'd need more to prove it.

As her research efforts continued, she had made additional discoveries and had started to fill in the gaps, learning more about Mark, who he was, and what he did. She realized she was feeling an increased state of suspicion and growing fear. After his first five years, starting at birth, of homeschooling from Alice, Mark was young of age, yet smarter than others at every school he attended. His mother paid so much attention to Mark that he had a broad knowledge of a variety of subjects. This started early in his life, the attention from his mother and his grasp of knowledge. The impact was evident through his entire scholastic career. His experiences were vast, he only needed exposure to things just one time and sometimes knew things without exposure, but everyone just assumed he picked it up somewhere, or made deductive conclusions quickly, almost like an adult, even though he was seven years old in sixth grade. She had found and read everything she could about Mark Solier. He made a few headlines, Mary had carefully printed each, noting in the upper right corner, the year, location, category, and keywords with her meticulous taxonomy system. A lot of these paper printouts, still warm from the library's old printer, were related to his outstanding, at a young age, academic skills and the ancient biblical languages he spoke. This got her attention, and also a new category in Mary's research system, using 'ODD' and the keyword, 'Biblical'. Mary recognized that Mark was special, even as a child, yet he grew up in a small town, so very little publicity came his way. Being from a small town herself, she assumed he didn't desire any publicity nor did it ever cross his mother's mind, it probably felt normal to her, and Mary was sure Alice was just glad a young boy like Mark could adjust without his father. Mary didn't know that Mark nor Alice ever spoke of Jim's death after the day he died. Mary had found Jim Solier's obituary online using the LDS Church's website for genealogy research called FamilySearch.org. Mary now had the details for three supposed accidental deaths connected to Mark Solier. She needed more.

Mary left the library late at night again. She was getting strange looks and realized it was closing time. She went home to continue her efforts. She no longer needed access to the ancient microfiche she could only find at this library.

She ran up the narrow stairs, unlocked her apartment door, and plugged her computer in as its battery didn't last long. She brewed coffee and quickly got back to her research of Mark Solier, becoming more mysterious and guilty the more she learned. She knew she needed more details. She summarized that his detailed knowledge, and quick learning skills, did allow him to select early what he wanted to do with his life, as often many people struggle with and can even more often get trapped by success in one area. Mark selected religion, not that 'selected' was the word he used. She had learned this by watching a highly edited corporate video on the website of his current employer, Baxter Enterprises. Each executive had a video with their bio page. He said "I had been called to serve," this part was highly edited as Mary noticed the multiple audio cuts and choppy changes in Mark's posture. She needed to see it again, opening the link again from her organized research bookmarks in her computer browser, she turned up her audio, now echoing in her apartment, and played it again, "I had been called to serve (audio cut), helping others and leading by example like (audio cut)." She watched the bio videos of the other corporate executives, and there were no weird edits. Why was Mr. Soliers video so choppy? It seems he must have said things that didn't match the corporate profile. She marked it as 'ODD'. Which gave her another task, she needed to interview Mr. Solier. She set her alarm to wake up early.

Her alarm went off as planned, she reached for her phone. Her morning routine was disrupted. She could barely see without at least one cup of coffee. She blinked a few times and looked up Mr. Solier's phone number in her phone. She was glad she had the forethought to add it to her contacts when Louise gave her the phone directory. She called to set up an appointment with Mark and a new voice at Baxter learned of Mary Morgan. Audrey Barnols, Mary wrote down her name, she did her job, and scheduled the meeting.

Mary continued her detailed efforts via web and interviews to connect the timeline of Mark's life and experiences. She found out more about Mark by making calls to a few people listed in his high school yearbook that had been in the same after-school clubs. She learned that the other regular-aged high school students were jealous of Mark; he had it made, recruiters, scholarships, and clear direction. The majority of boomer kids didn't have it so well. Things were scary in the early eighties, the world was unpredictable, bomb shelters still existed, Arab control of the world's most valuable oil resources, and people were worried the cold war would turn hot at any moment. The classmates she talked with told Mary that nothing seemed to bother Mark. He was at peace when no one else was. A lot of people felt his religion was brainwashing him as it looked like that from the outside. If you didn't know Mark, whom a lot of people didn't, you would think he was raised in a strict house of religion. He preached and spoke to everyone about his faith and little else, often sharing innate details of biblical stories not often known by even the most experienced scholars.

20

Give, and it will be given to you. Good measure, pressed down, shaken together, running over, will be put into your lap. For with the measure you use it will be measured back to you.
   - Luke 6:38

Mark got more of Alice than he did of Jim. His physical makeup was one that mirrored pieces of his mother and then there were common traits that you see in any Virginian. His mental makeup was neither. Jim, the father Mark never knew, was known as a one-way, my-way, type of man. He was honest, but as the path of compromise was started with Jim, regardless of subject, no one could remember any movement. A one-way compromise with Jim was considered a success, some would joke. The one thing that kept him as one of the most respected men in town, was not his approach, but more his commitment. He was first to show up when help was needed, even before he was asked. This was the common link between Alice and Jim. They met when Jim was with the local handyman, Danny Waterson, fixing her mother's downspouts. Alice's father, known by all by just his last name, Ritter, had fallen in his attempt to fix them, and that afternoon, while her father was still at the doctor, Jim and Danny had arrived to finish the spouts. There was no waiting in Jim's world, it was now or now, that was it.

Alice was at home in her early twenties when her father fell. Her mother accompanied the fire truck, which picked up her father and transported him to the doctor in lieu of the ambulance the town didn't have. A broken leg seemed to be the prognosis that the fireman gave. It had been about an hour and Alice was alarmed at a sudden noise in the Ritter house, and then voices from the front. She observed two men, one she knew to be Danny Waterson, who had fixed some things for his mother before, and the other was Jim Solier she thought, recently returned from the Army. She didn't recognize him at first; he had changed from the days at the schoolhouse.

Jim, of course, even at his young age had his own way of doing things. Lucky for Jim, he had a friend in Danny, someone that looked after his attitude. Danny grew up here, being a hometown boy, grown into a man, he served as the only volunteer constable. Danny looked after others and over a course of months, had set up coincidental meetings between Jim and Alice. She eventually got accustomed to Jim's constant use of the Army slang for agreement, "Hooah". It scared her as he often said it very loud.

Jim married Alice after three months of courtship. It was more sudden than most of the small town, or any town would have expected, but Jim's move to find work outside of Ackerford prompted the occasion. Jim was recruited to work for a shipping company in Norfolk bay. An Army friend let him know about the opportunity, where preference was being given to veterans. Ironically, Jim got hired and his Army pal didn't. Jim couldn't and wouldn't pass it up; there really wasn't room for compromise. The marriage and the move to Norfolk occurred in the same month. Alice would lose her maiden name of Ritter and take Jim's surname of Solier. The new couple would be getting started in the nearby, yet not too close, per Jim, military town of Norfolk. Alice and Jim started their life together and it would soon end, through a sudden ending to Jim's uncompromising approach.

Jim had worked too hard and seen too much violence while in the Army to believe in much beside himself. Mark didn't get much of Jim, other than half his genetic code, surely no memory, as he had been a baby when his father died. Mark had nothing more than a few weeks of time, where Jim was often more angry and resentful than normal. It was only after his death that Alice finally did what she wanted to do. Moving back to her hometown of Ackerford was her first step towards her new life with baby Mark. Her second was changing her name back. She would again be known as Alice Ritter.

After Jim Solier died, and after Alice moved back to Ackerford, the local community wrapped themselves around Alice, an unfortunate young widowed wife, and her new baby. The community learned his name was Mark and he just had his first birthday. The support came from the local church. It had just been recently built. Even though Alice didn't express the need for help, the newly built church and the growing congregation delivered the support without being asked. There were bake sales and special offerings, volunteer lists for lawn mowing, house maintenance, and handyman needs. The town of Ackerford was like that, small, supportive, and responsive to needs before they were needed.

21

Casting all your anxieties on him, because he cares for you.
- 1 Peter 5:7

Already short of breath in the Denver mile-high air, Lori regretted climbing the stairs instead of taking the posh elevator, she unlocked her door with the keypad, "I am now so fancy I no longer need a key," she thought. Sleeping well the night before, a shower and a short walk to the post office, what seemed like a workout carrying the bundles of mail and climbing the narrow stairs, didn't help Lori acclimate to the new elevation, nor to her new environment in her new apartment. The apartment had most of her stuff. Angela did a great job getting it moved so fast, setting it up nearly identical to her old apartment in Ackerford, but it all still felt unfamiliar to her. Lori had undone the rubber bands around the tightly wrapped mail bundles and it nearly spread itself all over the table, some had dropped on the floor. She was busy tossing aside the mail she knew to be a waste, credit card inquiries of all sorts. Most addressed to this other person she was trying to forget, her former self Mary Morgan, a person she recently knew well. That was all to change. A few days, maybe weeks from this discovery of her mail volume and she would be Lori Philbus forever. A hard decision, but one Jack strongly advised so there was no alternative. She found very little mail of interest, sorting solicitations from others, knowing she'd have to shred it all. She would rely upon Jack's office for most of her cleanup work. Angela would help, and Jack would order the steps to create a neat, near clean slate of her past life, her old life as Mary Morgan. Her mind drifted a bit as the monotonous process took over. She focused on her future, organizing her to-do list and sorting the mail. She didn't see the letter, addressed by hand, a man's handwriting and no return address. She aimlessly tossed it in the read later pile. If only she had mistakenly sorted it to the shred pile, her life would have moved on to her lifelong dreams, instead, it moved closer to a discovery, a revelation she would never forget, and always regret.

22

If I whet my glittering sword, and mine hand take hold
on judgement; I will render vengeance to mine enemies,
and will reward them that hate me.
  - Deuteronomy 32:41

Hours of work and research often produced results, Mary knew, that it took a combination of curiosity, effort, and often what Mary called logical guessing to come up with the puzzle pieces that made no sense by themselves, but after getting a few that were even loosely connected, it leads you to more that filled in the overall picture.

Mark Solier didn't do much during his college years, which was the overall conclusion made by Mary. He was younger than everyone, entering college as a sixteen-year-old after she did some simple math from his birthday and his admission date from his school records. The rest of what she could find of Mark's historical records told the story or lack of story. It was inconclusive was her first thought, and boring was her second. She sighed. She felt desperate to find something, anything to bulk up her brief, slowly becoming an unsupported theory, on the background of the supposed killer. Mary planned a visit tomorrow to Mark's college, not that she would find anything from more than twenty years ago, the late eighties was just the beginning of digitizing the past, but it was worth a shot. She would get a tenure list, look for professors over twenty years of tenure and start asking questions. She had very little else.

Mary had her list, four professors were still at Mark's college. Her first thought should have been a relief that she didn't hit a dead end, but it was more related to what kind of professor stays thirty years at a college like Averett, once a woman's college and converted in the early seventies to become coed. Her first visit, without an appointment, was with Wilber Bradferst, tenured thirty-eight years, his name even sounded old to Mary, likely his memory was also layered with dust.

Mary was listening to Dr. Bradferst, she needed something, anything to provide some meat or even filler to her legal brief. It was obvious to Mary after only a few minutes that the reason Wilbur had been there so long, was he couldn't survive doing anything else. At least he was smart enough to know his limitations. Mary was dealing with his other limitation, making a succinct point, she felt bad for the last thirty-eight years of students who actually paid to listen to him. Dr. Bradferst only remembered Mark from his first year, a young man as he entered the college at the age of sixteen, remarkable, however even more remarkable, and what made him remember Mark was that this was his second degree. Wilbur remembered that Mark had it difficult at first. It was a rough time for him in our country's initial battle with the Gay and Lesbian movement, it was in full swing. Some other kids, punk kids is what Wilbur called them, hassled Mark the first month he was there, Mark being younger and smaller. The punk kids being the rich kids of overtly ignorant families from the Christian south. Dr. Bradferst didn't hold back, and Mary noted his opinion, his details, and what he said next, "those punk kids got what they deserved."

Mary searched online and found what she was looking for in the local news. The article detailed the deaths of three college students dying in a car crash. They were classmates of Mark's at the time, Mary checked the dates. They died drowning in the river. There was no alcohol involved. Mary wrote down their names; Gilbert Maximillian, Rick Saxon, and Fred Jully.

She now had three more freakish accidental deaths associated with Mark Solier. That totaled five. His father Jim Solier, his Aunt, Jessica Bonley, and now these three college bullies. How many more would she find?

23

*Whoever goes about slandering reveals secrets, but he
who is trustworthy in spirit keeps a thing covered.*
   – Proverbs 11:13

The thing that made Stephen C. Canner most proud of himself was his ability to connect two weak facts into a real story. The reality is that he had run his well dry by just plain pissing too many people off in this city. His once sensational fact-based reporting became wrong. He went from being the good guy to being a pompous idiot in a lot of people's views. The opinion section of the paper was full of non-fans of Stephen C. Canner. The same media company that owned Channel 5 owned the paper and they didn't really like him either, but the viewership on TV and the spark it provided to the struggling paper was not to be overlooked. The actual cost of the ongoing Canner antics was small with a lower level office, a worthless low paid admin, and his dedicated producer, who many thought they were romantically involved, and a waiting room full of months-old hand-me-down magazines.

The story that he had ready for tonight was relating the

local college and the Backson accident in Ackerford. The interest from the station was that the college, infamous for its recent growth from a small locals-only college to a more value add program-based college, now taking taxpayer money, was involved with Stephen C. Canner. Supposedly, their law department was doing research for Channel 5 at the prompting of Stephen C. Canner. This was shocking to the producers and the anchorman, who graduated from the college and was considered a local boy done "good" in this city. The anchorman's shock, as he couldn't hide on his face, turned to surprise and then optimism to hear this connection, as this was a breakthrough for the defaced reporter, often neglected in his first-floor office, whose stories only seemed to get worse. No doubt the college could help him get his stature back; maybe Stephen C. Canner was capable of change.

John was watching the evening's late Channel 5 nightly news, like always, from his couch. Tonight was slightly different, he was sitting on the edge, more closely glued than any night before. His nightly beer was sitting unopened on his coffee table. He was excited, and a little nervous, as earlier, when he was eating at his local bar, eating the same bad food as he did last week, at what was becoming his normal bar stool, he saw the preview to the Stephen C. Canner Ackerford story for the nightly news. He saw the preview on one of the bar's large TV's, but couldn't hear the sound. He was anxious to see it, left the bar early. In his quiet apartment, he now was hearing every word.

The story was presented very well thought Alan, as he sat in the anchor chair and watched the feed from the Ackerford story. The local college and Stephen C. Canner have joined forces in a collaborative effort to apply some joint resources to the investigation of the Backson Accident. The team from the University, college is what Alan knew to be true, but most people didn't know the difference, was applying their legal team from the advanced law courses offered to review potential survivor benefits for the widow and fatherless children.

The phones starting going again in Ackerford, and Billy called the Chief.

Stephen C. Canner just gloated; he did it again, what his hero William Randolph Hearst had done, converting disconnected facts into news. Stephen didn't know it was called the Yellow Press.

John shut his television off, making a loud click and the quiet enveloped the entirety of his small apartment. His ears started to ring from his age and his stress level going beyond what he could handle. He didn't even know what to think, he quickly reviewed his monthly expenses in his head, as he was pretty sure he wouldn't have a job tomorrow. He sat down, he recognized his breathing was fast and his pulse was noticeable without even measuring it, he could feel it in his neck. He tried to calm down, it only got faster.

In another part of the city, a nicer part that didn't have one-bedroom apartments, the phone rang. Jack picked it up without saying hello as he recognized the number, things were said and Jack pushed a button on the TV remote and was now watching the news too. He caught only the last part of the Stephen C. Canner story.

The phone call was from someone who was also on that outside boundary, however different from Jack, in that he was actively doing something about it. Ralph Stoufer ran the legal department at the college. He wasn't in charge, but his influence was great. He wanted it that way. The actual head of the college legal department was a former DA and was so worn down with the misaligned intentions of today's lawyers; he did little more than put a face to the college when they needed him. This gave Ralph freedom to drive grassroots like change. The phone call was short and the idea was intelligent of using this story and the ambitious reporter to initiate a grassroots movement from the people about the need for fact-based law, instead of the now corrupt, confusing use of precedent-based case law. It supported what Jack and Ralph believed, it helped the school and it could help drive campaign funds, at least in Virginia, a state that was always on the fence during presidential elections.

"Get to work, let me know what you uncover," Jack stated to Ralph. He knew Ralph was energized, and giving objection or counsel never worked, so he said OK and let him run with it.

"I'll get it done, it's a long shot, but the spark is there, let's add some fuel."

Jack hung up with one thought. The small town of Ackerford, Virginia, his hometown, a town he once owned as a youth, was about to be put on the map.

Jack kept in touch with what many called the outside boundary of the law. Many law scholars were disgusted with the progress or rather lack of progress the judicial system has made. As the law is based on facts and precedents, it would only make sense that more lawyers, more cases, more prece-dent is a recipe for disaster. The outside boundary approached law from a fact-only methodology, disregarding the entire concept of case law. There was a belief that so much of the precedent was shit, so much of the news was a distraction. Jack knew what most didn't, it was called the Yellow Press, used as a weapon by some defense attorneys, and it often influenced the public, the judges, and juries. More and more cases even contradicted each other due to too many judges and lawyers taking the easy way out, that precedent was, or as Jack and many others thought, needed to be, a dying form of law. Even the recently Republican nominated presidential candidate, Joe Callahan, made the case for reform within the judicial system. Jack had called his old friend just the day before to talk about bringing back core values to the legal system, by core values, Jack meant facts, but Joe didn't want to disturb too much of his campaign funds. Jack agreed with him, to take a softer message on his first upcoming national campaign speech.

He remembered Joe said, "Using facts is a scary thing for most people, lawyers or laymen."

The phone call had barely just disconnected, Ralph stopped pacing in his bedroom, his wife watching him now, as he sat down, excited, opening his laptop. Ralph went to work. The news continued on other unimportant topics, Ralph typed on his keyboard and clicked his mouse as his wife drifted off to sleep. Ralph heard her say something, but only realized she was probably talking to him after she was already asleep. One product of twenty-five years of marriage was selective hearing and the other was the ability to accept it. His wife's quiet snores were her way of acceptance of his passion for finding the details, the unsorted facts that almost always led to the truth. He got up, shut off the television. It was quiet. His brain was on fire. Ralph was excited to get started, 11:36 pm or not, he softly closed his aging laptop, low on battery, and quietly left their bedroom, hustling his fifty-eight-year-old, also aging and low on battery, body down the steps, both flights, to his basement getaway, also known and claimed to the IRS as his home office. He was older, but he was connected. A life of curiosity created a life of inquiry. Being organized, he established some research methods using technology and good old deduction process to fill in the gaps when no one else could. Often filling in the gaps with multiple scenarios, allowing Jack's cases over the last forty years to shift on the fly as they, or rather he, was always prepared. For this new case, if that's what it was, being fueled by the media, he knew he had to find the facts. Equipped with high-speed internet and a plethora of public, paid and government-only research sites he started the process. Establishing the case objective, he reviewed what he knew, as his connected home office came to life and the equipment started to hum.

24

Learn to do good; seek justice, correct oppression; bring justice to the fatherless, plead the widow's cause.
– Isaiah 1:17

R alph's internet search found a lot. He knew it would, and was glad it did. In research, specifically legal research; more was better. Most of his colleagues looked for precedent as most cases were created and proven, based on previous judgment. The judgment part was the problem. As a judge could decide, set a precedent and the future judges would find it hard to overturn, therefore giving the law new life, as now two cases were proven making it even harder, virtually impossible to have facts mean anything the next time.

Ralph had been working with Jack since college. At Yale, Jack was what would today be called an "influencer". He was involved in nearly every wave of change at the school and created some himself. Ralph was a recluse, but Jack respected his skills. They were aligned then, and now, on making sure the details and the facts drove the outcome. Simply said, if you didn't know, don't assume, go find out. The years of fighting the fight, identifying the injustice, and then driving the actions towards justice, Ralph loved it. If Jack was upfront, the face of the effort, Ralph was the foundation of their cause, the work that got done to rework cases, the work that would drive national change, or like now, local justice.

Ralph looked at the facts, not the outcome of the cases that came up in his search. He added them to his database. They often cross-referenced themselves, as Ralph had been at this for a while. One thing Ralph never did is assume he captured the details. Nothing wrong with review, he thought, so he often spent time on the same cases, some, he's seen more than once, some enough he could probably try the case again by memory.

Ralph went to bed late and was up early reviewing his work from the night before. He started every case with a profile of everyone involved. Who they were, where they were from, who was their inner circle, credit reports, background checks. He leaned back feeling the relief that he was well connected, both to the public internet databases and many private resources. He and Jack had relationships built over the last forty years. He had access no ordinary citizen had. Access to databases that had information about individual citizens. The program launched after the terrorist attacks of 9/11. The FVEY, officially called the Five Eyes was a joint program between Australia, Canada, New Zealand, the United Kingdom, and the United States. Jack helped write the law, Ralph got access to facts. Access to PRISM, XKeyscore, Tempora, MUSCULAR, and STATEROOM. From start to now, less than ten hours and he had a complete profile of everyone involved, or so he thought, he didn't yet know the name Mark Solier.

Ralph's focus was on the victim, a Charles Backson as Ralph checked his name and correct spelling. Charles Backson was someone who was in a high-stress job at Baxter Enterprises, married twelve years based on the marriage certificate filed with the state of Virginia, to a Susan, formally Susan Richards, he had two children, a seven-year-old daughter, named Jamie, middle name, Susan, likely after her mother, a son of twelve, Adam, middle name Charles. They were consistent if nothing else thought Ralph. Charles Backson was a transplant from city life to rural life, three years ago, based on the real estate filing found online. Ralph knew something else, Charles Backson was born a city boy, his birth certificate noted he was born at Retreat Doctors' Hospital, the oldest hospital at more than one hundred and forty years old. Everyone that was from Richmond and older than forty, was born there. It also told Ralph the move to the far suburbs was not his choice or was at least rationalized. City people stayed in the city, they needed the noise.

Charles had worked at Baxter Enterprises since the beginning. He no doubt helped grow it and had given part of his health in the form of stress to the growth of the company. He was committed. He was promoted a little less than a year ago, per the companies press releases Ralph found online for the last twenty years. Charles' promotion was unique as he was leaping over a couple of typical corporate promotions to be named, Head of Research for Consumer Pharmaceuticals. He bought the white Mercedes the same week he was promoted, as Ralph compared the Baxter press release with the DMV documents he retrieved. A minivan to a Mercedes was a big move.

Ralph didn't see it last night, he had just printed it for review today, but he looked over the VIN report he got from his online source. The first thing he noticed was that the car had a salvage title. He highlighted this, took a note, and knew he'd revisit that one in the future. Ralph enjoyed when insurance companies fought each other, the life insurance versus the car insurance. No doubt the two insurance companies would have a field day with this.

He shook off the unproductive smile and started to dig again, his office was still humming.

His wife noticed his late nights and early mornings but said nothing. There was more activity than normal in the basement of Ralph's house, old enough to be on the city registry as being historic. The walls were brick from the original construction, created by hand, laid by other hands, and painted every year by Ralph, his favorite color, tan. Ralph had spent the previous four days, from sun up to when he could no longer think straight, immersed in the growing potential of this case to search, find, and highlight the need for facts. He took his hands off his keyboard, stared as he normally did at the clean, smooth tan walls, the moment occurred to him that he had everything but he really had nothing.

He had found more about the case than he would have initially thought, but even with the stretch of the legal system, no facts to support anything other than a single-car accident and a potential fight between the life and car insurance industries. Ralph sighed his last sigh of hope. He knew that they were two ugly industries, both of which stabilized themselves through investment in lobbyists and relationships, which means there were legal bribes that have occurred that would make this angle useless as nobody would get near it, they were untouchable.

He leaned back in his chair, took a deep breath, and called Rucker with a message of fact, but one that put this case, if that's what it was, off his desk and in the storage file.

"Jack, there is no precedent here, and the facts to convict someone of murder using only their mind are circumstantial at best."

Ralph would soon discover he was wrong.

25

Why do you pass judgment on your brother? Or you,
why do you despise your brother? For we will all stand
before the judgment seat of God.
  – Romans 14:10–12

Mary had taken no additional time than normal to get ready for the discussion with Mr. Solier today. Audrey, Mary remembering this was Mark's executive admin, had called that morning, luckily before Mary had taken the time to be ready and leave. Audrey asked if it was all right to modify the morning meeting to a lunch appointment, which didn't really matter to Mary, and she accepted. Audrey sounded nice, an instant yellow flag as Mary was skeptical to start. She was too nice, it felt like something else was going on, Mary turned it into a red flag and decided to be cautious. Audrey nicely said she would set it up and call her back. Audrey represented Mark well, but Mary having met this type many times, couldn't help but feel a little suspicious, moving towards defensive. She always felt it was better to question everything than accept the circumstances as they seemed on the surface. Especially after the openness of

Louise at the reception desk, and now the way too professional reservation she sensed from Mark's executive admin.

Deciding to wear a simple ensemble of jeans and a dressy blue blazer, she showed up a little late. Mr. Solier was waiting at the hostess station with a smile, one that was almost uncomfortable for Mary.

He immediately said, "Hi, good to see you, glad you could change your plans to meet my schedule."

Mary replied only after listening, making eye contact to make sure he took her seriously, many people didn't and that was frustrating.

She thanked him, "That is OK, my schedule is my own while I'm in school." Then a little defensively, "I have plenty to do though, probably too much."

She then told him, in her most serious tone, "Mr. Solier, I wanted to ask you..."

Mark interrupted her and said, "I'm too young to be called 'mister'," as he smiled.

She was now uncomfortable and filled the silence, "OK, sorry, but thanks for being available to talk about," she paused to be deliberate in her tone, " The Charles Backson incident." Looking for a reaction.

"No problem," said Mark.

She saw no reaction, he was stone-faced and his tone flat.

Mary had spent the short time she had scheduled with Mark Solier on the questions she wanted to ask. She knew them by memory and even had multiple avenues to pursue, depending on where his answers took her. The trick to this investigative interview, as she determined when she started the process, was to ask questions that would frame her case, without giving away the purpose. She did tell him she was a law student and her instructor had assigned the incident, she was careful not to say accident, as a case to prepare compensation to the victim's family. Again, she was very careful to avoid any monetary reference in her wording. To anyone listening, and hopefully, to Mark, it was just normal dialogue, not wanting to sound like a lawyer, or worse, a journalist. She practiced her tone in the car on the way over to sound like what she was, a college kid doing a required paper. Everyone was willing to help with that, it often broke down their defenses and allowed her to get more information, more facts. She felt she only had one chance and knew she had less than a week not to make a fool of herself.

"I know that Louise can be a handful," Mark apologized. "I used to spend the first hour of my day with her once we moved into the new building and hired Louise as our company greeter. It took me about three weeks of this laborious commitment, even for someone like me, to hear every story twice."

Mary laughed and considered the 'someone like me' comment, she wanted to know more, Mark laughed with her.

Mark thought Mary was nice in person and his first observation from a few weeks ago was back at the office from
his desk on one of the high definition security cameras with
bidirectional rotation and 10x zoom. He knew it was her from
the online image search he did the day before. Baxter had
great technology, the cameras covered the entire parking lot,
on all sides of the building, the executive parking garage, and
Mark was good at operating them. His initial observation
assessment was now confirmed; she was a talented, beautiful
woman. Mark had a difficult time meeting women, due to
his position at Baxter and his generally, what others called
monk lifestyle. He liked it though, living a simple life, not
needing material things, not having a television, being mostly
by himself, reading, helping others. This type of life was like
his destiny extended from his isolated childhood, but it did
have its limitations. One of those limitations was now sitting
in the restaurant with him.

Besides meeting women, his other limitation was his openness and honesty towards everyone, as was apparent by
Mary's first reaction to his comment about seeing her on the
security cameras a few weeks ago when she visited Baxter
Enterprises for the first time. She was instantly repulsed,
as too many times the stereotype is a creepy motive. Mark
explained that he was reviewing Baxter procedures for visitor
traffic when she had arrived and his only intention after the
required procedural audit was to bail her out from Louise, from
what others have called the Louise effect. Mary arrived in the
parking lot at the start of the security audit and after complete
review, the security officer told Mark she was still there, now
in the lobby. Mark continued in detail about the security audit

and testing steps. Mary realized her reaction was nonverbal negative, with arms crossed and no doubt a scowl of some type and directly staring at the person offending her. As he continued, her posture went from defensive to aggressive, after being told she was being watched by two men she didn't know. If nothing else, she realized one of Mark's weaknesses was he was too open and honest. This was something she could use to get the info she wanted. Mark continued with telling her every detail.

"Sam was the name of the security officer, he has been there for more than ten years and we are friends," Mark droned on, "and I am also on-site during each review. Which is the procedure."

Mark took his job seriously and so did Sam. Sam also knew Louise, he didn't have the three weeks of patience needed to hear her stories multiple times that Mark had and Sam knew he wasn't probably on the shortlist of Louise's friends. Sam suggested that Mark might be able to help out with this one, and besides it would be a good time to audit the visitor notification process, as the Police Chief from Ackerford was coming by later that day.

Mary listened closely, Mark was genuine and the overall creep feeling went away. It was clear he was telling the truth and the camera spying was truly a coincidence, nothing more.

She didn't forget her mission and started where any discussion should start, nothing flashy and nothing to indicate her true motives.

"So Mark, what do your duties entail at Baxter?" and a quick second question without waiting for the answer to the first, "What does your normal day look like?" asked Mary.

Mark started with his title, which was impressive for a what she guessed was a late-thirties man, as he was the Executive President for Baxter Ethics and Standards.

"The security audits are a serious part of the standards functions within my duties," stated Mark.

Mary knew in print, this statement would look like an excuse, but Mary noted he rolled facts off like they were the gospel truth. A talent that she noticed even back at the Baxter lobby with Louise, but she chalked it up to 'charm' then, but now she confirmed it was genuine. She let her mind drift to the upcoming hopeful court scene and how well he would show for the defense in front of a jury. She now took it further, thinking how he would react in court. He'd probably have a new haircut, a new suit. Of course, when stating the truth, you should look truthful, who knows if he was capable of doing this under oath, charged with murder. This thought abruptly pulled her out of the fantasy of a murder trial, as if the case would actually go to court, she sighed and continue to listen for facts.

Mark continued as Mary now quickly took notes via old school shorthand, on purpose as most people couldn't read it, "The ethics board is very active at Baxter, it was taken seriously even before I was put in the position of regulating our policy with religious culture, both historical and mainstream philosophy."

He had Mary's attention now, as she had never heard of any ethics board playing to the religious community, especially a drug research company invested in saving lives with what most saw as exotic, not God friendly science, either by treat- ment or pain reduction to prolong their quality of life. Her memory was doing its job, as she recalled every detail. His words, nonverbal actions, his tone, the security cameras. This revelation caused her to write something down, Mark paused as she picked up her pen again. She pressed her pen harder than she realized, writing a few question marks and something that would later get her attention, "???? LEARN MORE", knowing she needed more information about Mark's religious background.

26

I said in my heart, God will judge the righteous and the wicked, for there is a time for every matter and for every work.
  - Ecclesiastes 3:17

Mary was in her apartment, tired from her full day preparing for, then interviewing Mark, and afterword, sorting out the seemingly endless, discombobulated information she wrote down. She was tired from her need to see and hear everything, even more from having written it all down. Just talking to overtly professional Audrey for the second time in just a few days was enough to waste her time and sap her energy. Learning she was watched by two men on a security camera, under the guise of a security audit, creeped her out even more now. Meeting with Mark, having lunch she didn't enjoy, and listening to details she didn't need, was exhausting. Her brain was spent, her hands were cramped from writing more than ten pages of shorthand notes. She took the creaky, dusty, always dirty stairs because the building elevator was still broken. It had been broken so long the sign wasn't even there telling the residents anymore.

Everybody knew it was broken and had no hope it was ever to be fixed. Low-income apartments were full of people without money. As a college student, she qualified to be there. She had a bad dinner, and an even worse latte she picked up on her way home. The coffee was the one fancy thing she rewarded herself. The local coffee shop just couldn't keep people employed to keep the coffee consistent. She mentally moved on, smiled, and took her second sip. The to-go window was open late, and at least it was hot. She checked the time as it approached 11:40 pm. She sat on her couch and took inventory of what she thought she knew. A week ago, she sighed and shook her head, boy has that much time passed, a man with a wife and two kids was killed right near the Ackerford city limits, but still in the county. She pulled out the newspaper article from her folder and reviewed it. Charles Backson was killed at 5:42 pm on Highway 603 going east. His late-model Mercedes sedan had skidded off the road by crossing the westbound lane and going into the culvert. Mary had stopped at the accident site on her way to Baxter Enterprises the other day, or as she had written in her notes, using all caps, 'MURDER SCENE'. She only took a few pictures and knew she'd have to come back the next day. She then powered up her laptop to download the pictures she took on her way to Baxter Enterprises, she hit the OK button and downloaded the pictures labeled MS 1-8, MS was for Murder Scene, she had to remember to not label any pictures of Mark Solier, MS, a simple coincidence she disregarded. As she downloaded the pictures from her low-grade digital camera, she thought about what could've happened. She leaned back in her chair, she had time as her computer, like her camera, was also old, and slow. It was now making some concerning noises during what now seemed like

116

was a longer than normal boot-up time. She forced her mind back to the murder scene, maybe someone had cut him off and escaped the scene? She wondered if there was any damage to the car that wasn't from the accident, something that would support her foul play, murder accusation. She wrote down to go see the car tomorrow. The first picture was done, and she saw the preview of the tire tracks that started in the victim's own lane and went to the left. The second picture started to download and covered her laptop screen. She wrote down on her legal pad to check the Mercedes brake options, she had to assume it had anti-lock brakes, which would prevent the skid marks and make a hard stop controllable, but she didn't know for sure, just what she stored from the abundance of car commercials she'd seen. It's not like her Toyota wagon actually had them, she laughed out loud that she felt lucky just to have brakes, let alone anything related to anti-lock. Her camera showed only 33% download complete of the next picture, she checked her clock and it showed 11:55 pm, five minutes from being one day closer to the due date of her assignment. The picture download progress bar now showed 34%, it would be a long night as she took another needed sip of the getting more stale fancy coffee.

As Mary continued her camera download, she started her mental one. She examined her detailed notes and started to organize the facts in an order that made sense. She quickly realized there were large gaps in the story of murder, missing facts, missing points, just plain missing the proof, not even close. There was beyond a reasonable doubt her case, barely a theory would fail. She kept going. Mark's life was remarkable, yet plain. He had visited Brazil in his early twenties, going on his mission, as he described it. But Mary learned it was a solo mission, he just went by himself, to help people he read about in Life magazine. It was about a village near the Amazon river, in Anori, she learned he flew into Manaus and took a boat, hopefully with a guide which she didn't ask, thinking now, as she read her own notes, Mark was either stupid or determined. He had been there for seven months. She had written it all down and confirmed the spelling earlier. She found the name of the mission in her notes and searched online. She quickly found the mission group's contact information online and quickly typed off an email to their current director. Mary noted it was a hotmail.com email, not realizing that the Hotmail email company even existed anymore, losing some hope she'd ever get a reply.

Her energy slowed, the caffeine she used to keep going could no longer overcome her long day. She caught sight of herself in the mirror she kept in her room. The story there was one of a struggling student who couldn't let the truth go, or at least the truth she wanted to believe. She had felt this way often, and when she did, she did the same thing, she forced herself to fix her posture, bring her optimism for the facts back to the surface, and continue her work. It had never failed her before, she had needed to do it often, as she found herself often on an island of ideals, instead of being part of a group or even leading the majority. She didn't always like the island of ideals but had once been pressured to the mainland, which she thought of as the blind acceptance of normal. She had regretted it ever since and now used it to gain her energy and optimism that her efforts were worth it. She turned back to her notes, saw the gaps again, and this time started asking herself questions, questions about the missing facts and the actions to obtain the rest of the story, island or not, she moved forward, just like she always did. Saying to herself out loud, exhausted but determined, it echoed in her silent apartment, "If not me, then who, to get justice for the injustice."

27

He will wipe away every tear from their eyes, and death shall be no more, neither shall there be mourning, nor crying, nor pain anymore, for the former things have passed away.
  – Revelations 21:4

When she fell asleep due to exhaustion, the next day was always torture to get things done. Mary felt like she hadn't slept as her alarm went off at 7:29 am, she always gave herself that one minute to get motivated. She organized her thoughts from the night before, as she had pulled together what she knew. The framework for her case had begun. Today, she had a few critical appointments, the first with Susan Backson, then she planned to go see the impounded wrecked Mercedes, and finally a visit with her law professor, Mr. Stacker. She sighed at the last one, knowing it was a waste of time.

She drove out to the Backson house. On the way she took the route that had her go past the murder scene, she didn't even notice she'd become so convinced of her efforts, that she now thought of it as a murder scene. The drive was about forty-five minutes, but going this way extended the route versus the freeway, so she intended to leave early. Her morning happened fast, she was motivated. Shower first, breakfast next. Thinking so much about her day, she was delayed by the shock she saw on the morning news. The shock that they were covering the same story she was investigating. Such a shock, Channel 5 almost made her scald herself with her morning coffee, a lawsuit though, not murder, she thought, as the shock wore off and she put the morning facts in place. As she was getting dressed, this time in her best lawyer outfit, as she calculatingly chose to impress upon Ms. Backson she was more than a student. The news was broadcasting the story about the accident in Ackerford. They had the same facts she had, recapping the things she already knew. Must be a slow news day to talk about a single-car accident in the suburbs. She clicked the off button on the TV remote on the way out the door, grabbing her keys and hoping her car would start.

She was now out on the road, the scenery not noticed as it blurred by her, she was accidentally speeding. She had slept hard, but not well, not that she remembered it, but she felt it driving west towards the Backson residence, the morning news story playing over and over in her mind. She didn't have a list of questions for this interview, but more an abyss of facts. She wanted to know more and she wanted to start with the source, the Backson house. She checked her speed, her watch, and dialed Susan Backson, hopefully getting the right number from the web, as it was the last thing she remembered doing last evening, which was really the morning she thought, as her time to bed was well after 2 am. Her phone connected and it started to ring.

"Hello?" was the first word as was expected, but immediately Mary could tell Susan Backson was hesitant. Mary realized the morning news may have been the source of her hesitancy, little was she aware of the things that had already been part of the poor widow's morning.

Mary told Susan the truth over the phone, she wouldn't have it any other way. Mary was surprised a little at the positive tone and the acceptance of her request to meet up.

"I've had too many inquiries, all of which have been too direct and less than meaningful," said Susan, without prompting.

Susan's response was not really very surprising to Mary, "I'm sorry to hear that," Mary knew most people would be callous, their self-interest out front. Mary intended to suppress hers in order to get the facts.

"I look forward to a discussion with you about Charlie," Susan said.

"I'm on my way and will be there in about fifty minutes," Mary said to keep the conversation flowing.

Susan immediately commented that she was only thirty minutes away, "Is there traffic?"

Mary sensed some hesitancy in her voice, and not seeing her non-verbal queues, she now needed to lie, she said there was traffic and she wanted to take her time.

"OK, be safe and I'll see you soon, goodbye," and Susan Backson's voice was gone, for now.

Driving was a time for Mary to focus, especially as the roads to meet Susan Backson were void of cars. Mary recognized her anxiety was translating to her foot, pushing the gas more than she wanted to; she now slowed to be sure she arrived in the stated fifty minutes but also to give her time to review what she knew already. She didn't trust Susan Backson, but she realized she didn't really trust anyone, even after she met them, so Susan Backson was no different than others.

Mary had obtained a copy of the police report filed by a Billy Jackson, odd he wouldn't use his official name on an official document, maybe his name was Billy instead of William, as these were small towns with country people.

The police report was long, twelve pages, Mary counted that morning as she initially skimmed it over breakfast, interrupted by the news, she finished it but skimmed at best. She wanted the details, but first needed context on what happened. After finishing the twelve pages, skimming or not, she identified some things that seemed to be disconnected from normal.

The presence of the gun, the peculiar specifics in the report about the gun, being a Glock 17 with a large round capacity clip. Mary, being educated on guns, but not a fanatic about them, easily picked out this detail that was clearly not normal.

This was a professional weapon, carefully selected.

The details of the body were there as well, although not a topic for today. Not sure how much Susan Backson knew about her husband's death and condition of his body, which Billy (William?) detailed, but it wasn't Mary's plan to share them, nor did she really care about how, but more about why.

The other misplaced and hard-to-understand detail was the direction and time of the travel. Why was Charles Backson going east, towards the city? He was traveling opposite to the flow of commuters, which normally he was one of them, coming from the city to their homes in the rural suburbs, getting more and more rural as Mary followed the directions to meet Susan Backson.

The directions were easy and got easier as there wasn't much to get confused about as Mary got closer to the Backson's home address.

She gave herself time, as part of the fifty minutes estimate included, unbeknownst to Susan Backson a stop at the site of where her husband died. It was on the way, as there were few roads to travel between the city and the rural homes often purchased by those with money. The murder scene as Mary thought of it, the crash site, as was written on the overly lengthy report was unrevealing, but it did remind her of the scope of her hypothesis and solidified her approach with Susan Backson. She approached the scene, measured by her trip odometer, which she had set based on the police report measurements taken by the deputy Billy Jackson. She expected to see the distinct yellow crime scene tape, blowing in the wind, alongside this country road. She slowed her car as the correct mileage showed on her odometer, she realized, once again, she was the only one thinking murder. To everyone else, it was an accident. To most, already forgotten, it doesn't affect me, it was yesterday's news. She looked out the window of her car and could still see the long and scarring tire marks. She was initially surprised they were still there from the now week-old crash, calculating that Ackerford rural had not had enough rain or traffic to wear them off yet.

Mary had pulled her car to the rural roads almost non-existent shoulder and carefully set her hazards on even though there was no traffic. She didn't want to become a news story as Charles Backson had. She parked next to the long skid marks, she guessed they were about thirty feet in length, confirming on page nine of the police report, that they were exactly forty feet-zero inches in length. Its author, Deputy Billy Jackson didn't seem to miss any details.

She set aside the report and grabbed the folder full of copied pictures of the crash site (crime scene). The day before, she visited the police department, talked with the young as she, purposefully calling him by his formal title Deputy Jackson, the report's author. He allowed her to copy the report at the police station, which was public information, she took the opportunity to put the official police photos along with the lengthy police report in the sheet feeder on the police department's taxpayer-purchased fancy copier. They were just copies and only in black and white, but they were all there, and she needed to be careful to not expose Susan Backson to any of them, they were detailed and they were gruesome. She initially looked away, from her instinct of being human, at some as she went through all of them. She now went through again without emotion to find those she could use to make sense of what happened.

No one witnessed her standing in the middle of the road holding up the images to align the perspective, thinking about what happened, not "how it happened" as she realized Deputy Jackson had that covered, but why. Why did the car crash? Why did this man die? She looked at the worst of the worst pictures. Even without color, she could see the stains of blood. He looked almost normal like he was sitting at a traffic light, except for the deployed airbag, his obvious broken neck, and the blood. She knew it was murder, just couldn't put it together, yet. She walked slowly back to her car, compiling and mentally editing the questions she would ask Susan Backson. She would not shy away from the missing questions not asked by the young Deputy Jackson or the recent visit to the Backson home by Chief Daniel Waterson. She knew about that too as Deputy Jackson told her yesterday when she was making copies. If this was just an accident, why a visit from the Chief? Yesterday when she was there, Mary saw the police department was busy when she made the copies. She was casually looking around, yet watching for someone checking on her. She saw everything, they were busy. So why was the Chief making a visit only a few days after? The report was detailed, no unanswered questions. The pictures were plenty, even maybe too many. What could concern this long-tenured Chief? He had grown up in these parts, knew everyone, knew everything. Mary had learned a lot about the Chief the night before. She knew exhaustive research pays off. The best never quit looking.

As she slowly drove down the street, she made quick glances for nonconsistent house numbers. The Backson house was what you may think would be owned by a previously mid-level manager. Mary learned about his recent promotion to Head of Research for Consumer Pharmaceuticals, she filed that under the category, LEARN MORE the night before. She had no idea what a position like that did. She did know he bought a Mercedes and she aligned this with the day after his promotion. She learned this online from the DMV and from the Baxter press release. Nice, but not overly gaudy. No doubt they had plans for a new fancy house, to go along with the fancy Mercedes. Mary sighed, let her emotions pass, as she struggled with her own finances. Looking back at the Backson home, it was an older home, that was probably gaudy when it was built but now looked normal. As she pulled into the driveway, she noticed some refinishing was done, and although once professionally done, the landscape had lapsed. The house's age could be seen by the barn on the property, near the house, in good condition but not of the recent times. Mary guessed the 1940's and wrote it down as she brought the car to a sliding stop at the end of the gravel driveway. She noted a few other items, but noted more than anything the amount of tire tracks in the soft grass, now mostly mud. Some of the tracks were from obvious large trucks, more than one.

"Hello," Susan Backson said. This startled Mary as Susan Backson had met her in the driveway, nearly yelling it through Mary's half-open car window. Susan Backson was now standing at her car window, casting a shadow over Mary's lap, covered with the thick police report and stack of copied photos. Mary was nervously looking over one final time, looking for any fact, or clue that could help her learn more. Susan was unnecessarily close.

"Hi there, good morning," Mary said in almost a stutter and was clearly startled.

"I'm sorry to have startled you!" said Susan. "Would you like some breakfast?"

Mary had looked past Susan and saw a table, on the wide wrap-around porch, set up like a tea party. A full setup of plates, pitchers full of juice, and of course, some steam coming off of miniature teacups.

Mary accepted. "That would be nice." Nice? Mary reminded herself to stay focused.

The two women, in different stages of life, sat for what looked like to anyone watching was a normal weekly tea party. Mary wasn't one for small talk, and couldn't remember the last time if ever, she had fancy tea. She often didn't, or ever have time, her crowded schedule and overfilled task list didn't give her the opportunity, nor did she like it.

Susan started with questions, "How was your drive?" "Did you find us ok?"

Mary gave the obligatory answers and recognized how nervous

Susan Backson was, shaking, using both hands, as she poured more tea, although Mary had only taken a small sip and didn't need, ask, or want more tea. She didn't like it.

In an attempt to calm her, for the end goal of getting clear and more answers she didn't already have, Mary let her know the purpose.

"Ms. Backson, I'm writing a paper for a college class, I'm not from the news nor am I part of law enforcement," Mary said as she pointed to the tracks on the front lawn, concluding there have been many visitors, mostly rude parking in the previously well-manicured grass.

"It's been a tough time since Charlie died, nobody has really listened," Susan trailed off and looked down at her hands, still shaking as she put them on her knees to steady them and her escalating emotions.

Mary was planning on the fast track form of interviewing: ask, answer, take notes, often interrupting the witness, follow-up. She switched without Susan knowing it, ready to listen and potentially get details others would have missed.

"I have plenty of time, let's just enjoy breakfast and this won-derfully strong tea," Mary put her at ease. Mary recognized non-verbals, it was a natural talent, and Susan was giving off every signal, moving from intense stress to the initial steps of relaxation; a long sigh, a reset of posture, and a genuine smile.

"Sounds great," said Susan.

Mary wrote sparingly so as not to disrupt the flow of a grieving widow and now a single mother, but mentally noted everything. She had practiced the art of memorization, a real thing she first was skeptical about. The art is using visuals, colors, and the practice of snapping a picture with your mind. She often repeated keywords that were said, back to the witness, as these solidified a place in her brain. Storing it for use later. She did this with Susan Backson, going unnoticed as she listened and repeated some of the words out loud. They were now stored in her memory, Mary would recount and update her notes later.

Over the next hour, and three more cups of tea, Susan kept talking. "It was called Typhoo tea, the second most popular brand in England," Susan Backson shared. She also shared the detailed story of her late husband, Charles Backson, typical in many ways, atypical in many others.

Mary learned that her husband had a temper, one that was slow to show but was there. He would often be slow to act, or more specific, slow to decide to act. She was somewhat embarrassed when sharing the hidden, unknown anger side of her husband, no doubt feeling shame in talking negatively about the dead.

Mary noted words like anger, revenge, rage, spite, and stronger definitions put forth by Susan that he was vindictive to her, to others, and often vengeful. Planning it and then acting on it.

130

"He was such a good father, son, husband and very predictable in the way he lived his life," Susan shared in a nearly excited tone. "There were only a few things that triggered him," in a much more cautious tone, as she broke eye contact and instantly looked distant from her present. Mary took a few mental pictures.

Mary started to ask a follow-up, attempting to repeat a few keywords for her memory, but Susan interrupted her, not hearing anything Mary said. Susan seemed to grab ahold of her emotions and restarted herself, and kept talking.

"He couldn't even hurt the raccoons, he tried to build them a new habitat, he looked up online. He tried to build it in the woods so they would leave the cover of our barn, he was equally concerned for their health and ours," Susan said, now near tears.

Mary had what she needed, except one pressing curiosity. She concluded, that Charles Backson was who the local press presented, but there were a few more things. A few important things, Susan didn't share, nor did the "in a hurry press" ask. These things were also not on the police report addendum filed by the "give me only the facts" police Chief, Daniel Waterson.

"It seemed an odd time of day to be driving to the city, where was he going?" Mary asked as casually as she could.

"He came home after lunch, which was something he never did," Susan looked down.

Mary was about to further define her question but Susan continued. Mary could see she was hesitating, then it came out.

"He was upset, I could tell by the way he barely touched his lunch, and his quick pace around the house."

Mary was writing now. This was too much information flowing, too fast for her trained mind to capture. Her physical approach took over for her mental hardware.

Susan continued, barely taking a breath, "He was talking about the raccoons, in anger, he went out the back door in a hurry and retrieved his gun from the garage."

"I watched him shuffle the trash cans a bit, holding the gun in his hand, even though we never saw the raccoons during the day and then he got back in his car."

The sadness on her face, and moisture in her eyes, told Mary that Susan might have tried to say goodbye. Mary reached out to hold her hand and Susan accepted it.

Susan gave Mary an open invitation to come back or call anytime, something she likely didn't give to the reporters or the police. Mary would follow up in a week, even if she didn't have to, or need to. Mary wanted the relationship open just in case.

Mary felt both accomplishment and sadness as she backed out the driveway. Susan was waving and continued until Mary pulled away, slowly up the street, adding a new address into her GPS. She had more to do today.

The things about a small town that are often the source of frustration are also the source of what makes a small town so attractive; the trust of strangers. Mary had no problems getting access to the salvage yard where the white Mercedes was stored. She had an elaborate story ready, knowing she wouldn't need it, but wanted to be prepared anyway. She smiled a few times and took more than twenty pictures. She had to be a little conspicuous as her cover story was she was a college journalist doing a story on seat belts, even the lazy junkyard dog would be curious why anyone needed so many pictures for such a simple story. She would look at the pictures later in detail, but during the visit, nothing of value was apparent, maybe it was the site of a human's blood, now in color, a darkened red, on the leather seats that clouded her instincts. It all looked like a crime scene, untouched, except for the removal of the body. Mary was glad she didn't see the body in the flesh. Pictures were one thing, Mary considered herself tough and ready, yet she had never seen a dead body. She also knew she never wanted to, she had no interest in death.

Mary was on a schedule still, leaving the mangled sadness and seeing other past scenes of death in the salvage yard, full of wrecked cars, and destroyed lives. She had an appointment with her professor, Mr. Stacker, she had facts and details, but probably not any topics he was expecting.

28

How long will you lie there, O sluggard? When will you arise from your sleep?
  – Proverbs 6:9

John had been up most of the night, his insomnia coming from the lack of exercise his brain was getting on a daily basis, the bad food he ate every day, and the fixation he had in late-night television, endlessly flipping channels without watching anything. He also was stressed about the reaction to the Canner story. He rubbed his eyes and yawned. He rolled out of bed, feeling the aches and pains of midlife. He got dressed in yesterday's clothes and had to blink a few times to see the calendar on his old, getting dumber every day, smartphone. He had one appointment today, couldn't see it, would check it again after some coffee.

After a few minutes and a few sips of too hot, from an un-known brand, brew coffee, he realized today was his meeting with Mary Morgan. He looked at his current outfit, knew it represented him poorly, and only had enough motivation and barely enough caffeine to change his t-shirt, he poured his to-go coffee and left his apartment for the school. His car barely started, but like him, it got moving.

John was in the building early today, for him, a few staff were there as he walked through the large front doors of the old building, shuffling to the back stairs. The elevator was broken, he actually never remembered it working in his ten years at the school. He sat at his desk in his corner office. Corner of the basement he thought. He took a few more sips of his now lukewarm coffee and waited on his first student meeting in a while. He used to hold them regularly, thinking the students wanted them. The "factless" allegation from a few female students put an end to all of these one on one meetings. The claims went nowhere, but the school didn't like the publicity back then, it wanted to stay small. It's also the reason John joined back then, not for the women, but the size of the school was a place to make change, now more than ten years ago. His thoughts and frustrations towards the new administration's "value add" marketing approach were interrupted by the door and what John thought to be one of his only bright students, Mary Morgan.

"Hi, Mr. Stacker," Mary, not on purpose, making John feel old as she called him "mister", with a too serious tone for John's, still too early, low level of alertness. Any small thoughts or hope of even a short-term relationship ran from his groin. He sighed deeply, sat down, and randomly shuffled and stacked the things on his cluttered, government surplus-looking desk.

"Hi Mary, I've been looking forward to this meeting," John said and thought about its implications if she made a claim. He would be careful, he reminded himself to keep the door open and the desk between them at all times, sexual harassment training taught him one thing, protect yourself, although the basement was empty anyway, it would be his word against hers and he'd lose.

"Well, I wanted to come and talk about the Backson Case assignment."

"OK," almost relieved as he was semi-prepared for something not school-related.

Mary picked up the surprise in his simple response.

"I've decided to not follow the norm, as you probably would have suspected." She said with a hint of nervousness, which John took as flirting. It wasn't.

"I've done multiple interviews with Mr. Backson's co-workers, Ms. Backson, and researched every detail of this case. I've developed a hypothesis that I think has some initial merit."

"OK," said John, with an attempt to look in her eyes and not show any emotion. He was still catching up, trying to listen and drop his thoughts on what he was prepared to hear.

Mary thought she was doing the right thing. Not only soliciting an early opinion but also following the unwritten protocol. Going to the press or outside counsel would have made John look really bad and potentially embarrass the school, the latter she cared more about as she couldn't make it without the partial scholarship she was receiving.

"I've got some details that show motive (this caught John's attention) for the Backson case being a murder."

John sat up straight, he felt young again.

She got what she expected, even though she always had some hope about other's ability to provide insight or value, she often just walked away with her lowered expectations being barely met. John did just that. He listened, gave her the typical rhetoric questions, and didn't take a single note. He was not interested and even showed a strong disinterest, likely sourced in that he might have to do something. Mary didn't think he was the type to have a photographic memory or use memory discipline as she did.

The moment the door latched, John nearly shit himself, he jumped out of his chair, pushing it back and it hit the wall. He grabbed his pen, put his hands to his head, and paced the office, in circles, then he grabbed his desk. He grabbed the first paper he could find, from the mess of his desk, this was easy. He furiously wrote down everything he could remember about Mary's research. He knew if he asked for copies of her work, it would show more interest than he wanted her to know, for now anyway.

He also knew the shit storm was coming. There would be a witch hunt to find out who was talking to the news, specifically to Canner. He knew someone at the school would find out.

Likely they'd think it was him, he knew he wasn't well-liked and easy to blame. He was undecided about how he felt about that. He was scared and even more excited about the last forty minutes of well-done research and professional case review from Mary Morgan. A murder case in Ackerford, and one that a surprisingly bright college student in his class was chasing the facts, the truth. One that he assigned to her, one that had biblical proportions, her words, making reference to Mark's character and the perception of him. John was nervous, he realized now his heart rate and his short breaths. He grabbed the desk again, this time to steady himself. He was beyond nervous, he was scared.

29

*A false witness will not go unpunished, and he who
breathes out lies will not escape.*
   – Proverbs 19:5

Mary had never quit anything in her life and
although everything was against her, she didn't
plan on impacting her flawless record. She was
upset, but not emotionally upset the way other college girls
could get, she was pissed, a few levels above angry. She had
done the work, used her brain, and did ten times the value,
she was pissed the school had her using that word too. She
received a grade of a C+ on her case analysis. She was a person
of action, deciding that action would take some time. What
was the legal system coming to? The schools were creating
trained monkeys afraid of anything outside of the norm and
the norm was rooted in history, a precedent that was never
challenged, what if it was wrong? She knew case law driving
bias. She saw too much laziness and not enough altruism.
The importance of facts were diminished, discounted, and
sometimes not included. It made guilty people innocent, and
in this case, the seemingly innocent, not guilty. She was trying

to hide her disgust, as she didn't want the attention, she didn't care what grades other people had received and left without discussion.

She didn't see it, but John watched her closely as he was still exhausted from last night, the late-night debate with himself in his quiet apartment, in silence, with his after ten o'clock microwave dinner and generic brand beer. This individual debate went at least three beers, and four hours, about her grade, not from the quality of work, which was excellent for even a seasoned lawyer. He didn't want the attention, he liked his life now, doing what he wanted when he wanted. It was sad he gave up his promising career, but he realized after the third beer, he no longer wanted the life of someone that cared. He couldn't decide what grade could he give that would discourage her from pursuing it further, but one that would not create alarm from her, or unneeded escalation past him. Watching her in class now, flipping through the pages of her own paper, reading his notes and suggestions he made last night. Her reaction was blank. He thought he achieved his goal as her reaction was one he wanted, enough to give it up and one that would cause inaction towards him. He put it behind him, having no instinct or inclination that it would come back to bite him, hard. Mary escalated it, following the process, and contacted the school board, all of them, email made that part easy.

The school board met monthly. There were not many things to discuss or decide. This was not the normal monthly meeting, that would be next week, this was special. There were two items on the agenda for the day, the first, the school was in the news. Every school board member was present and they knew and it was the sole purpose of this special meeting. The second, what they didn't yet know, was the related escalation from a fourth-year law student, Mary Morgan on her grade given by John Stacker. Ralph knew more importantly than her grade, it was her accusations of suppression of her remarkable findings. Both issues, the news story, and the average grade were based on what seemed to be a simple single-car accident. Soon it would be revealed to be not that simple. Ralph confirmed as much in his own research of Mary's theory, supporting facts, and her brilliant conclusions. Ralph knew it was not going to be simple.

Ralph attended every board meeting, as his role was ensuring the direction of the school was true to its values and not one that became a corporate enterprise. This was a worry of many with the new initiatives related to only focus on revenue growth, disguised as the phrasing "value add." Ralph was experienced and old enough to know what he could and could not influence. He never, nor would he ever give up on the education of local kids, Ralph called anyone young, kids. He was old, or older as he said. He cared about the past and was committed to the future. He put himself last, there were many things to do.

He had seen the news stories and probably knew them better than the others as Stephen C. Canner was one of his research subjects during his case review last week. He knew them well. It was being overblown was Ralph's instinctual conclusion. Canner was reaching out at the end of a sorry career. Ignoring actual facts and perpetuating the now century-old practice of "yellow journalism". Ralph knew Canner, his history, and he knew this was his way, it always had been, the majority of his stories died due to weak facts or lawsuits.

An hour passed, every minute of it was just process and protocols to the board members, yet more exciting to Ralph. The board reviewed the PR response to the news story, celebrating the gains it had made in the quality of its value. The review of the escalation was focused on the grade, not the content. Several board members flipped through the well-prepared brief but didn't take notes. Ralph was watching them. It was decided to recommend giving this student a B instead of C. Ralph kept his frustration, yet relief they didn't read it closer, to himself. He carefully collected the paper copies of Ms. Morgan's extraordinary yet impressive conclusions at the end of the session. He had volunteered to distribute them at the beginning, noting how many copies he handed out. There were nine board members, and he counted twice, he had all nine copies in his hands again, he counted twice, some he pulled from the open blue recycling bin. Ralph's plan to guarantee their destruction was to do it himself, in his own commercial-grade shredder in his basement.

Ralph called Jack, this time more energized than he'd been in a while. Jack answered and he sensed it immediately, Ralph was on to something. What others thought was a simple case of a car accident and possible insurance lawsuit, Mary had identified that there was too much coincidence to be just an accident. She wanted a better grade, she would get much more. This coincidence was now a smoking gun.

30

But the one who looks into the perfect law, the law of
liberty, and perseveres, being no hearer who forgets but
a doer who acts, he will be blessed in his doing.
  – James 1:25

J oe Callahan had a history, one he felt proud of for being consistent and based on principals. These principles were not something he decided upon himself, but something he learned, researched, and then decided to align with. A choice, he thought to himself. One based on those before him, like Thomas Jefferson for one. Joe thought if you were going to have principals and take big risks to not only stand by them, but to broadcast them proactively to others, they better be solid. Joe was never short on pushing judicial restraint and using Jefferson's approach to calling out 'despotic behavior' of judges. Joe stood firm with his voice, his position in every level of government he ever held, and his earned reputation against opinions turning into bias, turning in decisions without regard for the law. Activism of this kind had no place in America. Joe promoted his agenda, which had started to influence others as well. Young lawyers not yet beat down, breakaway law firms, taking the hard road, looking to use the actual law, and academic institutions bold enough to try. It was being fought at every level.

New Mexico was small enough to build a consensus but big enough to still get the attention of the entire nation alongside things happening in the larger cities. Having been born in the east, Joe was of the character to get things done. This started early in his life being raised in Springfield, Massachusetts. At the time, without choice, he had to make things happen, from an early age. Growing up without a mother, and later in life having guilt that she died as he was born, he turned this into motivation as to his importance on making big things happen. He felt he was never short on effort, and no justice for an injustice was not worth pursuing.

Coming back from the Army, serving as part policeman and part intelligence officer in Vietnam, he enrolled at Yale to pursue what he saw then and still sees as the ultimate profession of lawyer. Joe was so passionate about the law, true justice, that his lips moved quietly talking out his thoughts. He was not one that pushes papers and gets paid, but one that upholds the law, the one written by those elected by the people, for the people.

Joe now sat in his New Mexico office in Albuquerque, nothing too special for one of its two allocated US Senators, his office buried in the center of a modest office complex. The position-ing within the narrow, drab-tiled hallways was purposeful as it enabled his security team to limit the traffic and use the location as a preventative measure for those constituents that might not agree with his often unpopular approach. Joe whispered to himself, "popular be damned." He knew it was seen as an altruistic approach, that was the point. Leadership is not appeasement, it is often not popular. It is taking people where they didn't know they needed to go. Joe leaned back, checked his gun as a reminder he owned his own security too, and then started the daily necessary routine of going through his email, already filtered by importance by his staff, morning briefing documents, and polished up on his speech for the afternoon.

He still had the black eye from the years ago case of missing prostitutes, and the now recently uncovered bodies in the West Mesa area. The investigation was ongoing. He brought in Jack Rucker to help. Joe had labeled the killer of the eleven women found, one with an unborn fetus, the 'Bone Collector'. The investigation was on track. There was DNA found on all the victims under their fingernails, they had all put up a fight in their final moments. There was one killer, there was no match in the CODIS database. With Jack's quiet, behind-the-scenes, non-public guidance, the team also looked closely at when the killing stopped and another case. The case of an older man who was killed by a teenager, who was the boyfriend of the older man's final female victim lying dead. There were no records on the teenage hero. The body of the suspect was cremated, no DNA was on record. These missing person cases were unresolved and surely would come up in his campaign for president.

Of all the good he did, what he didn't do stood out front and tried to define him. When he did stand tall, he was judged then too. He remembered another fight for what was right, as a young sheriff, when the local school boards were to ban his favorite book, *Slaughterhouse-Five*, he learned his first lesson of how what is right, and what is popular, often are at odds. He remembered winning that one, allowing kids in New Mexico to have the right to read what he read, in 1969, coming back from Vietnam, having seen what he wish he didn't. War. This was a different war, not violent in a physical sense, it was a political war. One of words and perceptions. Joe prepared his mental state, wanting to combine the reality with the political needs of the people he represented in New Mexico and the people he wanted to lead, the citizens of the United States.

Todays' speech was of similar flavor to his locally known principals, both in written form and prior television appearances. Although he knew he was only one of one hundred senators and the other side of congress, four hundred thirty-five representatives, all with their own agendas, speeches, and television appearances. He had gained some national-level attention beyond his words and more from his actions; often received by the public in a love it or hate it opinion; nobody in the middle. True justice didn't have a middle.

He took every word he said seriously, not to sway opinions or that he even cared what people thought of him, but more to make an impact on the future. He took his responsibility seriously. He knew too that he was a senator from New Mexico, ranked fourteenth in population, which surprised most people it was that populated. New Mexico was a mystery to most, seen as barren desert on television shows, a place to die in western movies, and didn't have anything to offer. It was barely noted

146

for its three-digit heat index on low-value national weather maps. He knew no one cared much about New Mexico. He knew his vote, out of one hundred Senators decided for a country of more than three hundred million, counted and he took that seriously, every day.

Today's speech would reach the entire country, near-simulta neously, as state and national media would be in attendance. New Mexico had grown in population during his time as the Office of the Director for the state police and district attorney. People liked the way New Mexico was run, attracting more and more conservative minds. Joe was proud of this, the state growing 40% during his time from 1990 to 2000, and continuing to grow since then. People wanted to live where the law meant something and the follow-through to uphold it was based on principle, not opinion, not judicial activism. He was making this a cornerstone of his speech and campaign, the age-old behavior despised by Thomas Jefferson himself, 'Despotic'.

Joe used his proven approach by identifying the most impor- tant part of the speech and then worked backward to align everything with making the point and making it clear. It was a serious day, but Joe in his office, protected by the unseen security team and of course his own personal weapon, allowed himself to smile, knowing today would be a point of before and after. The before, he would be known as Senator Callahan, or even Sheriff Joe by some, Governor by others, but after today, he'd be known as Presidential Candidate Callahan running on judicial reform, a correction back to the intent of the law, the importance of the facts and the elimination of case law opinions.

The text of the speech was just words, but Joe knew every word had a history that was going to be told today about not only the virtue of the basis of our government but the people who have upheld it since the beginning, during difficult times and how he was the next step in future adherence to judicial restraint. Not popular at times, but not popular by those that broke the law or wanted to do it. Reading quietly, yet aloud in his own head, Joe practiced the critical annunciations needed to impact those that would hear him today, and the replays likely to be in rotations for weeks or hopefully months. The speech was completed, and yet full of purposeful sound bites.

"The law was the law. It was put in place by those you elected," he heard himself saying.

As was his known style and the point of his campaign, he wanted to bring forth what was the truth, communicate it and then enable people to decide on their truth, based on real sourceable facts, not his ability to ignite their emotion, to a version of a malformed political truth. He knew though, reciting the alphabet with some enthusiasm could get some people going on their own.

His speechwriter knew this, he knew to bring in something Joe could deliver with conviction, not from a point of performance, but from a deep source of commitment and passion.

Once Joe started speaking to millions there would be no turning back now. The lights were on, the camera red lights indicated they were ready and the microphone was hot. He got the thumbs up from the television producer and looked the American public in the eye.

"Black's Law dictionary is the truth of truths. It is the reference of choice for all legal briefs and court opinions, and it defines the practice of Judicial Activism, a philosophy of judicial decision-making whereby judges allow their personal views about public policy, among other factors, to guide their decisions." He was practiced from his past, and constant rehearsals to pause here, make meaningful eye contact, the start of an emotional bond with the people in the room, and hopefully, the millions watching on TV.

Joe knew this was important as the definition needed to be trusted, not his opinion on what it was, but what it was defined by the independent source for all law.

"Overturning laws as unconstitutional, overturning judicial precedent, and ruling against a preferred interpretation of the constitution is NOT what YOU deserve." Joe annunciated both 'not' and 'you' as his speechwriter knew the approach to capitalize those words that would impact the listeners.

Joe knew this would get most people's attention and provide some inside humor for Jack too. Jack was coming in from Virginia, he probably was already here as he preferred to fly commercial and come in the day before. Jack could be counted on, he was Joe's friend.

31

If we claim to have fellowship with him and yet walk
in the darkness, we lie and do not live out the truth.
– 1 John 1:6

J ack was on the Yale campus, with limited classes in his senior year and his grades in the top ten of his class, not knowing for sure the other nine; he was spending the day doing what any good Bonesman would do; spying on possible new recruits.

A recent transfer to Yale was also a Vietnam veteran, but not one you would know by looking at him. Jack had been watching and following him all day, albeit undetected. Jack was careful, he knew this recruit was both trained in police activities and spent the last two years in special investigations, trained in deception and spycraft. The recruit had been deployed for two consecutive tours in what was being called the worst place in the world; Vietnam.

This year of 1969, the Bonesman recruitment engine was in full force as a definition had been put in place to find the right mix, as stated by the Bonesman himself, Lanny Davis, and later documented in the yearbook:

> *"If the society had a good year, this is what the "ideal" group will consist of: a football captain; a Chairman of the* Yale Daily News; *a conspicuous radical; a Whiffen-poof; a swimming captain; a notorious drunk with a 94 average; a film-maker; a political columnist; a religious group leader; a Chairman of the Lit; a foreigner; a ladies' man with two motorcycles; an ex-service man; a negro, if there are enough to go around; a guy nobody else in the group had heard of, ever..."*

Jack, like other Bonesman, knew it by memory.

Startled, Jack turned quickly to see this new transfer in his face and looking serious.

"I see the book you are reading, I'm reading the same one," said the spycraft-trained new recruit.

Jack held up the book with a smile on his face, "This one?" Jack held up his fresh copy of the just-published Kurt Vonnegut's *Slaughterhouse-Five.*

Jack didn't break his eye contact and started to ask him his name.

The new recruit replied, "I know you already know my name." Jack realized Joseph Harrison Callahan was not the normal freshman and knew he'd be a perfect addition to Yale's secret club. Being named after two presidents and a founding father of the country, a Vietnam veteran, trained in spycraft didn't hurt his chances. Jack knew he'd make his own history.

Jack also assumed Joe was on to him, confirmed by Joe's confident and direct expression as he started to confirm what Jack assumed.

"I also know you," Joe said. He went on.

"In my selection of schools, I wanted to get an education, but more important to me is to follow in the footsteps of leaders who could be considered revolutionaries."

Jack also knew Joe had decided on a double major in criminology and forensic science. Joe knew Jack already knew it too. They shared both the desire to bring justice and do it with details.

Jack added this to what he already knew about the new recruit, one Jack would introduce tonight, not only to the Skulls but also to the Colonel. His mission had accomplished his duties as a Bonesman, finding those worthy of a society so secret, its members didn't know everything, although they thought they did.

Jack didn't know or care to know more about the Colonel, he cared about their mission, to bring justice to the injustice. It was informal, yet serious. Serious enough to act. To take on what others didn't notice or care about. To seek out injustice and correct it. The Colonel would be pleased with the inclusion of Joe Callahan.

Jack and Joe moved on to what most did at Yale, early afternoon beers. They didn't know it, but their lives would be bonded for life, interwoven to make a difference, sometimes an accidental one.

32

That we should be saved from our enemies, and from the hand of all that hate us.
  - Luke 1:71

J ack's email was specific, Ralph expected it. It was really just a subject line; 'Find the Leak'.

Ralph shredded the other eight copies of Mary's well-written conclusions he had collected, keeping the one on which he made his usually copious notes. Giving that one to Jack with a one-page summary attached. Jack could read Ralph's notes after years together, but Ralph knew he didn't like to.

Ralph went through his progression of options, of whom could or would want to feed the press about the unreported details of the Backson case. He considered even those he knew couldn't be true. The other eight school board members might have been motivated individually, but the risk was too high professionally by bringing attention to your personal opinions while serving as a volunteer on the board of the local college.

He knew the middle of the road was the goal of the school board, those making waves avoided all-volunteer boards like these. Besides, he collected and destroyed any copies of the legal analysis distributed in the meeting. That he knew, he did it himself.

His other options were the author herself, Mary Morgan, her professor who assigned it to the class, whom Ralph embarrassingly didn't know his name (yet), Jack himself, as Ralph filtered no one from the facts, his quest to know the source. Ralph didn't know who Jack talked to before his upcoming meeting with the Chief. Of course, there was the district attorney Dale Johnson, but Ralph knew he was both too lazy and apathetic to care enough to share, or likely remember the details the news somehow knew.

Ralph trusted people, but he didn't trust people with information. He knew the speed of opinions often turned into facts, which was the problem as he saw it. Not only with people, but with the judicial system. He couldn't trust, even though he was sometimes tired of not giving the benefit of the doubt.

Ralph made the list longer, adding names from the office; the disabled Stuart Wilson, the new kid Thomas Williams, the widow of the victim (is that what he was?), and even Angela who knew everything Jack knew. He paused to think of others and put his pen down.

33

The LORD taketh my part with them that help me;
therefore shall I see my desire upon them that hate
me.
   – Psalms 118:7

T he Chief's office phone, his direct line, never rings, unless it is something bad. His wife learned a long time ago, don't call, just wait and he'd call her. But here it was, ringing away. He answered the same way he's been answering for the last twenty years, "Chief Waterson, Ackerford Police." The caller was Jack Rucker, always a friend, and never a foe, and they knew each other well. The press had taken pride in watching Rucker bring his reputation and his hotshot, big-city lawyer tactics to the Chief's cases over the years. Billy had more than half his arrests turned over his first year due to Rucker pulling dusty old laws off his shelf, and Billy was a good detailed cop. The guy was pure law and surprisingly right on the money every time. Miranda became Billy's middle name. Jack was one of the few lawyers that, even in his self-proclaimed retirement, still believed in the law, and this is the only reason Chief continued the relationship. They were both very detail-oriented, all the details, not just the obvious important ones. Mutual respect was evident, being childhood friends didn't hurt.

The call was rare, come to think of it; the Chief could never remember a call from Rucker, lots of legal documents the DA would get upset about, but never a phone call. So the Chief replied, "Hi Jack, for what do I deserve a first time ever phone call?" Jack replied pretty simple, "Danny, I have something I've never seen before in any recorded case in the history of the United States, and it occurred in Ackerford," Jack continued, "I'll need your help along with Johnson if he's around." Dale Johnson was the current DA, and as stated, he was never around.

Chief set up to meet with Jack later that day, his schedule was pretty open and Jack's sense of urgency could be heard through the phone, he knew this voice from their time as kids, ruling the town. Just getting the phone call was enough and the Chief coupled that with Jack's tone, and he knew it was a right now, clear your already open schedule thing. Jack didn't ask, nor did he care about the Chief's other responsibilities. Who knew where Dale was. Jack said he would take care of finding him, which was fine with Chief, as he and Dale were from different worlds.

Dan Waterson and Jack Rucker have been around a while, both in the world of life and together in Ackerford. Their backgrounds couldn't have been more the same as young boys, and more different as grown men, however, today they were face to face talking about something neither of them could believe. A man accused of murder, using his mind as his weapon, was being discussed. The Chief and Jack had done this before, not together, but the facts were real facts then, motive, means, and real clues. This time was different; Jack knew the details, he wasn't yet in the sharing mode, and Chief only knew there was a lack of them.

Danny knew he and Jack go way back. They share more in common than any outsider could imagine. From saving each other's lives on separate occasions as kids, rowdy ones at that, to going on double dates in high school. They also share the need for privacy, even though they are in highly public positions, to serve the community they used to terrorize as youths.

They spoke a language that seemed almost not to be English, and couldn't be followed even if someone was listening. Jack made sure that no one was, keeping his calendar booked with other appointments, albeit fake, only Angela his trusted admin knew they were all fake, as he prepped her with responses. Trusted yes, but not on a need to know that Jack was involved, more than known, in the Backson case. He wanted to talk with Danny about how this may go, and prepare him for the worst, but more importantly, prepare him for the best, as the opportunity to drive the right thing rarely happens. Jack knew Danny, and he knew he would do the right thing, what he didn't know is if Danny knew what the right thing was. Danny, being smart, knew he was in over his head and welcomed Jack's help. The other factor was that Danny knew Jack would do the right thing, he always had. Too many times Danny witnessed Jack bloody himself over the defense of his brother Mikey, both physically bloody, fighting harder than Danny did, and politically bloody during the trial for Mikey's death.

Jack reviewed the case with the Chief. Jack's style was to always work through the difficult issues with people he respected and trusted, although Chief didn't know this from his legal past, he knew this was true from his boyhood memories of their youthful adventures.

Jack continued, "The Backson case seemed simple, at first, a man was killed in Ackerford jurisdiction."

Danny gave him a quick look of concern, one that reflected the years of their childhood and the years since. Jack returned it and continued his details, knowing Danny needed them and wanted them.

"A motive was established earlier in the day, as discovered by Mary Morgan, at the suspect and victim's place of work, Baxter Enterprises. A verbal threat, and threatening posture to kill, was witnessed by three people, independently corroborated." Jack knew the interviews would have to be redone or the court would kill the evidence. Mary wasn't part of the system and Jack didn't want anything to be missed. Jack would talk with Dale soon, he already texted Angela to get it on Dale's calendar. He knew he'd need to talk to him in short sentences that Dale would understand. He would be specific with Dale, giving him a checklist and he'd send Dale out to get it done. There was no need now to interrupt this long-overdue reunion of old friends. Jack knew that Dale didn't like the peon work, but oh well, this case was unique, and Jack was the only one that knew why, for now anyway. When done, Danny would know why too. Not needing any leverage, Jack did know that Danny, being a fan of the famous Joe Callahan, didn't hurt anyone's motivation.

The television in the Chief's office was on, but the volume was muted. It was easier to ignore this way. As he stood, the wooden office chair rolled on the old floors, and Jack saw a picture on the TV change. It changed to the recognizable destroyed Mercedes of Charles Backson. The picture was one from the junkyard, not the accident location, and a picture of the victim, the man Jack had never met. Charles Backson's corporate photo, alongside the Baxter Enterprises logo and his title, Head of Research for Consumer Pharmaceuticals.

Chief saw it too, rolled his chair a bit, grabbed the remote to the television, fumbled with it, pressed one button, unmuted it at its previously set high volume, and the word "murder" echoed in the office.

Jack leveraged the relationship he had with Danny, and Danny with Jack. A few words, a handshake, and a synchronized urgency. They now knew their actions would need to be fast, both in process and protocols to control the narrative, forcing Channel 5 and this obtuse, aggressive reporter, Canner to get in alignment with the real facts.

Chief drew up the paperwork, Jack would find Dale, get him to agree, and get it filed. They needed to get Mark Solier in custody, now, today.

34

But in your hearts honor Christ the Lord as holy, always being prepared to make a defense to anyone who asks you for a reason for the hope that is in you; yet do it with gentleness and respect.
  –1 Peter 3:15

Dale was prepared. He was brought into the investigation at the beginning, something usually left for the detectives, and then the DA is brought up to speed. Usually, Dale was brought up to speed on the way to the courtroom, which was an annoyance to the detectives, but he was good, when he wanted to be, and everyone knew it. He could capture, process, and decide on actions before most could even physically process the information from their ears to their brain, everybody knew this too, so he didn't get much flak. The cases he dealt with in Ackerford were pretty normal, there was a lot of precedent or the case was full of facts.

When Rucker called him, directly using no admins to coordinate, Dale was caught off guard and surprised. His number was private and secure. Part of the surprise was that Rucker called him directly, but more mysterious and concerning was how Rucker, who was not officially a state or federal employee could get the number or the access code to have the call be connected to Dale. He dealt with Rucker before when Jack came home, he officially, and supposedly, retired to Ackerford and took on a few cases pro bono to support the local community and clean up the Ackerford legal process, getting off more than a few due to sloppy police work and lazy prosecution. Both the sloppiness and laziness came from a past that was full of cases with clear-cut facts, so the process was often misused, or even abused. Case law making it easy. Dale himself didn't realize the details of the law until Rucker beat him almost without lifting a finger and without even having a full staff to help him. Jack only had his admin, Angela, and the old guy from the college, Ralph somebody, to help him.

The call from Jack was short, referencing an afternoon meeting Dale didn't know he had until looking at his online calendar, he saw it. Jack told him it was to discuss an upcoming case. Dale knew Jack had been dormant for a few years, even formally announcing his retirement to the relief of many. This was exciting and a little nerving as Dale had probably gone back to some of his lazy, less than perfect methods. Jack had asked Dale to keep it silent, not just quiet, but completely silent. If he wanted to be involved, teaming with Jack, silence was required. Dale agreed and Jack said he would see him in an hour. Dale didn't know how the meeting got on his calendar without his approval. He had nothing to prepare for the meeting with Jack as he had no details.

Dale got back to work on the lawsuit against a local man's

insurance company. The case against the insurance company came to him from John Stacker, a local college professor who gave him a well written legal brief on a case for, Dale had to look up the plaintiff's name online as he didn't recognize it, uh, he fumbled with the keyboard while trying to read quickly too, Charles Backson who had been killed in his car and had left a widow and two young kids. Dale put it aside as it would have to wait, along with everything else he was working on, as he prepared to meet with Jack Rucker. He had no details, which made him nervous, so he got a cup of coffee and read some online sports news to kill some time.

Regardless of his influence, one thing Jack couldn't do is pick the judge. He thought about making an attempt, to at least influence it with his words, or have Ralph do it like they had on previous, less public cases. Jack knew it would corrupt the case. Jack wasn't interested in winning, he was interested in justice, the real law, and by even attempting to pick the judge, he would compromise his values, the things that caused him to pursue this case, to begin with, in addition to the brilliant investigative work done by Mary Morgan. Jack knew, he could feel really, that this small case was going to be big soon. It would likely influence the future of law. It would be a moment of before and after, where the approach to justice would be different. Less injustice, less case law, more facts, if it went the way Jack and others had planned.

II

It Continues

35

And repayeth they that hate him to their face, to destroy them; he will not be slack to him that hateth him, he will repay him to his face.
  - Deuteronomy 7:10

J udge Ford was handed the written affidavit upon his arrival at the courthouse. It was not waiting in his office on his desk, in his inbox as normal. He was both frustrated and intrigued by its importance. There was a business card attached, he recognized it as Jack Rucker's immediately.

Judge Ford knew Jack Rucker well. Jack had a reputation he had earned. He was not wrong. His preparation, his experience, and his instinct allowed him to choose the fight he not only could win but those he would win.

An affidavit was part of the process, rarely declined by even the most biased judges, acting in their duty-bound neutral roles. The police knew how to do their work, as a declined affidavit was a black mark on your badge. They also knew anything but facts would open them up to perjury charges, a

167

permanent removal of their badge.

As the Judge closed his door, hung up his jacket, he reviewed the summary. What he read had no precedent. He knew prior to 1983, this case would have been thrown out. Since 1983, Judge Ford recalled, it was the same Jack Rucker that challenged the law and influenced the US Supreme Court to change the definition of probable cause. Rucker had the law altered from a stricter requirement of proof, called 'bright-line rules', to the judge alone determining if there was enough support to conclude probable cause. This is called 'totality of the circumstance's which a judge, and only that judge, uses to determine if there is enough evidence to arrest a suspect. Judge Ford sighed, as he didn't really have to recall it, Jack had attached documents that detailed the 1983 ruling as well. The complete writing from Justice William Rehnquist defined the totality test being superior to the bright line ruling. Judge Ford knew that Rehnquist was writing for the majority of the court even as an Associate Justice. He also knew that all the way up to his death in 2005, he was a mentor to Jack Rucker. As he was now, in 1983 Jack could be persuasive with his opinions. Judge Ford found his pen where he left it, signed it as it was in his power to decide and he didn't want Jack distracting him from the rest of his inbox. It was full.

Jack was notified by Judge Ford's judicial clerk. The same one Jack required to hand the document to him that same morning. Jack called someone he trusted to do it right. Gary Barker. He then called Dale and Dan to keep them in the loop.

Over the years, Gary Barker served at all levels of law enforcement and now as a US Marshal, he had seen very few surprises. He had seen his share of guilty before innocent judgments. He made most of these preliminary, without due process, guilty judgments, himself. It's easy after a few years doing it every day, as the person arrested tells his own tale. Innocent people are surprised, guilty people are not. Guilty people have a pre-planned story that is regurgitated almost before the Miranda Rights are finished.

Gary was completely surprised, not by Mark Solier's words, or lack of them, but by his genuine lack of emotions. He was one of the calmest men Gary had ever arrested. Two of Gary's best officers actually did the duties, but Jack had asked personally that Gary be there to oversee the process and make it perfect, Jack's exact words.

Mark's only reaction was the ultimate surprise of when the charge of murder was read aloud. His co-workers let out a collective gasp, most of them picking up the phone, texting, or using their social media accounts to bring the day's events to their immediate circle of friends.

One of these friends was new to Chris. Chris was fresh out of school, needed a job, and started with Baxter about three weeks ago. His new friend was a local reporter he recognized from the few times he watched the late-night TV news. Chris recalled the day, a few weeks ago, he got his new secret mission. Chris, who had started at Baxter Enterprises just that day, was on lunch from his first-day orientation and was approached by this guy he recognized from television. The reporter approached him in the parking lot, far from the building as this is where Chris was told to park as a new trainee. The reporter caught him off guard, flashing his badge which Chris, after his initial fear, was relieved it was not a law enforcement one. After the relief of not being law enforcement, what got all of Chris's attention was the roll of cash the guy was showing him. He was now being paid to keep his eyes open for anything interesting surrounding Mark Solier. Chris was getting paid by this guy, in cash, for doing next to nothing, and Chris saw his new job at Baxter as just a paycheck, so how could he say no. When Mark was arrested at Baxter, in public, this was something interesting. Chris stepped into a private hallway, pulled out the newsman's card, and called the number. After about five rings, the belabored, smoke decayed voice of a severely burned out secretary answered. She labored to say with any enthusiasm, "Canner News Service."

36

Give strong drink to the one who is perishing, and wine to those in bitter distress; let them drink and forget their poverty and remember their misery no more.
  – Proverbs 31:6–7

There were seven people in the room, one more than Jack had wanted. Six were expected, the Judge, the honorable James Ford, the suspect, Mark Solier, the recorder, the DA, Dale Johnson, himself, and the defense attorney, Richard Palmett. The seventh was a priest. Not invited by Jack but requested by Mark and allowed by Judge Ford. Jack, casually enough not to be noticed, wrote down the priest's name and texted it to Ralph. Jack knew that Ralph knew, when he just got a name sent from Jack, it meant it was urgent and for Ralph to do what he did best; dig in, research, learn, put together the facts into something valuable. Jack knew in a few short hours, he would likely know more about the priest than the priest remembered about himself. Ralph was that good.

Jack and Dale had decided to allow bail, as a fight would cause more details to be shared than needed. The proceedings were simple, the Judge asked for the crime, upon what grounds, and then bail was set. The crime was murder, the grounds were not that easy, but Jack and Dale had spent time on the details. The sworn testimony, taken two weeks ago by three independent co-workers of Mark, stated that he hated the victim and both had testified that Mark was in a rage, looking at the victim with a blank, non-blinking stare. What they would both describe as a look that could kill. He had also used words neither witness had recognized as English or any other language. Dale noted that both sworn testimonies, were independent, were corroborative in nature, and both included the statement that Mark gave Charlie (Charles) a "look that could kill".

Jack wasn't worried that the initial evidence was weak, as he knew the law and he also knew that motive and means were the only two things needed to get a trial. The Judge even commented to Jack about his disappointment in the details, as his review of his docket last night. The Judge expected more. The Judge also knew Jack wasn't sharing all he knew just yet, he just didn't know why.

The defense attorney was court-appointed, as Mark had not hired one on his own, and Baxter Enterprises was distancing themselves from their soon-to-be infamous, former Executive President for Baxter Ethics and Standards. The overwhelmed, yet nonetheless motivated, defense attorney was following the process. The priest was there as a character witness for Mark, although not needed, as Dale made it clear that bail was not an issue in this case. The defense attorney called him anyway to the stand to the annoyance of the Judge, but Jack was impressed just a little with the perseverance of the defense attorney to do it right. The priest spoke eloquently about Mark, sighting many references to Mark's character and, more specifically his actions within the community for the past twenty years, noting his solo mission to Brazil and the results he produced for that community. Reducing the drug trade and saving hundreds, if not thousands in the following days, months, and years. Jack knew all this, down to the drug dealer's middle names that died during the time Mark was in Brazil. Ralph didn't miss anything. Dale was a little worried, as the specifics were impressive, even the Judge was interested, which caught Jack's attention too. Without a doubt, on record, even though it was just the preliminary hearing, Mark Solier was an upstanding person. Some have called him a saint, although now as a charged murderer, others would see this as an abuse of the religious symbol. Nonetheless, he was described as one, not only in the community with his service acts, but as a human being as stated by a respected local priest. Bail was waived, without an objection or even a glance up from Dale, as this is what Rucker told him to do the night before. Jack directed him to show no interest in the ruling, do nothing to prevent bail. Jack knew the documents were going to be made public and Canner would no doubt get them the moment they were available online. Mark was released with a trial to be set in the next coming weeks, maybe months.

Rucker knew that the work was now to begin. Legal work, work that had no precedent and when completed, could change the way our country's founding father's vision for a free society's judicial system would work. Jack's thoughts were not about the work, but about what was right, what were the facts, and what was the proof. He needed time. The process gave him time. His urgency was fueled by wanting to keep the killings as low as possible. He suspected Mark's power and wanted to minimize it now, and ultimately eliminate it forever.

37

But I say unto you which hear, Love your enemies, do good to them which hate you.
  – Luke 6:27

D ale knew that some information had been collected from the three witnesses at Baxter Enterprises, of which he'd have to refer to the many pages of notes given to him by Angela. He did know this, the first witness was with their corporate lawyer, a guy named Rupert, the other two he'd have to check-in for appointments, and the documents for their names.

Dale Johnson could be a total ass. His childhood friends even nicknamed him such. They openly called him 'ass' as if it was his name and Dale was almost proud of it, even at eight years old. To an outsider, it would have been funny to hear little kids say "hey 'ass' you comin' over on Saturday," or "did you hear that 'ass' was dating whoever," but long ago didn't matter now. Dale hadn't been called 'ass' for a while, not as his nickname, but it did consistently define his adult behavior.

The adult and educated version of 'ass' was now at Baxter Enterprises with his patience at zero talking with Louise, although she was the one doing all the talking. He had made an appointment, or rather Jack's admin did, and he was on a schedule. Dale didn't have anything else to do but nothing, of course, Louise didn't need to know that, so he was his normal 'ass' self.

Louise already decided she wasn't going to help him because of his attitude, appointment or not, but Dale showed his official justice department badge, with its fancy logo, hologram image, and security bar code. He made some idle threat. Louise had a life of her own and didn't need any district attorney on her bad side, especially an asshole one like this guy as she dialed the phone for the first appointment. Eric Rupert, the Baxter attorney, who required, even with an appointment, a call anytime any law enforcement or justice department showed up. It happened more often than the press knew, more than Louise liked. Louise knew him well as they had been together before. Rupert answered and they exchanged ex-lover type flirtations, as Dale became more annoyed with only hearing the Louise half. She hung up and said he would be there in a moment, through the double doors, she was aggressively pointing with her recently manicured bright pink fingernail. Dale was looking at her instead of where she was pointing and there was this silence, as she jerked her finger again towards the doors, as to exercise her only real power of control. 'Ass' was just looking at her and she didn't like it. Dale looked now as the doors opened and Rupert came through, fixing his tie and pulling up his pants. Dale made a huge sigh as to visually express to both of them that they were a waste of his time.

Louise attempted to get him to sign in and take a badge as was required, but she was more than ignored, it was like this 'ass' was deaf or something. She had her ways, as he needed her for his next appointment. She hoped he had patience because she sure did. Two can play the 'ass' game as he and Rupert disappeared behind the double doors with the echoing click of the security latch, leaving the expensive, impressive lobby empty, except for Louise. She went back to her computer, no real work to do, but plenty of time for online shopping.

"Mr. Rupert, I'm Dale Johnson, the DA responsible for Ackerford felony cases and I'm here today to review some information provided to a college student who talked with you last week."

Eric Rupert, a smart, but still just a corporate lawyer at a very large (largest?) pharma company, didn't like these pay your dues like assignments, dealing with the local, ego-based district attorneys. He knew this guy, Dale Johnson, by name only. Before coming to the lobby, Eric barely recognized Dale on the security camera video now streaming to his computer monitor, even after zooming in on his face. The person standing in the lobby, looking disheveled, with poor posture, was almost not recognizable from the more polished government photo on the website research he had done the day he was notified of the meeting request. Eric Rupert was detailed in everything he did to protect his company. He also read Johnson's list of overt accomplishments next to his photo on his government prepared bio a few times again, the night before. Now face to face with Dale Johnson, Rupert shifted his weight, paused a bit, and using his well-established non-verbal "code" with Louise, he already knew this guy was a down-talking asshole. So, his emotions got the best of his memory, his motivation was to answer the questions and keep the unneeded information to himself. Why help out the enemy? Not really knowing, but his attitude was reflected by most Americans, the law and more specifically the lawyers were considered the enemy until you needed one.

Dale asked some expected questions and got expected answers. Eric noted Dale didn't take notes. Probably just checking the boxes. The last question, not a box to be checked normally, was Dale asked and then requested any history of disciplinary action against Mr. Solier. Eric knew there was some, not typical for a Baxter executive, but he'd not only have to review it, he'd also have to share it with this new asshole, Dale Johnson. He made a note to do both in the next few days. They shook hands as lawyers do, out of necessity, ending the short relationship and hoping not to see each other again. They wouldn't.

Dale took in a deep breath outside the now slow closing doors of the Baxter main entrance. He looked around, concluded it was all good, overtly landscaped grounds, some birds, some bees, some people grooming the grass, and the relief that he was done with Mr. Rupert. He had a few more boxes to check, keep down the noise of this case, and get back to doing nothing. As others saw it, back to being Dale Johnson.

The one advantage among many disadvantages of working

near and with Jack Rucker is that his administration team was incredibly efficient. Dale had in the past his own secretaries, Dale reminded himself they were executive assistants now. In the past, he could never find or keep anyone around. They either took other jobs before he hired them or quit a few weeks after. Either way, Jack's team was his. They didn't always respond, if ever, to his requests, but they definitely took care of the incoming noise from the public.

Picking up his phone, he saw he had six calls in his voice mailbox. He hadn't missed any actual calls, so he knew these were from Angela; she left messages directly to his voicemail box, as he had asked her to not call him unless it was important, she learned nothing was really important to Dale, so she used this method for every one of his messages. What Dale didn't know, is that Angela informed Jack too. Using the same voice message system for things that were not confidential and protected by law, and other methods, usually verbal for those things she knew Jack wanted to know. Angela worked for Jack, Dale just thought she worked for him too. Angela knew who she worked for, she had been with Jack for many years, serving both him and her country.

Dale listened to the first message transcribed by Angela, as he also ordered his food verbally, from the drive-through fast-food restaurant half working speaker. He hadn't eaten breakfast and all the work this morning made him hungry. He didn't really hear the message, just the name of the person who called the office, John Stacker. Probably a nobody.

The other six messages, were treated the same, unimportant,

or at least just less important than the hastily spread burger, fries, and drink Dale had across his lap as he pulled out into traffic, reaching for the radio dials as traffic parted in his favor.

If he took notes, he would have listed the following callers, John Stacker, the professor who started it all, Stephen C. Canner, the one who couldn't help but fuel it, Gary Barker who wanted to know how the Mercedes went off the road, Ralph Stoufer who's mission was always suspect, Thomas Williams a nosy new guy and Stuart Wilson, the overprotective, nothing better to do, campaign manager for Joe Callahan.

Without the notes and without the need to care, Dale finished his food, parked his car far away from his office, in an abandoned parking lot, and took his daily nap, forgetting it all before he even dozed off.

Ralph took notes, even on his own call to Dale, what Angela sent to Jack, she sent to him. She knew they were a team, led by Jack, solidified by Ralph.

Ralph now knew the source of the leak; everyone, and no one. Canner just put it together and couldn't resist the temptation to put it on air, he usually got it half right, this time, he got it right, he just didn't know it, yet.

38

Even a fool who keeps silent is considered wise; when
he closes his lips, he is deemed intelligent.
  – Proverbs 17:28

After the arrest was done, sadly in public, Gary thought it went smoothly as expected, and the suspect was now in Gary's government-issued, nondescriptive, yet obvious, all-purpose black shiny sedan. As Gary sat down in the passenger seat, amid a variety of computers, and other government-only electronic devices mounted on the dash, he closed the passenger car door and reached for his phone. Gary glanced in the rear seat, the suspect staring back at him. Gary looked at his phone, opened his favorites list, and pushed the listing for Jack Rucker. Jack answered, in his normal, anticipated by Gary, Rucker way, with nothing but "Hello." Then after Gary shared the facts, Jack said "Thanks." He then hung up. Gary had seen Rucker in high profile yet discreet action many times and was happy to be part of this case. He didn't know exactly what was happening just yet, and he judged Mark as innocent, but he knew if Rucker was involved, it was something big. Rucker faded by choice from the limelight about five years ago. He was known for taking high profile cases, not those of high profile crimes, but those that were a mystery, requiring a deep understanding and determination to defend or prosecute. Rucker often took either side, not a preference for the prosecution or defense, often as it turned out, the more difficult side. It was always about the facts for Rucker, what was right for getting real justice. He picked the battles others didn't, getting justice for the injustice. That is what Gary was about too.

Tim Hopper had worked for Gary for just over a year, spending more than a year in the application process to become a US Marshal. Tim had been driving patrol cars and making arrests most of his career. He liked it, he felt a daily fulfillment in delivering justice. He had the chance to stop crime, and prevent crime. During the years, he's had all kinds of criminals in the back of his car, but not like this. This was by far, the quietest, most saintly-looking suspect he had ever seen. Gary asked him, even though Tim knew them from memory, to read the Miranda rights from the standard-issued laminate card. Other than knowing he arrested him for murder, Tim didn't know anything else. Tim sat quietly, as Gary sat next to him on the phone, hanging up after only a minute or less. Gary sat up with a sense of pride and stowed his phone on the dash. Gary put on his sunglasses looking forward in silence. Tim started the car, looked in his mirrors for cars and other threats, a necessary habit from his previous role with the Secret Service. He adjusted the large, multi-view, extended rearview mirror from the suspect he was watching, who was now staring straight ahead, a blank look on his face. As Tim observed the suspect through the mirror and occasional glances during right turns, he noted the silence, but also the almost meditative state, as the suspect seemed to be almost asleep, with his eyes open. He couldn't help but wonder what kind of weirdo he had in his car, thankful for the barrier between them, accused of murder, displaying almost no reaction, and then falling asleep, eyes wide, now shut, on the way to the jail. Tim knew the way and they were only a few turns away from the destination.

Mark was sitting silently in the squad car, moving only slightly as the car made starts, stops, and turns. He was in his own world, he was in full-blown prayer mode. His silent prayers, if said aloud would be heard as odd one-way discussions, almost conversational, and were never complete sentences. Even now, during this very confusing time, as he calmed himself, he was silent. He only knew he was accused of murder, and being transported to where he did not know.

Jack was in disguise, no suit, no tie, blending in on purpose. He was completely concealed in the daily happenings of the county jail. He knew there would be enough people that no one would notice his presence as he was out of character, dressed casually with a baseball cap, the Yankee's he thought, as he didn't have a priority for sports and wasn't sure. His plan was to observe and to get a look at the killer instead of just the data he had, and the many photos his out of sight, off the payroll, investigative team had taken. The important part, as Jack knew this man's power to kill, was that he not see him. Jack was sure he could blend in and get what he needed, a solid look at the man that would help him change the United States Justice System.

Jack had been to this jailhouse many times in an official, public, capacity either through the support of others or related to something he himself cared about. He had never been here as an observer, and he noticed things he never noticed before. The security seemed upfront to be a lot more robust, either because of the events on 9/11 or maybe the escape attempt and success last year, Jack didn't know, but it was definitely more on the surface. As he sat in the waiting chairs, he immediately saw the discussion, probably a little more, as there started to be a collection of officers forming in front of the jail. Jack rose as he expected to blend farther back into the environment as the suspect arrived, but instead, he saw the Channel 5 news van, and as he watched he only hoped it was not, and then he saw him. Mr. Canner, who was being worked into this case by Jack's team from a different angle, but his sudden presence now was not part of the plan, a rare surprise to Jack at this time. The next thing Jack saw were the cameras, destroying his plan to observe the killer from his disguised attendance. This prompted Jack to slip out the one-way side door giving a brief wave, a purposeful tip of the cap, hiding his face as he did so, to the security guard there, guarding the entrance to the exit.

Tim and Gary were on camera and they knew it. They've dealt with this Canner guy before and you knew, if you saw him, a camera and mic were coming next. Gary wondered how his edit crew ever created a story out of so much crap, the microphone was then thrust in his face and Canner was there with his cameraman, and the red light was on. This was expected, the presence of the camera at the station upon their arrival was not. Gary asked Tim to get the suspect inside, expecting Mark to do what suspects do, and cooperate and even cover their face. But Mark didn't, his exposure was all of fifteen seconds from the patrol car to the private entrance to the jail, only used on these types of cases, as the muggers, hookers, and others were brought right through the front door. This Canner guy was a pain and his timing and exposure to the suspect couldn't have been worse in Gary's eyes. Gary knew Canner was proud of himself as he came back to Gary's stare with a smug smile, reflecting how he felt on the inside knowing he surprised the scene. The smug face, of course, was off-camera.

Gary must have said the standard cop phrase "no comment" about a hundred times. Not only was it in his training, but Rucker was strict. Not a word. Not a word beyond the phrase "no comment". Rucker even repeated his expectation, more like a command, as he looked Gary in the eyes before they left a few hours ago to arrest Mark Solier.

"I don't care if you have to say it a hundred times 'till they get the point, say it."

Gary was starting to feel like an idiot, repeating it so many times until Tim could get Mark inside and the other officers dissipated. Once that happened, the only other people besides Gary and the Channel 5 news crew were those meaningless, nosy onlookers. Gary abruptly walked away from Canner and Canner protested but the final "no comment" from Gary hit home and Canner realized he had been worked. Canner also realized that his arrival was a surprise, but they seemed to be prepared. He was also surprised to see Gary Barker, a US

Marshal involved in the arrest, the use of Federal resources, the black sedans gave it away, they always did. This was an inside job, only a few knew about this murder charge, there was no public outcry for a suspect as nobody even knew that this accident was being considered a murder. Only a few knew, and Canner was glad he was one of them. He wondered how connected this Stacker guy from the college was into this, but his initial thought was that he was a burned-out, washed-up, small college professor, who couldn't get a real lawyer job. He knew someone else was driving, organizing not only Gary Barker as the lead detective but someone who had the power to arrest for murder upon such seemingly, flimsy evidence. There was something he was missing and this was the thrill he lived for, and why he became a journalist, not this two-bit storytelling he's been doing to flame his ego and pay the bills.

39

It is the glory of God to conceal things, but the glory of kings is to search things out.
  – Proverbs 25:2

The video equipment arrived the day before and a contractor was in within hours of the delivery to set it up. The jail had two interrogation rooms, one used to be a closet until last year, but the other was set up nice. It was freshly painted, the smell combined with the new furniture placed just that morning. It was out of place with the rest of the jail, but the cameras were only focused here. And now the jail also had digital video recording as of this morning. Barker had signed off on it, so it got done.

The video camera started recording even before the suspect was brought in, the light was now flashing red. A specialist, with no badge or name tag, was brought in to script the entire interrogation and essentially "produce" the video. He instructed the detective, named Michael, to follow the script. Gary could see the specialist using director-like actions with the interrogator doing the interview. The specialist came back into the remote room where Gary was watching, he looked at Gary, noting the overtly pressed uniform and shiny, prominently placed, US Marshal badge. Along with the interrogator, who was called Michael, there were others in the interview room. The specialist knew they were not part of the script and had told them to remain silent. They agreed with head nods only. Gary assumed they were members of the interrogation team similar to this unknown specialist, looking, yet now realizing, that everyone had removed their name tag. Watching from the remote room, Gary didn't recognize any of them.

Mark was brought into the interview room, sat down, and was silent. He stared at each person, one by one like he was memorizing their faces. He was purposely moving his eyes from person to person, which was noted at the time and confirmed by the review of the digital video later.

The questions were simple, short, and direct. "Do you know why you are here?"

Mark answered "Yes," as he knew he was here because he was being "charged with a sin," his own words, also noted. The interesting part is the unusual use and requirement of a script that drove the interrogation, so the training and experience the interrogator had, was useless, he didn't even know any facts to manipulate and catch this man in a conflict of issues, known in less technical terms as lying. A little frustrating, but he was told by Rucker himself to follow the script, period, without modification. The other questions related to facts around his name, his address, and his lifelong residence history. It was noted also that his residence history was an odd one, including his solo mission trip to the Brazilian jungle. All these questions the interrogator knew were already on record from the research group.

Michael paused, as the next part was both to capture information but to also capture the non-verbal reactions for what the digital capture system would provide.

"Do you know how your father died?" asking in a direct tone.

"He died in his sleep a few weeks after I was born, I don't know how."

Michael knew that the death certificate, which was now public as it was older than 25 years stated the cause as unknown even after a lengthy detailed autopsy.

"Do you know how your Aunt," Michael looked at his script to get the name right, "Jessica, died?"

"My mother told me she was killed by a bear," Mark then added, "That scared me as a kid."

"What about Greg?"

Mark looked up, asking "Who? I don't know anyone named Greg that died."

"Greg was your stepdad, he died in a car accident, he was hit by an elderly man who had an epileptic seizure."

Mark realized this was the mean boyfriend his mother had when he was a boy. His face impulsively contorted into sadness remembering the beatings he took, then stated the truth, "He was mean to my mother and me when we were not in public."

Michael continued, "Tell me about Gilbert, Rick and Fred?" purposely leaving off their last names.

"It was sad, they didn't need to die. Their car accident into the river could have been avoided." Mark answered as he put his hands together and bowed his head. All of which was caught on camera.

"How did you know them?"

Mark looked up, not blinking as he put his hands on the table, "They were in the same college when I was there my first year. I was young, they were older and they wouldn't leave me alone. I asked them many times to stop and finally reported them to Professor Bradferst."

"Did you kill them?" Michael finally asked the question everyone wanted to know.

"They killed themselves," Mark answered and then a long uncomfortable pause.

Michael knew to wait, the pause would often cause the truth to come out next. The suspect sat still, staring at him. His eyes were dark.

"I have a list of criminals in Brazil that died when you were there. Did you know how many died?"

"I don't know the number."

"Seven," Michael said as quickly as Mark answered. Looking to force a reaction.

"I only knew the town celebrated and thanked me. It made me uncomfortable."

Michael read the names, the purpose was to get a reaction, all of which was being watched through the one-way glass and being recorded in 240 frames per second.

"Hermes Sousza, Marcos Youseff, Marcelo Bispo de Oliveria, Tiago Silva, Paulo Batista, Maria Gracie, and Alberto Bonita." The names echoed off the walls.

Mark had no reaction as he continued to stare at Michael.

"The people were blessed to no longer be controlled by them." The pressure in the room seemed to increase as Mark made this matter-of-fact statement. Not denying he did it.

"Charles Backson left two kids and a wife, did you know that before you killed him?" Michael now purposely put his hands on the table, disrupting the silence with the slapping of flesh to metal.

"It is sad that Charlie is gone." Mark again put his hands

together and looked down.

It was obvious to everyone watching, he didn't deny it. People who are innocent, react emotionally and deny it. People who are guilty, react defensively and deny it. Mark was doing neither.

The last question on the script was the most intriguing, both as it didn't fit with the other questions, short and direct, but also because the interrogator had never before asked it and didn't know its purpose.

"Do you know anyone in this room?"

Mark answered quickly with a "No."

The interrogator had introduced himself as Michael, not his real name, as was specific to the script and made clear by Rucker, that no names were to be used, stick to the script, no exceptions.

As the interview ended, the interrogator noted one more thing, in the room, he didn't recognize anyone himself. This was very odd. This made him frustrated, almost angry. He had been doing this for years, he had success and was considered the best, called in on the most important interrogations. Now he was being forced to read a script. He kept his negative thoughts to himself, outwardly being the professional he always was and was expected to be. The digital camera continued to capture the scene as the room dispersed and Mark looked to the sky and visibly was having a conversation with someone, although he made only a mumbling noise. Only later during a review of the high frame rate video and audio was it determined to be structured but an unknown language. The state-of-the-art language translation software kept coming back with a result of unknown origin. One thing the video did catch when he was exiting the room, a direct, never blinking, seemingly cold stare that Mark gave "Michael". Michael, not even his real name, stared back until like a scared dog, the suspect looked away.

Michael, his real name was Robert Lourlet, never saw it coming, traveling towards his home, a truck had its brakes disintegrate in normal conditions on the freeway. Two factors played a role in this one car, one death accident, the first were the failed brakes, and the second was the interrogation of Mark Solier.

Jack had read about the death of his friend Bob, his full name was Robert Lourlet, in the paper. Jack realized that he himself could be accused of murder if people knew what he knew. Jack picked up the paper this morning and purposely looked, knowing he would find it, the accidental death of Robert Lourlet. Jack selected Bob himself, as he knew this outcome could be possible, for his unique life situation. Not only was Bob an incredible interrogator, doing some of the most critical work with Jack, post 9/11 on terrorists, Bob had no family. He had no surviving kin either, Ralph had checked twice. Jack didn't want it to happen, but he needed the video, and he needed to take the risk, with someone else's life.

40

Jesus answered them, "Did I not choose you, the Twelve? And yet one of you is a devil."
  - John 6:70

J ack and Ralph had the initial list of jurors, separated by those that had responded and those still missing. Those nonrespondents would get an automated phone call follow-up every day from the courthouse. The process of selecting a jury was complex, bureaucratic, necessary, and the most important part of Jack and Ralph's success for the past forty years of their legal achievements. They got started the moment the juror list was available. They both knew it would be an early morning on the day the court provided the list. They also knew the defense attorney was still asleep, they always were. Ralph invited Dale, although he was probably asleep as well. As the district attorney, he owned the case, but without even a thought about it, Jack and Ralph knew they would puppet Dale through this, and obviously, Dale knew it too.

Jack and Ralph had known each other for a while. Ralph had

been the silent partner of the two, working with Jack for more than twenty years. He liked the silent part, did his job but didn't have to worry or deal with the press or death threats, debatable which one he liked less. Jack had tried cases at all levels of the court system; it was always surprising to most by the cases that he selected, but not to Ralph. He knew Jack was all about the passion for the law. Enthusiasm was there, but it was deeper. Jack had all the common knowledge, and, what often puzzled Ralph over the years, he knew Jack had specific facts and information about the history of law going back to times before Christ. Ralph had wondered at times over the years, both where it came from and how Jack remembered it all; using it at the right time, when needed. The changes in times, over the last few thousand years, were driven by the more recent cultural changes in laws from the decades before now. This occurred in every century and sometimes more than once. The immersion in the underlying impact of legal proceedings and the subsequent impacts to human beings is where Jack felt his calling was formed. Ralph learned this by being Jacks' closest friend. Ralph often wondered what Jack didn't share, but he knew one thing, Jack had his mind on the future and the daily impacts he could make today to change it.

The initial list from the courthouse was due this morning to both the prosecution and defense attorneys, Ralph predicted it would be a mess, he knew it was being rushed and as predicted, it was in poor shape. The courthouse delivered on time, as they knew it was Rucker and Angela, who was Jack's relentlessly detailed personal assistant. She was a compliment to Jack's missions over the years, a combination of skills that made her equally a watchdog and attack dog simultaneously. She had left messages and even personally visited the clerk's office the day before. Always pleasant and always specific about what Jack needed. The list showed up with two hundred names on it, some had been crossed out with poorly handwritten notes on the copy. Cleaning up the delivered mess of a juror list, Angela had cleaned up the initial list of all two hundred, even the names that had been crossed out. She had organized them into a spreadsheet from those that had detail, to those that were quite empty. Of course empty was still not empty, as Angela could find even the smallest details. Jack's success depended on it.

Ralph was ready, knowing that his part of the jury selection process was next. He uploaded the spreadsheet of the juror list he received from Angela into the new proprietary software program that Jack provided to him. Jack had it built by an unknown software engineer and enhanced over his five years of public retirement.

The juror details uploaded, included all of their basic info, name, social security number, phone number, and address. He clicked the 'create profiles' button and quickly he could see profiles being populated with information that would have taken Ralph weeks, even with his secret access to government databases, to find, if at all. It was now done and Ralph didn't care whether or not it was legal. He was just glad to have it and relieved he didn't have to do it himself. He now started to filter the list using the built-in probability algorithms to pre-determine how a juror would make decisions.

Ralph finalized the chosen juror profiles and began to build a jury questionnaire that would determine the twelve jurors to convict Mark Solier. For the first time in his career, he had included questions about paranormal beliefs, the existence of evil, and personal definitions of Heaven and Hell.

41

Do not I hate them, O LORD, that hate thee? And am
not I grieved with those that rise up against thee?
  - Psalms 139:21

I n every courtroom, there are moments. They vary depending on region, and even between neighboring cities. The founding father's concept of a jury of your peers really was a jury that was selected by a process of elimination by both the district attorney and defense lawyer. This was supposed to create a jury of peers, as the outliers were quickly excused by each side. A moment in every courtroom that is the same, is when the Judge enters. The perception, and even more the reality, is that a Judge is a very powerful human who has real power over process and people. When the Judge enters, people stand, with good reason. Nobody wants an upset Judge, not the jury, attorneys, and especially not the defendant.

Judge James Ford was known in this region as a grandfatherly type, although only in his early sixties, and he had no children. Virginia law forced retirement at seventy-three and he had already served three terms of eight years each, the third coming to an end this year. He routinely handed out two dollar bills to kids of parents he met at breakfast, farmers markets, and public events. He was known as Judge Jim by the public, only called that by those that were never in his courtroom. He was always proactive in keeping the public on his side, as Virginia was one of only two states where the state judges were selected by the legislature. Virginia had done this even before it was a state, and was one of only two states that still was aligned with the public's opinion, good or bad, the people's choice.

Negative people influenced often weak politicians, so Judge Ford took care of the people, both in the local towns and in his courtroom.

As the jury arrived, it was both normal and abnormal at times as mentally noted by the court reporter. She did double duty as the primary clerk for Judge Ford as well. Now what felt like an eternity ago, she was the one who handed the Judge the affidavit, instead of placing it in his inbox as normal, she was the one who called Jack Rucker after the Judge had signed it. This was going to be different. She could feel the tension at the arrival of every person into the courtroom. The air tastes different, more stale as the time slowly went by progressing towards the next part of the process. She had seen everything in this town, having grown up here, and she'd been writing down every word, every day, for now, twenty years in this courtroom, at the same desk she now sat. She used to replay the facts, then she learned not to care. This was different, it had her attention, but she didn't know why just yet. Her breathing was quickening and she wasn't following her regular routine of testing her machine, backing up the paper, checking the power cords. She realized she couldn't seem to get enough air and was overwhelmed with a feeling of fear. She grabbed her desk, not noticed by others, steadied herself, took some deep breaths, and tested her machine, it worked fine, as it always had. She let the Judge's assistant know her ready status, and she, in turn, updated the Judge that he had the normal ten minutes to get prepared.

Judge James Ford was a reader; living alone and being alone most nights, he often read anything he could on the topics he cared about. Currently, his focus was on the historical and recent attention to the conflicts between judicial activism and judicial restraint. Since being assigned this case, one he sought out after signing the arrest warrant and then secured in the back rooms of the judicial bureaucracy, he had immersed himself in the details. Beyond the documents and the research his team provided on the unique charges being made against the defendant, James also called Jack Rucker directly yesterday. Out of protocol, but the Judge knew Jack and Jack likely expected the call.

The conversation was short but effective. James wanted to know what Jack thought, and as important, why he was choosing this case, after five years of retirement.

"Why now?" he had asked Jack more than once.

The why was almost more important than the what when it came to Jack Rucker; James knew this, Judge Ford followed

Jack Rucker's career his whole life. They had once been close to friends, running in similar circles but went different paths after a few disagreements at Yale. Jack would often take on missions, defined as causes in the late sixties, usually public in nature to rebel against the norm. It was more than just words, as he would act in many different ways, to coordinate his efforts to make his point, and drive change, or try to. James Ford, was a senior advisor to the Bonesman, being a few years ahead of Jack. Yet, he couldn't get through to the younger Jack Rucker. Since, through years of picking the battles, James realized his friend (is that what he was?) turned his rebel ways, into renegade-like causes. The difference, is Jack now knew what he was doing, and rarely chose unworthy fights, and even more rare, he no longer lost any. James remembered clearly what caused his mentorship back then to cease, stopping any time spent with the younger Jack Rucker. It was when he found out Jack's involvement in a secret group who thought they were above the law. It was a secret even to his fellow Bonesman. The involvement in getting justice for injustice. James knew some of the actions this group took, originally calling themselves the "Court of Vehm". It was at this time that the Bonesman gave Jack his nickname, "Robin Hood". As a senior at Yale, James saw some more actions and evidence from afar, then it went completely underground, more quiet, invisible to even those that were watching, it was more secret than the Skull & Bones.

The jurors are first to rise, as they have been coached, as Judge Ford made his way to the bench, depending on the case, it could sometimes be seen as a pulpit to preach from, as Judge Ford had often extended his advice to the defendants, convicted or not. The Judge settled and people took their seats. As the preliminary reading was taking place, the Judge scanned the room as he often did, from the jury to defendant, then checking out the counsel and district attorney. All seemed normal, even as the case was not. Judge Ford stopped and evaluated the defendant more than he normally had. The charge was unique, so the Judge figured the defendant would be as well. From the outside, Mark Solier looked simple. His posture was stiffer than most, his build, haircut, was the same; stiff. Simple was the best word to describe him. The Judge scanned the attendees, which today included a class from the local college, their professor, who the Judge remembered as a slacker of sorts, and of course the news team. It used to be journalists, interested in writing a story, but more and more it was the news, the yellow news, where facts didn't matter. The Judge had watched the recent Canner episodes, he recorded them, watched them late at night after the live broadcast was over. He recorded them to skip the other news of low value, and the commercials, but he wanted to have them to review later. It seemed this case had a leak, and he didn't know where it was coming from nor how Canner knew what he shouldn't. He recognized the Canner guy, now sitting in his courtroom, who sensationalized even the smallest story, even now, with heavy makeup on, focused more on ratings than facts. Judge Ford sighed, and refocused on what he knew was to be a long proceeding that day and would get even longer throughout the trial. He knew Jack and his team would be detailed, tenacious, and looking to not only win but make a point.

This jury was a diverse group, with a diverse understanding and analysis of what they were hearing. Both sides brought to the table facts but also a cloud of mystery. The talk among the jurors was inconsistent with any Jerry had ever been a part of or heard about. Jerry Russell was not a veteran of being a juror but also not ignorant either, more than enough hours of lonely nights of TV educated him on crime scene investigations, courtrooms, and the last-minute surprises. He lived the life of analysis, albeit a more real-time analysis. He was now a Federal Air Marshal, as he, like many, were inspired after 9/11 to make a difference. Being from New Mexico, he then sought in late September of 2001 and got sponsorship from then-Sheriff Joe Callahan to attend the thirty-six-day course called FAMTP, the Federal Air Marshal Training Program. It was located in his hometown of Artesia, New Mexico. He graduated first in his class. Even prior to 9/11 he routinely kept up with his investigative roots. He was an independent contractor investigator for a few companies, including insurance, which really sucked, as Jerry often found fraud, and when he didn't, he often found despair in those whose lives had been accidentally ruined. He felt he knew how to investigate, he knew details.

Jerry's experience and his visual awareness of what was happening now were how this group of jurors collaborated. It didn't adhere to the normal world, but normal is what had been changing and maybe this is a catalyst to continue it. Even Jerry agreed that the evidence and coincidence was more fact than just an accidental chance. The talk continued about what was right, what was fact, and what was fantasy.

Julie had a complex life and two kids. She also shared too much, Jerry noted. She often was relieved that things went ok, more out of luck than anything else. Most mothers planned some things, and for sure Julie wanted to, but having two kids and an unpredictable, violent ex-husband, just made it impossible to have a plan. Her divorce was not normal. If someone was to write about it, and someone was to actually read it, she knew it looked bad on paper. Everyone who knew her agreed, it was bad luck. Her ex-husband, Pete, eventually died of cancer. They were divorced before he died, as he had gone crazy. He'd been assessed for mental stability twice before he was finally institutionalized, against his will, in a psychiatric hospital, diagnosed with bipolar disorder. Julie had loved him, even though people close to her judged her for it, she married him for love, as her closest friends were persistent in their advice not to. She had both her daughter Elizabeth and her son, Stuart with him. Tragedy impacted her son Stuart too, as he was only ten years old when he was paralyzed in a football game accident, never to walk again. They were known by most as two good kids. Elizabeth and Stuart didn't know their father that well, only the bad part. She had no idea how she survived, she thought more luck than anything she actually did. Even the man that saved her from the final beating in Wal-Mart had been luck. Pete was twice as mean after he got his cancer. It started the day after being diagnosed and ended the day he died, in between, Julie was lucky to be alive, she knew it and everyone knew it. If the beginning was based on love, the middle was complex with the unpredictable nature of his bipolar disorder, which was only fueled by him getting cancer, the end of the story was simple and violent. Pete hit her in the back. He had been released from the hospital that day, only the hour before is what the police report would show. She didn't even know what happened until her trip to the hospital. Someone attending to her medical needs and someone else holding her hand that she knew wasn't Pete. She would never see Pete again. He had been arrested for the assault, incarcerated as he was guilty, and put in a prison hospital. Her last image of Pete was that horrible picture on TV, the one you see of others, a distraught face, an orange jumpsuit, a plaque with a name in those white misaligned letters, also likely surprised by the overworked police photographer just doing their job. This was the last time Pete was heard from, sadly also her kid's last memory. The cancer killed him later. She told Jerry, who was the jury foreman, and the rest all of this in just her introduction.

The first day was always longest, not in time, but in the lack of variance from the norm. It was balanced by the newness of the case, often first-time jurors, but to the Judge, and likely to the regular crowd, boring nonetheless. No one could have foreseen that the second day would start with anything but normal, the need to replace dead jurors. Juror Number Five, Julie Sanders, died first.

42

For we must all appear before the judgment seat of
Christ, so that each one may receive what is due for
what he has done in the body, whether good or evil.
  - 2 Corinthians 5:10

C anner grabbed for his gun, loaded and off safety, rolled off the bed, and positioned himself at a low-risk angle to his always locked bedroom door. He refocused on the time, the red numbers, glowing in the dark room, blurry, yet becoming clearer as he blinked and rubbed his eyes. His bedside clock said 2:23. The noise in his apartment that initially awakened him and was now escalating, moving towards the door to his bedroom, causing his current state of readiness to increase, his blood pumping fast as he regripped his handgun. He was used to it, and ready for anything due to the numerous, and never-ending death threats in public, by email, by phone, and even once by a letter using the classic ransom note lettering, but never a physical break-in. He unloaded a few shots into the ceiling, sounding like an explosion in the small room, and initially panicked Canner as this was the first time Canner fired his gun not at the range and without ear protection. The noise that woke him, that was right next to his door, outside the room stopped. Then a voice started yelling his name, "CANNER!" out of surprise, and a few "WHAT THE FUCKS?" and "ARE YOU JESUS FUCKIN' CRAZY!?!" This specific phrase and now the voice, Canner recognized as his producer. He lowered the pointed barrel of his gun away from the door, his aim now pointed towards the floor, but not yet that far away from the door; an abundance of caution he learned to have, having a firm grip with his trigger finger in the ready position.

"What the hell Sandi?!?" Canner yelled.

"You could have Jesus fucking killed me!" said Sandi.

Opening the door slowly with his own abundance of caution.

"Why are you here breaking into my house? I was going to kill you."

Sandi now calmer, but still energized by both the potential of being killed by her boss, and by what she was about to share with him.

"Six of the Jurors have died, all of them in strange accidents in the last eight hours."

Canner was rarely without words; this news took his breath away. His first reaction as he flipped on the lights, blinding him, was to put the gun on safety, eject the round from the chamber, caught it naturally, as he had done it many times before, and put his gun away.

As he had for more than ten years with Sandi, he said what he always said, "Tell me more."

Sandi started, first talking, then pacing herself from her notes, with the death of the jury foreman, Jerry Russell, he was the third to go, but the first she had heard about. She shared what she knew, he was killed by a mudslide on the way to his home, washing him and his large pickup over the side of the road and drowned him in thick mud, and only him; no other cars were hit. There was rain, but normal rain; it was a freak accident.

"No way this 'Mind Killer' douche, Mark Solier could orchestrate a perfectly timed mudslide!" said Canner. He was probably the only one calling him the "Mind Killer".

Sandi continued with the death of Julie Sanders, described as the Juror with the bad life. Canner knew which one right away.

"She died first, by an accidental discharge of her car airbag, she was putting on makeup and it went off, she was found in her driveway, broken neck, the initial report showed the car was struck by lightning."

Canner was speechless, a first, staring at Sandi. Wanting more, and not yet awake, gunshots still ringing in his head, he shook his head, he couldn't process what was happening. He loved being a journalist with a motivation to make public the facts, now he sat stunned and if he was to admit it; scared. As he tried to put together what was truly happening, no way these were a series of unconnected, unrelated accidents. He knew Sandi agreed, he could see the fear in her eyes too. It was the first time he'd ever seen it there, yet he knew the look.

Sandi continued and prepped Stephen for the next one; "You probably want to stay seated for this one, the juror who was the pilot, Dave Swenson, was killed at the airport by a small plane. But get this, it was on the ground and the prop exploded, cutting him in half, right there on the taxiway of William M. Tuck airport."

Canner knew that airport, it was far away from the courthouse, wondering, but not asking why he was there.

Canner could only mumble, "Jesus fucking Christ."

He jumped up, startled Sandi, then said "Let's go." as he grabbed his suit off of his bedside suit valet, ready to go, always. He grabbed his gun too, checked the safety, knowing he needed to reload his clip. Two bullets in the ceiling and one in his clenched fist. He rechecked the safety, and against his extensive gun training to always have the safety on, he confirmed it was still off, ready to fire. He wanted to be ready for what might come next. He was now relying on his survival instincts, his experience wouldn't help him now. Sandi stared at him as even after ten years, she knew this was not normal Canner behavior.

As they transitioned down the hall, elevator, and stairs to Sandi's poorly parked car, she filled him in on the other three deaths. All as incredible as the first three, all seemingly accidental, as it would be difficult to impossible to plan them. She also had the address and phone numbers of the remaining six jurors, if they were still alive.

Two of the jurors lived in gated communities preventing any access, let alone news reporters at nearly 4 am, and endless phone calls produced nothing, no answers. Sandi called one so many times, it filled the voicemail box, preventing any more messages.

One juror did answer and invited them to his home. They jumped in Sandi's car and she accelerated as Stephen closed his door and buckled his seatbelt, being thrust against his seat and to the side. The tires squealed, as they made the last corner, turning onto the street of the juror. They weren't the only ones disturbing the usual morning silence of the upscale neighborhood.

Sandi scared Canner from focus and thumb-typing on his phone, "A JESUS FUCKIN' FIRE!" The home on the left side of the street was on fire, and not a small fire, it was obviously being fueled by some type of ongoing accelerant. Canner was in shock as he counted the house quickly and realized it was their juror.

As they both were distracted by the enormous, uncontrolled fire, both their phones now ringing, and alert notifications going non-stop. The incredible set of circumstances happening faster than anyone could know in only the last few hours.

Sandi was suddenly and violently thrown against the seatbelt and her airbag exploded, the fire truck hit her car full force from the back thrusting it over the curb into the well-manicured yard hitting a large tree and flipping it, driver side down. Sandi knocked out or worse, Canner was awake but dazed as more and more sirens and lights appeared in his head and right in front of his now clearing up vision.

He was fighting to stay conscious as he tried to process what was happening. He knew he was hurt, he knew he was alive, he knew little more.

43

Be strong and courageous. Do not fear or be in dread of them, for it is the Lord your God who goes with you. He will not leave you or forsake you.
   – Deuteronomy 31:6

Ralph and Jack always arrived early. The courtroom was as they left it, ready for justice. Day two of any trial was the day it really started. Day one was full of emotion for most, as it was often their first time in the courtroom, and this case, even for veterans of the process, caused anxiety due to its premise and the overwhelming presence of the defendant.

The courtroom this early was mostly empty, Jack could tell the Judge was there as his personal items were on the higher rise bench and the court reporter was organizing the area. No jurors were present as they were held in the jury room until needed. Jack and Ralph set up on the prosecution side, Dale had not yet arrived. Ralph had called him, woke him up, but he still wasn't yet here. Ralph knew they didn't need him, but he also knew they did. Ralph nor Jack were formally representing the state. Dale was that figure, his role was to prosecute based on the law, in this case, he was doing what Rucker told him to do.

Judge Ford stepped out of the neatly disguised chamber's door, it was blended with the polished wood walls installed more than one hundred years ago. The courtroom was ornate then, from a time when the judicial process was at the core of our country and the rights of its private citizens. The Judge was bellowing to Jack and Ralph to join him quickly. As Jack and Ralph got up, the press area started to chatter, phones buzzing, ringing. Jack recognized their faces but he couldn't hear their words, something had happened. Jack noted he didn't see Canner; many years knowing he was the center of attention, but in the middle of this chaos, no Canner present. Ralph noticed it too, he also didn't see Canner's sidekick producer. That was odd for both to not be there. Ralph caught up to Jack, as they were on the edge of running towards the Judge.

Jack made direct eye contact with Judge Ford as the Judge shared what he knew, which was not much. Seven of the jurors were dead, the last of a gas explosion early this morning in an upscale neighborhood, about two hours ago. The other jurors were being located, none of which could be contacted. Ralph not normally known to speak first, repeated the judge's words, "None?"

Judge Ford said it again, slowly not to make a point, but because he too was stunned, while staring at Jack, "None."

The beginning of the next words were interrupted by a professional, yet escalated, knock on the chamber door. The knocking accelerated and in escalating intensity, as it sounded like two people wanted his attention. The Judge himself moved quickly to the door. Two people entered, first was the bailiff with his gun drawn, clearly looking to protect the judge, the next was Canner; or what looked like Canner.

Ralph stepped back, Jack stepped forward. Canner was in bad shape. Jack had seen Canner suffer unexplained black eyes and a few broken bones, but not this, he should have been in a hospital. What Jack didn't know, was that Canner was in the hospital. Upon his first conscious thought, just thirty minutes ago, Canner tore out his IV and forced his way out, walking the two miles to where he now stood. He came straight to the Judge's chambers.

Four experienced men stood in the chambers of a three-term elected judge, what now seemed a small room off the courtroom that typically processes domestic disputes and misdemeanors. They all knew it was the start of something that the law nor the press could control.

Dale and Ralph huddled, to refresh themselves on how re-placement jurors are called, but more focused on providing a motion to the Judge for these extraordinary circumstances. Jack had suggested something out of the standard practices, it was out loud, directly at Ralph, but with enough force in his voice for all to hear. As intended, it was a directive. Ralph knew it wasn't a suggestion and Dale too, not that he had a choice. Jack's direction was clear, "The new jurors need to be masked, hiding their identity from the defendant."

Canner answered his phone, taking the focus off of the needed legal activities; he only looked worse from what he was being told. He moved quickly towards the Judge as the bailiff reached for his gun, Canner grabbed the television remote, off the large desk of the Judge, glanced at the bailiff, the bailiff had removed the retention strap on his holster and had removed his gun halfway, ready for anything, Canner deliberately moved slowly now, showed the bailiff the remote, and hit the power button. The TV flicked, Canner changed it to channel 5 and there was a scene of chaos, shot from a helicopter, one flying low, below the buildings.

Less than five seconds passed, the attention from all four and now the bailiff too saw the scene. A car on fire, a large group of medical personnel, and the banner across the bottom; "Breaking News, Juror injured outside of courthouse." Only now were the sirens barely audible in the Judge's secure chambers. The bailiff, now fully in defense mode, pulled his gun completely out of its holster, positioned himself between the door and the judge, opened the door, and the sound of the chaos now blasted in the room. Sirens from multiple emergency vehicles and the rhythmic thumping of a low flying helicopter, its blades cutting open the morning air, echoing off the nearby buildings.

Next, the picture on the television flickered from the source, it wavered, spun, and quickly descended towards the street. The noise coming through the empty courtroom, echoing from the nearby street was synchronized with the audio coming from the now videoless television picture, a large explosion outside caused the television to now go silent and black. The bailiff turned and asked, more commanded, the Judge to stay in the chambers. Jack and Dale stayed, Canner didn't, he moved, quick. He was injured, with life-threatening injuries, and while most would not be able to move, he nearly beat the bailiff out the door on his way to the street.

The news went wild, the crash of the helicopter, the death of the last juror. Quickly the case details streamed online faster than the facts could be checked. The death of the jurors and the transformation of the defendant from geeky and likable, to stoic and scary; Mark Solier.

III

It Ends

44

Who hate the good, and love the evil; who pluck off their
skin from off them, and their flesh from off their bones.
   - Micah 3:2

Stuart was more frustrated today than most days. Every paper, national or local was full of the opposite of the message he has worked his whole life, since his accident, to deliver to the American people. His message of hope and trust went unheard. People only talked about despair and doubt. He was frustrated. His admin was late, he couldn't get the help he needed, as when others got busy, they forgot about the "courtesy" that he didn't want, but he accepted that he needed, to function. It's something he was used to in the regular world, as if he was invisible, being now overweight and in his wheelchair for the last eighteen years. He was now twenty-eight years old, but he felt and looked older. Most wore a look of shock when they learned his age, no doubt others thought he was older than he was. He'd gone through the ups and downs for years after his injury and had been incredibly productive at the side of Joe Callahan, even getting the right kind of public attention at times and being an excellent role model for paraplegics. At least in public, he mentally sighed. It was getting noisy in the outer office, which caused two more problems, one it was noisy and he couldn't shut the door the last two inches, and he couldn't get anyone's attention to help him get his day started. He was stuck with what he didn't want, the newspaper full of bad news. He hadn't yet heard the worst news, the accidental death of his mother.

Stuart Wilson was popular. Sometimes popular for negative reasons, but he was known by everyone. The press core wouldn't touch him, even the most aggressive ones as they knew two things, not even the press can attack a disabled politician (is that what he was?) and they needed him to give them the facts, the real story, and he was right, every time. He needed to be right this time, he reached for the most valuable tool he had, his phone, and touched the screen, hitting the digits quickly to a number very few people had, one that the receiver was always answered, as no call was ever placed that wasn't of the most important nature. Calls directly to Joe Callahan's office were not placed by accident.

45

We know that we are from God, and the whole world
lies in the power of the evil one.
  - 1 John 5:19

P eople were upset at the declaration of a mistrial, an unpopular motion made by the district attorney. Dale was just doing what he was told. Mark Solier was back on the street, in public, with the will and the power to kill. Although not an outright dismissal of the charges, the public didn't know or care. The suspect was guilty and yet free to kill again. Dale motioned on a manifest necessity, making it impossible for justice to be obtained. This time it was made impossible from the entire jury being killed in one night. The legal community was shocked and the campaign headquarters of Joseph Callahan was stunned. Watching this unfold, Joe was disappointed at the 24-hour news channel's actions, as he always was, but this one really dug deep as finding an expert on this subject didn't exist. The normal retirees were coming out of retirement, acting like experts with their old experience and older opinions. They were saying what people wanted to hear. Joe always thought they should publish their fee as part of the "expert" label they were given and brushed off the thought as he took stock of his current situation.

Callahan was associated with many things in his home state of New Mexico, where he worked hard to fill every public service in earning his way, paying his dues, to be a Senator, and a US Congressman, one of only two people New Mexico counted on to represent them. Now for twelve years. He was often considered a conservative; he's been called rebel, cowboy, and leader, sometimes within the same campaign week, regardless of whether it was city council, state governor, or his most recent reelection, to again be their Senator and represent the people of New Mexico at the national level.

Joe thought of his loyal team, Stuart always being on top of things. He had known Stuart since he coached his football team back when Stuart was just ten years old. Stuart Wilson became a well-known person in New Mexico, and often untouchable, as no one would go after a disabled person. Joe never saw him that way anymore, although it was difficult after his accident, Stuart needed the campaign, which was for Governor at the time as Joe remembered. Completely unintentional, but Joe's private actions, later made public towards Stuart, were what gave him the sympathy from some and the power from others about his message, doing the right thing, no matter the pressure. Joe didn't feel responsible as accidents happen, although he still remembers the ten-year-old version of Stuart saying, "Coach I can't feel my legs," as they were both trying to hold back tears.

Joe had been in Virginia all week campaigning for the election in November. The party convention was approaching, and being close to the "Hill" was important, of course, the week's agenda constructed by Stuart. Joe couldn't watch another minute of the 24-hour news and forced his tired body out of the hotel chair in an attempt to find the remote.

He found the off button. Hotels always having the big remotes with the big buttons. It was the big red button, a simple push silenced the room. His brain could not focus. It needed to focus, now. Something needed to be done and Joe slept little last night. His mind was his only distraction. He had lived a full life, full of many experiences. He often played them over and over in his mind, what could he have done better, what could he have done more. As he was now the Republican nominated presidential candidate, it came with some welcomed privileges, an army of aides to do the work, and the ability to gain true privacy were two he appreciated this early morning. He let his mind race, thinking of his impact on justice from the beginning of his career, staying the course to align facts with outcomes. He now had earned and would be responsible for what came next.

The call came at 8:00 am, he recognized the incoming number, and knowing its importance Joe answered without a greeting. He listened more than normal and acknowledged a few of the critical points. Going forward was no longer a choice but a requirement in this political process. He and his team had opened the discussion, one that had been needed for the last ten years (or more) and had been two to three years overdue. The United States judicial system was worth it, he closed his eyes as he laid back on the bed, listening to the next actions the campaign should take. He noted the emphasis by his trusted partner on the word "the." It was no longer his campaign, over ten million dollars and three hundred people were actively engaged in "the" campaign, but only a few would be involved in the actions. The call ended without goodbyes, with Joe needing to find his schedule manager, he needed to free up his lunch.

46

The plans of the diligent lead surely to abundance, but
everyone who is hasty comes only to poverty.
   – Proverbs 21:5

J ack got off the phone. He already had a busy morning,
being briefed by his team on a variety of media stories,
both those printed and those in the pipeline. He had
one of his teams dedicated to specifically leading the press,
a carefully orchestrated mix of leaks and misinformation,
although the press was arrogant enough to think they were
partners. He walked to the outer office, as the noise had gone
from active and chaotic to a quiet buzz. He was glad Stuart
was at it again, Jack knew him before the accident, as a young
star football player on the local fields of Ackerford, a boy
from a broken home but focused and energized towards his
goal. Jack watched from afar, as this hometown boy, who
reminded him of himself at that age, had opportunities taken
away through an accident that wasn't preventable. Jack had
watched Stuart grow, never making an excuse then and not
now. He was someone to be trusted. Jack called Angela, a few
things had to be arranged. As he waited for the phone to be

answered, he saw the polished new guy from the previously failed Jackson campaign go by with his phone glued to his ear. While waiting on Angela to answer, Jack looked through his one-way glass installed in his office. He observed the new staff member who started on the team today, whom Jack met a few weeks ago and hired yesterday. Jack vetted Thomas quickly as he was both an alumni of Yale and a fellow Bonesman. Thomas's start to life was more complex, yet it checked out in complete detail by the team Jack used to investigate everyone he worked with or wanted to know more about. The investigation uncovered detailed information about his family, read weeks ago, and before an offer was made to Thomas. The detailed information identified Thomas's father, born as a bastard from the war in Vietnam, Jack recalled the term, Amerasian. Thomas's father, and then Thomas himself, was heavily discriminated against, their South Asian looks caused those still angry about the war to treat them as if they were leftovers. Thomas was a grandchild of a Vietnamese Grandmother and the offspring of an American war-fighting patriot. He wasn't the only one, there were thousands, yet the real number never known. Jack knew their struggle, he led many cases that involved the mothers, those that didn't abandon their children, known in Vietnam as "children of the dust." Jack remembered when he first felt alone as a lawyer, as he took on these cases early in his career, as justice was not being served. He was triggered, motivated to do something, when his own government, on their own official statement dismissed them. "The care and welfare of these unfortunate children, has never been and is not now considered an area of government responsibility," the US Defense Department said in a 1970 statement. Jack remembered it clearly, as it

46

was one of his first actions of always getting justice for the injustice. The action was covert, outside the boundary of the law, as he used his secret Bonesmen relationships to pass on information to the often seen as competing, yet in reality, collaborative, group in the Freemasons. This influence started and then was relentlessly fueled by the young Bonesman, known as Robin Hood. It drove President Gerald Ford, the last known Masonic President, to announce plans in 1975 to begin Operation Babylift, its goal to evacuate these so-called, Amerasians, from their destiny of becoming unwanted beggars and criminals. Jack felt the power of serving and driving true justice.

Jack didn't know if Thomas's father was saved by this program, although likely he was saved as part of the action set in motion by Jack's relentless methods to drive what was right and those of President Ford. Thomas' father, who would have been around seven years old, surely wasn't part of the first flight, Jack remembered it had crashed and killed one hundred forty-four people, mostly children. There were no records of the remaining three thousand "relocated" to the United States as the government called it. Jack thought of it as being "saved" from what would have been a difficult life in Vietnam. Looking part Asian, yet easily recognized as the child of a blue-eyed American was not one most lived through. Jack knew that a lot of initial American foster parents, or even government officials who couldn't spell or pronounce the baby's given name, changed their names. These relocated children started new lives, with adoptive parents all over the United States. He also knew, that only three percent of those that were searching, found their fathers. Even the deep resources Jack had at his request, could find little of Thomas' father's beginning. Jack knew that when the Communists came to Vietnam in 1975, mothers of children born from Americans, destroyed or hid photographs. There was no documentation left. He didn't know if Thomas had found his American military grandfather. Jack thought he knew everything there was to be found about Thomas. Jack used multiple resources, including Ralph, to build a background on him. Thomas had a difficult upbringing for a street kid, with extended family in New Mexico. He lived with his birth father, then as a foster child upon his father's disappearance. He was the textbook definition of "at-risk", but though having temporary parents, and limited details on his own history, he became only strengthened by the challenges he faced. Thomas graduated from Yale, but he came from a desert town near Albuquerque, New Mexico. This was Jack's friend, Joe Callahan's, home state and recently Thomas was recruited from Joe's political competition, the now discontinued Jackson campaign. Jack smiled now.

The blue-eyed, young and fit, recently hired to the Callahan campaign, Thomas Williams was on a bee-line to Stuart Wilson's office. Angela finally answered her phone and Jack turned toward the outside window, his back to his office door. He was now looking over the US Supreme Court building, with the US Capitol in the background.

Having the newest model phone held to his ear, waiting for someone to pick up, Stuart was glad to see Thomas approaching his office. Stuart waved to Thomas, and then in his often overly direct ways, pointed and gestured with his hand at the intern sitting in front of him. In a nonverbal way, he indicated 'shut up' towards the recently added by Jack, talking intern, Mary somebody? Stuart couldn't remember. She shut down with a frown on her face, but was quiet, which is what he wanted. Stuart was annoyed with the lack of urgency by the team that was hired, some of which he hired himself, some were assigned to him by Rucker, including this new one today. She was sitting quietly, looking useless to him. Stuart was unaware of the value she had already provided to Jack.

Thomas came on board through a variety of recommendations, originally working for Robert Jackson, a popular southern candidate who was running a close second in the presidential primary, statistically the same, but people didn't understand or care about the margin of error anyway. He was a close second until some of his family history was uncovered and he lost the minority votes. It is difficult to recover when your forefathers, less than two generations ago, not only had slaves but had been convicted of killing some during the Civil War. Unfortunate, thought Stuart, some things are unable to be recovered from, even without an approved smear campaign, which Joe refused to do.

Stuart never thought of these tactics as more than political, not dirty. Facts were facts. Jackson's great grandfather did have slaves, he did kill them. These were facts, not dirty tricks. Joe Callahan refused to use them, yet he didn't prevent others from doing it. His professional conclusion assumed Thomas was driven and willing. Joe wouldn't do it, but Rucker would. Stuart knew Rucker chose the right fights, had the connections to execute the plan, and most importantly, the willingness to see it through. Rucker never shied away from the opportunity to right a wrong, getting justice for an injustice.

Stuart met Thomas just a week ago before he was officially hired, at the request of Rucker. You didn't not follow the requests, seen as direction, of Jack Rucker. Stuart thought Thomas was a cool cat though, both with the ladies and with the tongue. Even in such a short time of knowing each other, Thomas had helped Stuart smooth over his abrupt tone on multiple occasions and he was, even in the first informal week and today being his first official day, well respected by all the interns and seemingly by Rucker as well. Stuart could have been jealous, as Thomas was younger than Stuart by six years, had full use of his legs, with similar backgrounds, what he knew of him anyway, and was probably living the life that Stuart would be living without the wheelchair or the extra fifty pounds that came from being a prisoner to your disability.

Stuart ended the call, pushing the red hang-up button on his phone. He placed it face down hard on his desk, frustrated at the lack of anyone answering. He then looked at Mary (?), and her resume, which he held in his hand, getting her name right, Mary Morgan. He then waved again to Thomas as he got closer to the door, to come in, and said "Mary, here comes someone I'd like you to meet."

The door opened, a near gust of fresh air entered the stale office, full of law books, every political book ever written, the hint of a woman's perfume, and the slight stench of a wheelchair and its prisoner.

"Stuart, rough day yesterday, how crazy is it that the jurors all died? but we have the right team, never forget that," said Thomas, turning the grimace of the intern now paying attention into a quiet smile, an effect Stuart didn't have on people.

"Thomas, good to see you, how's your day looking, I could use some trusted help to run some things down," which caused the intern to collect her computer, her notes, and her books. She stood up, ignoring Stuart and Thomas, and started to walk away. Stuart quickly told her, not by name, as he still didn't recall, nor bother to look at her resume again, to "stay and help with other dealings."

Thomas took a seat to the right, while Stuart had the intern take down the name of the restaurant for lunch, the Old Ebbitt Grill, in his expected and normal condescending tone, he spelled it for her, E-B-B-I-T-T. He then told her to use the code word, "Harry" with the hostess to ensure the availability and the private table. Stuart knew this code word would get the little-known secure room reserved. It would also bump anyone from the schedule. When he called, he never had to wait. The code name made no sense to most others. Stuart felt his own pride in using it. He was the one that gave it to President-to-be Callahan.

"Make the reservation for three." Without saying please or sharing the names of the other two.

She frowned and shuffled out. Thomas stood up quickly and opened the door for her. Thomas and Stuart were both looking at her in surprise as she left. Stuart just saw another intern who was going to be a problem. Thomas saw an opportunity. Thomas then closed the door, and turned the spindle on the blinds, darkening the room from the outer office light and giving Thomas his desired privacy.

"So, Thomas, what's your take?"

"On what, the intern?" He said with sarcasm, just giving himself time to give a better answer to the expected question from Stuart.

"No, this crazy case and the jurors dying," Stuart said knowing Thomas was stalling.

"It sucks Stuart, but I know you are prepared, everyone is probably getting lazy because they know you had already planned the action we'd take, just in case," he smiled at Stuart. Thomas hadn't known the content of the early morning call directly to "Harry" but his assumptions were right, there was an action plan being created. He knew Stuart would have an important role in defining the next steps.

Thomas, using a well-rehearsed sleight of hand, replaced Stuart's leather binder with the replica he had made. The electronic device no one would see, placed in the embossed logo of the Callahan campaign. Powered by kinetic movements, the device used nearly no power until it was needed. The slow turn and effort Stuart needed to use in turning his custom office wheelchair, gave Thomas plenty of time to swap it without notice, transferring its contents and putting the original in his own bag, which Thomas concealed below the level of the desk. The interior blinds, casually, yet purposefully closed, prior to the swap by Thomas, making it even more possible and discrete.

Thomas was in awe of no one, having grown up on his own, hustling for everything he had, both material and his experiences. At times he escaped with his life and had to start again. His life experiences had trained him well. His former life had forced him to adapt, his experiences as an unwanted child, in unwanted foster homes, the torture from his unloving father who disappeared, or his unknown grandfather, even after an exhaustive search looking for him. Thomas had resources, even as a young adult, in addition to his own tenacious grit, he had technical resources. A self-taught hacker using his skills to find out what he needed, and to fund his bank accounts, from the easily stolen credit cards of strangers, to execute his missions. The only thing he knew about his grandfather was that he had been an American Army Captain in Vietnam. His grandfather was a ghost. If he died, he would have found him through his backdoor access to the Department of Defense DNA databases. He must still be alive, yet a ghost. Thomas couldn't find him and wouldn't give up. Thomas was fueled by a desire in his youth to make amends, avenge, and revenge. His goal, was first and foremost to do the right thing, using any and all, legal, illegal, and covert ways to get things done. It was all the same to him, his means always justified the ends. His training was not being wasted.

"Well," Stuart sighed and looked around the room, "I'll be out of the office today and likely too busy to manage the interns.

Can you take over and give them some type of direction?" Thomas knew the agenda was judicial reform, he knew it from the bottom of his being, getting justice was his life's mission. True justice. He had seen enough injustice for multiple lifetimes. He had and now was, being asked to take action. He was ready, willing, connected, and capable.

"I know that I'm new and we were once in competition just a short time ago, but our agendas were and still are the same, I appreciate your willingness to ask me," Thomas said as he looked Stuart in the eye without blinking.

Stuart liked being liked, it happened very infrequently, "No problem Thomas, you remind me of me, I hope you take that as a compliment."

Thomas was good at hiding his agenda, unlike Stuart who told the truth more with his facial expressions, lacking the regular non-verbal body language signals most people have. Thomas was the master at hiding his purpose, "Stuart, it is an honor to think I was done after Mr. Jackson's unfortunate history was revealed, and now I continue to work with professionals."

"Great, I'll send out an email letting the interns know they report to you. I need to leave in the car at 11:20 am, so I'll do it before then."

Thomas was about to reply as Stuart's phone vibrated on the wooden desk and then rang in the generic ringtone, Stuart grabbed it on the first ring and Thomas left providing the thumbs up response to Stuart's request. He left already knowing who was on the list. He was interested in what Mary Morgan knew. His training paid off again, and during lunch, he would know more in a few hours than he knew in months of his regular intelligence gathering.

Over his life, he found being proactive and knowing more than others benefited him. It is how he learned about his father's private life and why he decided to kill him.

He now needed to know what Stuart knew. He wanted to know what Jack Rucker was doing. He deserved to know what Joe Callahan was planning. He didn't know how'd he'd use the information, he just knew he would need it. Hopefully not to kill anyone, but he often moved in the direction the information pointed.

47

Know this, my beloved brothers: let every person be
quick to hear, slow to speak, slow to anger; for the anger
of man does not produce the righteousness of God.
  – James 1:19-20

A s in every society, there exist secrets. Some are those
that occurred in the past and people no longer talk
openly about them, or some occur every day, under
the cover of normalcy. This day was a nasty rainy one in
the suburbs of Richmond. This group of carefully selected
strangers, invited and each elected to join the mission, were all
quiet professionals in their own way. They all elected to join,
individually confirming via the secure network. The network
notified Doug, a senior member of the Group, only those
names who had confirmed to fulfill this particular mission.
Doug was chosen to be this mission's leader. He had lead
missions before. The confirmed team members were all on
the way and Doug just waited, the mission objective in his
hand. The Group was activated to accomplish it.

Jeff showed up first. His military training and years of

experience killing people always had him doing two things, the first was to show up and the second was to think violently. Jeff was a member of the Group for as long as Doug had been, not that they joined together, or even knew each other. They knew of each other only by code name and reputation, but Doug knew they were recruited about the same time.

What the others didn't know was that Doug Barlow was a teacher. Even Doug realized the chasm of difference between his regular world of being a teacher of the future, and the when needed role, of killing people who needed killing. They also didn't know or care, that Doug wasn't even his real name.

They all knew the history, as it was used to recruit them. The group formed due to the disgust of a Vietnam veteran, known personally by no one. He had disappeared years ago. The Colonel, as everyone referred to him, was only known to have earned the rank of Captain in the US Army. He had served in Vietnam and often was stuck between impossible policy and necessary war, where he had seen more good men killed by dumbed-down policy than the war itself. His reputation, real or not, preceded him and was a critical part of recruitment. Doug even remembered that it was the leadership of the Colonel that caused himself, a teacher in an inner-city public school, but former special ops to commit, commit to something important. The Group's origin was unknown. Some have thought, including Doug, its mission was born in medieval times. Being a teacher, Doug had researched what he could, finding that the mission of justice for the injustice was aligned with the secret society known as the Courts of Vehm. The Vehm Courts then, and the

Group now had a simple mission, and that was to identify and overturn wrongdoings by the United States Justice system. Doug had heard over the years about how people had received preferential treatment, or a mistrial was called due to poor lawyers or poor laws, sometimes both. Over the years, the Group had investigated and taken action to cure the faults of others. Doug bowed his head slightly and forgave himself for his private thoughts. He shook his head and realized that some killing, outside of war, needed to be done.

The Group kept no records, no formal covenants, just everyone knew their role, and Jeff's role was to show up first and bring the violence. He thought about Jeff's involvement over the last twenty years, coming in as young as he, doing things that normal people would regret after they age a little, but like him, Jeff had no regrets. The Colonel recruited them himself, identifying them as young men frustrated with the movement during the mid-seventies, frustrated with the gridlock of action, and the focus on the weak, those that knew no personal accountability. Even now, Doug remained focused, as the cycle of limited accountability has grown again in the last six or seven years. Doug laughed to himself about the hot coffee incident a few years back, where a millionaire was made from hot coffee, that was too hot, getting spilled in a drive-thru. Jeff looked over as he unpacked his belongings, as Doug didn't laugh to himself as much as he thought.

"What's so funny?" asked Jeff.

"Just having a hard time accepting the world, and reminding myself of our purpose," said Doug.

Jeff barely acknowledged the response. He was busy, both in his organization of his belongings and his own personal reminders of the situation. He left early that day, knowing the general population wouldn't be smart enough to know that rain causes traffic problems around Richmond. The forty-minute drive to the meeting place took up to an hour, so he got started early. Unlike others, he had no story to make up about his time away from work or his time away from his family, neither of which he had full time. This part was painful for Jeff, not that he let it drive his decisions, but he always thought about what could have been. He deployed to every war that had happened after Vietnam, to Grenada, Panama, Bosnia, Desert Storm, Afghanistan, and Iraq again. He was then discharged on a quiet day, about five years ago. His family, his wife, and young boy were killed while he was away in Iraq. He wasn't notified for more than a month after the accident as he was embedded deep into the front line, being in downtown Baghdad for target identification and what was called "illumination" by the USAF, illumination of the targets for termination. After so many years, Jeff knew this was the moment that the Colonel identified him to be part of the Group, adding him to an existing group of members that had been together since the early seventies. Learning a month in delay that the only thing you cared about and he knew too, the only thing that cared about him was gone. His wife and son were cremated before he could even be notified. Jeff's reaction was surprising to some, as his election to stay in the field instead of going home was amplified by his question to his superiors, "What good can I do there?" Jeff was head down now, focused, and stated clearly, "My job is now here full time." He continued cleaning and polishing the high-capacity magazines and reloading with 5.56mm ammo. Jeff didn't know the Colonel at that time but was reassigned within a few weeks, for his own good he was told at the time, but it was clear now, the Colonel called his name.

Jeff didn't look like he did back then. Part of the assignment was no longer to illuminate targets for the flyboys but to personally take them out with confirmation. The Colonel's team was anonymous, all of which went through personal changes, to both the physical and mental areas. Jeff had not been Jeff at the time, he was someone else and he had been transformed into Jeff Knowles, his former life and name almost now forgotten. As they were going undercover, deeper than even the military special forces, his physical appearance was changed to fit in, blend in, where questions wouldn't be asked nor any medals earned.

The Colonel was good to Jeff, he was constantly in the field, assigned to take care of injustice. He sometimes was a single-person team. He liked action not talk and he had the chance to deliver upon this, doing what he was asked to do, and never questioned when he felt he needed to do more. There are many things he did that no one would even know.

The door banged open as the person entering was carrying two large metal briefcases. As obtuse as possible, the looming figure said, "Don't get up, I'll do all the bullshit work myself," which caused Doug to laugh, as he wasn't getting up. He knew the Group personalities, even though he didn't know these members. They were all self-sufficient, motivated by the common goal of justice, not wanting help and only once in a while sarcastically pointing it out. Doug didn't look up, and replied as any member of the Group would have, saying nothing more than "OK," with the same, expected, self-sufficient sarcasm.

Paul Hammond didn't say a thing unless it was some type of undercut or sarcastic comment not even intended to have humor. He was a strong build, although he looked normal in his 'civvies', not being able to give up the military slang term for being dressed like a civilian. He didn't have a single military bone in his body or thought in his head. He was the expert at understanding people and knowing the spin to put on the outcome of each plan. Doug got up, to satisfy his own needs, curious to help him open the briefcases as he knew they contained some framework to the plan, all of which would be useless in the hands of others, but the Group had been together long enough to read between the lines. Jeff didn't budge, or even acknowledge the entrance of Paul and some of the other members, as they arrived to do their parts; he kept working within his own world, as he had done for years.

Paul gathered this particular group of experts, without words, as he opened and showed the hand-drawn documents. He had been doing this for the last ten years, not caring about the advances in technology, he knew if the plans were hand done on paper, with a pencil, there was no electronic way of infiltrating the data, besides, they were as good as any plans could be done. The goal was established, the timeline defined, and the assignments made. Paul knew everybody by reputation and he knew what they were capable of and willing to do for the Colonel, even in his permanent absence.

"You all know the target," Paul said, adding "the news you don't watch," Paul emphasized with the Group's typical sarcasm, "calls him the 'Mind Killer'."

As Paul was getting into the plan, Doug's secure pager, the same one they all had been issued and used for just one purpose, went off. As he checked it, he held it up and showed them, one by one, what the message said. They all knew it was coming from the control number, the true source could have been anyone, the source was never known, yet trusted. The message simply said, "Adam is Dead." If an outsider was there to witness the reaction, they would have seen nothing, not even a change in expression. Doug knew that the people here worked for their own reasons, working as individuals they functioned as a team, but that was as far as it went. Everyone knew Adam, or the person they called Adam, no one in the Group, past or present, had a real name. They all knew him from separate, past engagements, and they knew he brought the technical expertise to blow things up using electronics but no one knew or cared beyond that.

Paul continued on as he described the background of the case at hand. He defined the target, and defined the past and ongoing injustice, he started on the need for urgency as the beeps came through the room's only secure door. The secure lock buttons were being pushed from the outside. Doug paused, Paul looked up, Jeff pulled out his never-on safety sidearm, and they waited. The sixth beep was heard in the small, windowless, single-door room. The last number of the security lock entered, a slight pause and the door lock clicked loud. The door opened. Juan was the angry one and always last. Juan didn't speak English very well, often in short bursts only. It annoyed most of the team, but his willingness to do the tough work and his ability to engage in any environment, made him more valuable than any annoyance, again, known, but never talked about. He showed up and joined the Group around the table, not even slowing the progress of the plan briefing. Paul looked up, made eye contact with Juan, and continued communicating the mission, the facts, and the roles to each member of the Group. There was one missing member, Adam's duties were assigned to others.

The plan put forth by Paul was non-negotiable, if you didn't like it, then go home, the Group would go without you. The Group had never been a democracy, the Colonel set the rules and you followed, otherwise you were out, with no way to fulfill your need for justice, except by individual efforts. This happened once, that Doug knew about, there was a lot about this Group he knew he would never know.

What Doug did know was from a few years back. A member frustrated with emotion, wanting the Group to take action, separated themselves from Group, and took action independently. This previous Group member had killed a judge in Oregon in 1989. The Judge was from New Mexico, appointed by the Oregon governor, to expand and clean up the corruption in his state. "James", the former Group member, was caught by the police and charged with murder, for which he did commit and for which the police had plenty of evidence, justice was to be served. The Colonel made sure there was a plethora of evidence and a plea bargain was never offered, as he had more influence than most could imagine. Doug always remembered the Colonel had been at this his whole life before he disappeared. Not only did the member known as James get caught, he was quickly charged, and in record time convicted, with no attempt at a plea. Doug remembered the headlines as, during this time, his secure pager was silent, there were no missions. He remembered the case being prosecuted by the nationally known prosecutor, Jack Rucker. There was talk of a conspiracy as James was claiming his innocence and was only a petty criminal, a background no doubt forged to protect the Group. He was later killed in a prison riot. No one questioned or cared that it was orchestrated by the Colonel himself. Doug liked the feeling of justice, regardless of how it was done, it was needed.

Paul, taking non-verbal clues from Doug to wrap it up, finished the mission briefing, using names and his finger to point at each member, defining their role and setting the expectations. The orders were given as if the Colonel was there himself. Now everyone knew the mission. The "Mind Killer" that everyone saw on TV was free, not because of his innocence but because of his guilt. People were scared, the first set of jurors were all dead, everyone had seen the now multi-million views of the video posted online of the helicopter crash on live TV. The drama of the first jury encapsulated the attention of the entire country, both young and old. Everyone thought and most knew that the juror deaths were too coincidental to be accidents. The long-tenured Federal Judge James Ford was scared. He had gone into Federal protection and his whereabouts were unknown. He was scared in a way that no protection services could prevent. As members of the first jury died the night after the prosecuting lawyer's cross-examination, Doug, witnessing the last die on live television, started the planning process. Not that he got a secure message, or that he was asked, but he did it for all the injustice he saw, regardless of the size of the injustice. He knew his secure pager would start to go off. He knew others would too. The message from an unknown source to start the process of an unemotional revenge, justice for the injustice, as it was known by the Colonel's manifesto. Now going on for more years than Doug could know for sure. He also did it for his own bearing, it felt good to provide a plan for justice when someone else could not. He did it for everything he saw, local or national.

Doug even did a justice plan for when a driver fled the scene of a traffic accident which that driver caused, killing a family of five. Doug had tried to save the family, there was nothing he could do to help them then. It was initially an untouched case, slipping through a too busy judicial system. Doug witnessed the fleeing guilty suspect, with his own eyes from two car lengths behind it. Doug wouldn't let this injustice go, it was what Doug felt he was born to fix, getting justice for the injustice. He shared the details of his eye witness, using his real name, for the record, with just one, newly badged Federal US Marshal assigned, a sharp resource named Gary Barker. Doug remembered the then younger prosecutor who got the conviction of the runaway criminal, Jack Rucker. Doug also knew from the news he didn't watch, that it was the same Jack Rucker that was driving the law in this case, prosecuting the "Mind Killer", upfront in public, not hiding behind a mask or secret service protection. He was again taking on responsibilities that no one was asking of him, disregarding his personal safety, and everyone else was scared to pursue what was right per how the law was written. Doug Barlow, by his fake name, and Jack Rucker had never met, and it was unlikely to impossible that Jack even knew the Group existed, but Doug knew Jack existed and followed his cases. Often they would work cases Rucker didn't win, although not many, as Rucker was famous for proving beyond a reasonable doubt the guilt or innocence based on fact. Doug remembered a few cases, where the innocent was charged, and the Colonel took care of that too, it wasn't all bad work, one of the things that kept Doug in the game, as it was about justice.

"Let's go," Doug stated to the group and everyone started out the door. Before anyone said it, not that anyone intended to, Doug informed everyone that he would open the recruitment door for a replacement as Adam was now dead, no one knew how, they just got the short message. A look from Juan more to understand the English than anything else, however, no acknowledgments from anyone else. Doug knew they were here for their own reasons, none of which involved Adam. Doug knew his own and he knew without the mission of this important group, that he wasn't sure he could live life, he only assumed the others were somewhere near that target too.

The plan was simple; an accident was arranged as an ironic way to provide justice. The accident was a simple and masterful plan, Doug smiled, only slightly, not noticeable to others, as he started his car. Per his orders, he was headed for downtown to catch a plane to New York, to visit an international terrorism hub there. Doug knew he needed some intelligence and how to get it.

47

Paul was a man of mission. The rest of the Group didn't know Paul and he didn't know them. He did know the Colonel, as he had been around for a while. He met him during a trip to Washington D.C., on a security detail. A parade for returning Vietnam veterans was being held as a political statement of President Nixon. Paul remembered it vividly. The crowd was not there to celebrate, the democracy we knew had turned its back on the people that secured their freedom. The soldiers that fought the fight were blamed for the decision to fight to begin with. The politicians even had people placed in the crowd, dressed as normal folks to "enhance" the celebration, is what Paul remembered.

Paul would have forgotten that particular security detail, he had done so many, but was reminded of this specific D.C. security detail, years later, during the unofficial retirement ceremony of sorts for the Colonel. Even though the Colonel wasn't physically there to see it, a picture slide show was shown, of various public activities the Colonel was involved in. Paul recognized one of him, much younger than he was now, where there was a picture of the Colonel, then an Army Captain, and Paul, then an Army Private, initially holding back a group of peaceful protesters, there as part of the Moratorium to End the War in Vietnam. Paul remembered seeing all the signs, so he hadn't forgotten why they were all there. He hadn't forgotten the date either, October 15th, 1969. This was the day things changed. It began what President Nixon would label "the silent majority". People who kept quiet, but took action. The protestors were in front of the Lincoln Memorial building in Washington D.C. The second picture was of one of the protesters, which broke the line and attacked the Captain.

Paul recalled, the young protester, also in an Army uniform like his, more disheveled, was frantically yelling, directing his language directly at the Captain. Paul remembered subduing the man, but not quick enough, as the protester unsuccessfully threw a few punches, they were too close, but the Captain avoided them easily. Later, the Captain found Paul to thank him, nothing to do with defending the line, but more for his support of the country's ideals and to ensure it prevails. He also learned that the Colonel (Captain) ensured the protester, a former Army enlisted man, was not prosecuted. The Colonel (Captain) knew this protester was fighting for his version of justice. Paul remembered the details the Colonel somehow knew about the protester, shortly thereafter. This protester, a former Army Corporal, demoted to Private for conduct in Vietnam, had just moved to Norfolk, took a new job, had a new wife and new baby. He had no recall of attacking the Captain, nor anything he had said. The Colonel felt no need to make him pay for that. That was the beginning of the recruitment process for Paul to join the Group, as Paul realized later when the Colonel asked him to join the fight for justice. The then Captain disappeared the next day. It was 1969. Paul had never seen him again, nor had others. Only rumors of his existence persisted, often talked about only once by new recruits. His earned and given nomenclature of Colonel was the only way he was referenced. Paul remembered the name of the protester, Jim Solier, but didn't recall the last name of the Captain, nor had he remembered him wearing the required name tag on his uniform.

48

*Repay no one evil for evil, but give thought to do what
is honorable in the sight of all. If possible, so far as it
depends on you, live peaceably with all.*
  – Romans 12:17-18

Mary picked up her phone and it was her date from last night. She saw it was him, and let it ring a few times to show she wasn't so eager. She was glad he called that next morning. Their date (I wonder if that's what he thought it was) was more of a gathering of the Callahan admins, assistants, interns, and other staff, there were so many. They all reported to Thomas now, including her and he was keeping them busy. Mary was invited by Thomas, even though it was an informal gathering. She wanted to see Thomas. She also went to see some of the others and to hear the buzz about the trial's unexpected outcome. She hadn't yet seen the papers this morning, but she knew it had been a busy night for Thomas's team. The room's cell phones were in a constant state of ring last night during dinner. Some had the forethought to turn them off, others were more ambitious and answered every call. Thomas was on his phone a lot of the night. He needed to be, she understood, as he was a close confidant of Stuart and Stuart Wilson was directly orchestrating most of Joe Callahan's campaign's actions, under the increasingly watchful eye of Jack Rucker.

Thomas was the only thing that kept her mind off the horrific accidents that killed all the jurors, of what the press had sarcastically relabeled the Callahan campaign tagline into the "new judicial system." He was now filling her ear about the news in the press, the upsetting turn of events, and the start of the political process to rearrange the facts, in an order that provided momentum to the agenda, the one believed to be right, and worth the sacrifice, political and physical if necessary. Thomas asked her to lunch. He wanted to have her meet him at the book store across the street from the restaurant. He said what she wanted to hear, "They have good coffee."

She hung up the phone excited to be able to see Thomas again so quickly, lunch downtown was exciting. They decided on a place with history, yet known to very few. He knew it. She only learned about it when she called to set up the lunch for Stuart. She had needed a code word then, and she remembered the spelling too. E-B-B-I-T-T.

Thomas hung up the phone thinking the call went well. He could still work his magic. He had been manipulating others for so long, that the words came out effortlessly. Staring into the empty corner of his office, his clear thoughts of action, "Now is a time for leadership," he whispered before barking orders to another intern outside his door. He wanted to make sure his reservations synced with Stuart's. It took him a few dates over the last week with the younger hostess at the restaurant, but he had his own code word. He knew he'd get a table.

She was excited and completely overwhelmed. So many things were on her mind that she couldn't concentrate for more than a few seconds. She was trying to uncloud her mind from the upcoming school year, which she hadn't even registered for yet, the status of her bank account, which was helped by joining the Rucker team as one of the few paid interns and her new relationship, blossoming quickly. She knew she was tired of Mark Solier and blocked that out. Later she would realize it was only the beginning of her journey, one where she was an unknowing passenger, holding the controls in her own hands.

49

I hate them with perfect hatred; I count them mine enemies.
  – Psalms 139:22

D oug Barlow didn't like it. A second death in a week. The original group of five was now down to three and he felt the need to adjust the plan with Paul. Adam and now Juan, gone. He didn't know how Juan died, just that he did. The message on his pager was short. No explanation given. No one would ever know their service to the injustices of the past. The future need would miss them. Doug knew more would be called to service, more would follow, as he had years ago.

The two deaths, so far, were accidents. They had to be, Doug thought, as he counted his Glock 17 clips, checked that they were full again, verified the batteries in his equipment and the backups in his military-style cargo pants side pouch. He finished loading the last clip, his thirty-three round, it was literally called the 'big stick'. He put it in the special slot in his custom cargo pants. He wasn't planning on using it to kill people, it had a different purpose this time.

The planning and execution into killing a person, even making it look like an accident, always had the possibility of someone, likely a new investigator thinking it was foul play. As investigative techniques and new data sources, such as DNA came to the forefront, killing someone became exponentially more difficult.

The Group didn't communicate other than face to face. They were notified just once of an opportunity via a secure messaging page, there were no reminders. Each member, not knowing other members, were offered an opportunity to serve justice, as people were not obligated. The individuals made their own choice to participate, if so, they showed up, did their part, and went back to whatever life they lived when not fixing injustice.

The hotel door vibrated from a single knock, Doug knowing that was the sign of a former military member who still took things serious. The next step was to verify. Using the door peephole, with its expected wall eye magnification, he looked for what he expected to see. Whoever it was, was legit, holding up the nondescriptive card, nothing on it but the purposely blurred, pixelated image to the regular eye, yet clear to the proper magnified view. Doug opened the door, with his hand on his gun, verified or not, preparation was who Doug was, not some of the time, all of the time.

Paul made eye contact, extended his hand and Doug knew things were off-plan. Paul had been around, he knew the history of the Group and but didn't share it. Doug was new, or felt new, as no one knew the tenure of the others.

"Jeff is dead," Doug said.

Paul did little more than pause. "How?"

Doug shook his head, did it matter? "I don't know, I just got the message. Like before with Adam and Juan."

Paul didn't ask more, it didn't matter. Nor did he really care. He looked at Doug and nodded to ask, what now?

Paul was a planner, he simply took in the information when it happened and adjusted. He wasn't cold, just didn't care. He had a life full of tragedy, each one removing the ability to feel.

The last option in the plan Paul put in place was still on. The first options, now gone as others were dead, and no longer available to do it.

Doug knew Paul had many skills. Today, his sniper skills would be used. Not just his shooting, but his ability to get in place without detection, disguising the muzzle flash, and leaving the scene, taking only the part of the gun that could uniquely identify it, the barrel.

They prepared to leave, there was no reason to clean up as they didn't bring anything, or use anything, and as normal, they had gloves on and subtle flesh colored masks to prevent any face recognition software from capturing their face or identifying them, but not obvious to the general public that they were in disguise. Standard practice for the Group.

They left, took the stairs out the back door of the hotel, riding bicycles to their next destination. Clandestine operations were not what was shown in the movies or written about in books, it was much less interesting in real life.

They departed and then parted without a word, nor a look, in different directions. They both knew what they would do next, yet, neither knew where the other would be going.

Paul had the longer ride, to the train station. The remaining parts of his sniper rifle were in a locked locker. The important part, the thing that is matched with the bullet, the rifles barrel, his barrel, was kept with him at all times.

Doug waited for the signal from Paul as he knew he wouldn't hear the shot from Paul's silenced sniper rifle. Doug's job, from his position in the parking garage, was to identify when Mark Solier, who was the target, was on the street. Doug would then notify Paul with the code word from his one-way transmitter, which would then vibrate Paul's throw-away one-way receiver. Doug saw the target leave the church at the expected time based on their previous surveillance. He sent the electronic code word, sending it in Morse code. Dash-Dash, break, Dash, Dot, Dash. It was the letters MK, the shortest version for the person the press labeled the "Mind Killer." What he had not seen was the flash signal from Paul's signaling mirror. Doug knew it was to come from one of six possible FFP's. Doug could demilitarize himself on the outside but still thought in military terms. Paul didn't signal from any of his Final Firing Positions. No way Doug missed it. His polarized binoculars still covered with the glare shields from his mission to the middle east desert, where the sun shined brighter. He could see clearly from his position to each of the possible selected FFP's. Paul selected the final firing positions and provided each of the possible six locations GPS coordinates to Doug. No muzzle flash, no Paul. It didn't happen. Where was Paul? Doug destroyed his transmitter as planned, broke it in thirds, and deposited each piece in locations that would never be found or the piece combined again.

Doug didn't really care what happened to Paul. He wanted to finish this job. They were motivated for this one, they wanted justice. Including Paul. So many innocent people who were serving on the jury had died horrible deaths. Doug had seen the helicopter crash on live television. Paul was the only one Doug had worked with before, he knew him from the Colonel's retirement and they had been connected on a job in Missouri, some small town to kill the town bully. There had been many witnesses, forty-six of them Doug remembered, but nobody came forward.

The worst part of any covert job was the food. You ate at places that were not crowded, avoided places with cameras, and most times, places that had employees with the most to lose. This meant, bad food. He looked not at people but chose a focus, either reading something he didn't care about or in this case, the television hanging in the corner. His back to the wall, he faced the television. Breaking News: Train Derails at Union

Station, killing one person, but no injuries to the more than two hundred New York Bound passengers.

He saw what nobody else would notice, the specialized military boots. It was Paul.

Doug sat back, and for the first time, felt something, it was fear.

He did what he needed to do, plan his own exit. As he was now convinced someone knew the plan and was systemically taking them out. He knew them only by their made-up names, first Adam, then Jeff, Juan, and now Paul. He did one last thing, out of his commitment to justice, he wrote a letter. He would send it to the Callahan campaign office and disappear, to a new life, never again choosing to bring justice. He knew he could always go back to teaching full time.

50

Then one of the twelve, whose name was Judas Iscariot, went to the Chief priests and said, "What will you give me if I deliver him over to you?" And they paid him thirty pieces of silver. And from that moment he sought an opportunity to betray him.
- Matthew 26:14-16

T homas met Mary across the street from the Old Ebbitt Grill. The book store was busy as it was known to be full of bargains, not that price mattered in this part of town, but the bargains were more unique in nature instead of price. The store was infamous for people finding first editions, autographed, or even ones with personal notes. The most recent, a dialogue between Thomas Jefferson, Ben Franklin, and the original plans for the Lewis & Clark expedition. It was a crowded place with a lot of young people in nice suits. Thomas blended in perfectly, having the standard high-quality suit, shoeshine, and haircut similar to thousands.

Thomas felt some emotion as he saw Mary approach. She was added to the intern staff by Rucker, who added no one, he only approved the early interviews. Thomas was added by Jack as a recognition, and informal thank you for exposing candidate Jackson's family history. Thomas had Jack tagged as a non-political lawyer, so finding out he added Mary to the staff, he investigated. There had to be a reason, he also tagged Jack as someone who didn't do things based on his feelings, what was the motive?

"Hi there, thanks so much for seeing me today as I know it is so busy at the office," Mary said.

Thomas purposefully whirled as if he was surprised, which he never was, and made a witty comment that demonstrated balance in his life, "People have to eat, I know that for sure, so thanks for taking time too."

"The staff interns that were out last night, aren't going in until 2 pm today, knowing you guys would need the morning to get things straightened out." She said with a smile and a little bit of flirt.

Thomas noticed all the details. It was habit, he was forced his whole life never to relax. Over her shoulder, on time as he ex-pected, he noticed the government car pop the trunk, a signal he learned was a car that carried Stuart Wilson, his custom wheelchair was in the back. The political process, no matter how sensitive to minority groups, had yet to actually embrace in more than words the needs of the disabled, so executive-level government vans with disabled features didn't exist.

As he was listening to Mary talk about her experiences from

a late night with her intern peers, he noted the absence of Stuart's briefcase. Although not visible to even the most attentive detective, Thomas had an initial worry that Stuart had not brought his phone or leather binder, the binder Thomas had swapped that morning, or the phone that Thomas installed malware to both listen and record through the microphone. As Mary turned to go down the legal aisle of the store, Thomas grabbed a display book from the large "Back to College" display to peer over, as he covertly spied out the front window and watched the activity of the team across the street. Suddenly the driver, after receiving a few words from Stuart, returned to the car as Jack held onto Stuart's wheelchair. The briefcase appeared and Thomas turned his attention to Mary, as she was commenting on his selection.

"Nice choice, a classic, you probably should have read that when you were in college."

Thomas looked at the book in his hands and thought about his answer to Mary. He carefully placed the now required reading classic *Slaughterhouse-Five* back on the shelf where he found it.

His thought-out reply came out, "This book was banned in public schools in the early seventies and burned by others, not wanting to corrupt or inspire the youth of the time."

"It was the end of Vietnam and there were campaigns to ban it more than eighteen times. It only inspired me to read it when it was banned in my home state of New Mexico."

Thomas didn't tell her it was his favorite book, that would probably just invite more discussion he didn't have time for.

He knew the schedule; he had about five minutes to be seated.

There were two hostesses on duty at this small restaurant, one of which was young and attractive, serving customers, the other was attractive, but older, vetted with a security clearance, a civilian contractor, paid by the government as a GS-13, likely four times the pay of a regular hostess. She was ready and was waiting for this special group. She quietly, discreetly, led them to the back sitting room, years ago the office of the original restaurateur. The front room of the Old Ebbitt Grill was unforgettable, the large murals depicting the past, antiques of value not on display, but used, at the large mahogany bar. The heads of animals blended in, not even noticed anymore, even though they were hunted and killed by President Theodore Roosevelt. The grill had taken different shapes many times since 1856, being moved, bought, and sold, but never losing its purpose. Presidents visited, some for a drink, some for other matters. The grill, past its history and being recognized beyond its food, namely oysters, was known as a safe place with an easy, covert, near clandestine level of private drop off and pick up, a rear door if needed, and a steel-reinforced inner wall, not even the current owner knew about that, was the real lure of those needing it. It had been a mainstay for meetings of importance for the last twenty years. Thomas himself had been in that room, during a different time and for a radically different reason, as part of his efforts to collect the facts on the Jackson campaign, ultimately sabotaging Jackson's campaign. It is why he knew he needed the high-tech equipment, a Bluetooth low energy (LE) repeater, embedded in the replica leather binder Stuart carried everywhere. This simple device, designed for very low power operation, was now inside the room with Stuart and the others. The device built by Thomas, connected to Stuart's phone automatically. It extended Stuart's phone's Bluetooth feature from its class 2 range of thirty-three feet to class 1.5, increasing the range to a hundred feet. It was below the class 1 power, which Thomas learned would have been picked up by the sensors installed in the room. The Bluetooth 1.5 signal leverages a robust frequency-hopping spread spectrum approach that transmits data over forty channels. This transmitting low power Bluetooth connection, in combination with Thomas' successful mission, to hack Stuart's phone, and others, on the first day he met Stuart, put Thomas in the inner circle, allowing him to know what he wasn't supposed to know. This commonly available hack, yet to be patched by Google, the provider to Stuart's phone, provided him with access to the device's built-in microphone. Thomas knew that this location, the seemingly simple Old Ebbitt Grill was regularly checked for listening devices inside and outside the facility. Room access was restricted, a detector installed in the backroom doorway with alerts sent to the security detail nearby. He also knew the technicians didn't check beyond a fifty-foot radius. the bookstore where his server was set up was beyond their zone. He knew his repeater was made out of material not detectable by the hidden system in the backroom doorway. This hidden system to prevent unauthorized devices was installed just three years ago. Thomas learned this the previous week in his internet search and document crawl for any contract documents for the Old Ebbitt Grill location. He found what he needed from a government contractor website, which was sadly unsecured even to the amateur hacker, which Thomas knew he was not. He found the hardware used to detect devices through the door and in the room. The system installed in the door of the Old Ebbitt Grill back room was new by government security standards, but old enough not to keep up with the equipment Thomas had built himself. The signal from Thomas's hardware would broadcast on an encrypted channel, so the network connection he set up at the bookstore could receive the signal clearly enough for the microprocessor to record it into an audio file.

Thomas crossed the street with Mary, headed towards the entrance of the Old Ebbitt Grill. He moved quicker than he would have liked, but concerned more about his timing than safety, he playfully ran with Mary as if they were a couple in love. It also gave him the excuse to grab her hand, which made its mark on Mary as he passively observed her face.

The regular hostess, the younger of the two, the one not cleared for access to the backroom, guided Thomas and Mary to the Old Ebbitt Grill's reserved seating area. It was filled with a priceless collection of memorabilia. Mary was heedful as she looked at the multiple animal heads on the wall. The hostess seated them in the vacant booth against the wall. The young hostess recognized Thomas from last week when she went out to dinner and shared with him the password of an infrequent VIP restaurant guest. This would enable Thomas to secure a private table reservation. She remembered the instruction to keep this specific table open and his requested discreteness, as his job was very sensitive. She kept quiet and Mary didn't see the upset, near angry look she gave Thomas as he was with another, more attractive woman than she. She remembered Thomas's promise that he would come see her again during a time when he wasn't working. Mary reviewed the menu and then listened to the specials from the overdressed waitress, a change that was put in by the newest owner. Thomas checked his equipment, through an app on his phone he coded himself just last night. It was working, with a strong signal. Although he was always calm and always prepared, he shifted more towards his basic needs than his life's mission, and that need was to get some food, he had been up nearly thirty-six hours.

The plan Stuart laid out in detail impressed Jack, where Joe was treating it as if it needed work. Jack reminded himself that Joe had known Stuart for almost twenty years since he was a Coach and Stuart was a ten-year-old boy playing youth football. But the plan was brilliant. An approach that would find multiple small cases, that could be surely won using the "new judicial system." Jack even hated thinking the name the press labeled it. Jack listened to Stuart's plan, as it was obvious that it had been created, revised, and reviewed more than once. Stuart was a plug-and-play-like planner, regardless of circumstance there was a thought-out plan to meet the needs of any scenario. Jack was thankful, as he no longer had the energy to be in this level of detail, although it was his lifeblood during his career, the details and the challenge. Of all the things that Jack did know, one he didn't, was the current digital recording being transmitted from inside this supposed secure room to a digital server outside, creating a recording and a backup simultaneously. Even with the precautions installed at the Old Ebbitt Grill, just an hour before it was swept for any electronic bugs and devices by the Republican Party army of geeks, as Jack thought of them, although recognizing their importance in today's world. The food came after a delicate knock on the door. Stuart moved his leather binder to the side of the table, the place setting unoccupied at this four-person table. The seal, raised only slightly more than the original, installed by Thomas and swapped in Stuart's office just that morning. It was being powered by stored kinetic energy that was created by the small vibrations in its journey from Stuart's desk, his car ride and now sitting quietly, its true purpose unbeknownst to the table guests. It silently activated and started transmitting an encrypted digital audio signal, via class 1.5 Bluetooth to a radius of 100 feet. Thomas's portable computer server was close by, in the bookstore, hidden on a lower shelf full of books no one read. It started the secure electronic handshake, automatically connecting to the device when Stuart's briefcase was recovered from the back seat. Thomas had made it all happen in just a few minutes, using his technology skills, while waiting on Mary to arrive. He set up the computer, and prior to leaving, he confirmed the connection to the device now in Stuart's retrieved briefcase. As he reached down to put his favorite book back on the "Back to College" shelf, he saw what he expected, the light on the server changed from orange, flashing a few times to connect green, then a solid blue. It was connected.

Thomas was now sitting behind the wall to the secure back-room, occupied by powerful men, sharing what he did not yet know. He was less than twenty feet away from them, his smile impacting those around him, a smile he had been trained to deliver.

Mary interrupts his smile with an abruptness not yet appropriate for a relationship on their first real date.

"Thomas! Did you hear me?"

Thomas turned his gaze from the blank wall to Mary's face, continuing his smile in an attempt to recover from him not hearing a single thing she said.

"I'm sorry, what did you say? I'm overwhelmed by the trial."

"I just saw Stuart with Jack Rucker and Senator Callahan. They just got into a car together," as she casually pointed with her eyes out the front window of the Old Ebbitt Grill. She was surprised herself. She knew she made the reservation for Stuart and two others, but she didn't know the others were Jack Rucker and Joe Callahan.

Thomas smiled. Oh, how solutions present themselves when you often least expect it. This gave him an excuse to leave. He needed to ditch Mary and get to the audio file. He didn't want some nosy bookstore clerk finding his setup before he could get the file transferred.

Mary was talking, Thomas was syncing his Bluetooth with the server he set up across the street. It connected, secure and the download started. Thomas was pleased to see the length of the recording was the full length of the secret lunch. It all worked. Now he wanted to know what was said. What was the plan? what were they doing? How could he help?

"You are being rude Thomas!" Mary got his attention this time as he looked up from his phone, he was watching the download progress bar slowly move on his custom app. It was working, but it wasn't done yet.

He was a master at seeing what others couldn't see. Now he needed to find a way to cut this meeting short, and get to the audio file. He needed to learn more about what was said, what was happening, and how he could use his skills to contribute.

"I'm sorry, I was checking my calendar," he lied, but she didn't know. "I'm going to have to go, in case Stuart needs me at the office."

Mary understood, yet was disappointed with his lack of attention. He didn't even walk her to her car. Thomas was a good person, he seemed to always want to do the right thing, yet was distracted from normal things, such as walking her to her car. She waved goodbye as he made his way to the Old Ebbitt Grill bathroom. She wasn't in the mood to wait and left.

Thomas watched her leave and for once, took his time. He didn't want her seeing him. The download was completed and he disconnected the Bluetooth from the hidden server in the book store. After he was able to listen to it, he'd send the "Kill" command to the server and not just deleting the hard drive files, but adding in random text and encrypting it. It was a new digital hard drive, so impossible to recover any of the data.

He left. No one saw him. No one cared.

51

Be sober-minded; be watchful. Your adversary the devil prowls around like a roaring lion, seeking someone to devour.
   – 1 Peter 5:8

Thomas entered the bar which was two blocks east and more than a block off of the main street where Old Ebbitt was and where all the people were too. Mary was parked west of Old Ebbitt, as he knew he wanted less risk of her seeing him. This bar was a local bar, and he was a new customer. He had found it last week, as he knew he'd need a quiet place to listen to the secret recording and a place to be with his own thoughts.

The audio played into his Bluetooth earpiece, it was crystal clear. Thomas could easily hear who was who; Stuart, Jack, and Joe came across in a clear tone and he could tell they were worried. All of them.

The bartender put a cardboard coaster in front of him and said something Thomas didn't hear. He paused the audio, by tapping the button on his handsfree Bluetooth earpiece, "Sorry, what?"

"Would you like something to drink?"

"Yes, I didn't hear you." As he put his untraceable pre-paid credit card on the bar.

He ordered a drink that looked manly but was void of chemicals that would distract his mind and cause him to miss something. The bartender confirmed his order, with a look of judgment, as non-alcoholic drinks were rarely ordered in this part of town. Thomas's thoughts and ability to see many different points, also gave him the ability to stay ahead of others, even the smartest of them. He had already thought about it before it happened. The bartender delivered fast, as he didn't need to mix anything. Thomas took a sip and triggered his thoughts to start again. He tapped the button on his handsfree earpiece to turn it back on and clicked the button on his phone to restart the audio. He again heard their voices and their tone. They were definitely worried. They were talking about something Thomas knew a lot about. Killing another human.

Stuart had laid out a detailed plan to Jack and Joe. It involved a detailed plan to retry the "Mind Killer" for the murders of the jury, using new jurors with masks to prevent their accidental deaths. The proof was there in the list of people who died around Mark Solier. Stuart read the list, and Thomas wrote down the names, replaying it a few times to get them all. Thomas was both confused and interested in the list from

Brazil. Mark had killed Brazilian drug lords? Joe sounded hesitant, but Jack was pushing hard to move it forward. More than once, Thomas heard Jack say, "facts are the facts", "there is no case law for this" and one he had heard before, "justice for the injustice".

He had now listened to it three times, reviewing many parts over and over. Thomas put his phone in his pocket. He needed time to think. When he was alone, Thomas spent time with his own deep thoughts, easily keeping his phone in his pocket, limiting any distraction, knowing his phone was secure and not tied to him in any way.

He calmed himself by reviewing his problems, causing his stress to go down, unlike how others managed their feelings. He managed his by turning even the worst of them from feeling, into critical thinking. It is what he did best.

He had escaped New Mexico, leaving behind Casey, who he was then, and his birth name, Lanh Nguyen, no one would ever know that one. He attended Yale and started the long process of fooling those that were smarter than him, that he was an asset. Even Jack Rucker was convinced Thomas was Thomas.

He had learned technology, when he was young, working with his father before he died, who was a hard-core drug dealer, dealing meth in the Southwest. He started calling himself Casey then. Most suspected it wasn't his real name, it wasn't.

By accident, and out of necessity due to his father being a meth dealer, and in order to earn easy money, Casey was forced to learn technology. Casey was a natural. His ability to think and connect logic enabled him to quickly learn, and deploy technology in ways that kept him anonymous, yet active in doing what he did best. Getting what he wanted.

He sat at the end of the bar with his back to the wall, the lighting in the bar was dim on purpose, hiding who was there. He wasn't constantly watching the door, yet also not blind to who came and went, where they sat, and what they drank. He couldn't help it, the details just came, he let them. He needed to feel safe as he let his mind remember the past.

He remembered the energy created by the pain of being part Vietnamese in the desert town of Albuquerque, living on the edge of town, near West Mesa. Details were now coming fast. He'd often cross busy highway 345 into the Petroglyph National Monument. He was alone then, both in his life and his thoughts. Those hikes allowed him to be alone in nature, never on the paths the tourists took. This is where the energy would come out, as he devised actions towards things he knew were wrong. He had seen too much already, his father raping women, his real mother killed at the hands of his father after she lied about having an abortion. Casey was there when she took her last breath. He was also there when his father took his. Killing him was easy, poison was easy to come by, even for a thirteen-year-old. Casey knew his father deserved it. Casey deserved to see him die and his father deserved to die. Casey was careful to bury him where no one would find him. Months later, after others found out about his father's disappearance, he was put into the foster care system.

Living with his foster family now, Casey would see Clyde, his new foster father, leave late at night. Casey would follow him to Central Avenue in downtown Albuquerque. He already knew Central Avenue was full of prostitutes. He knew then, as a young teen of almost fourteen, that he would take action against women who did this. He didn't know why and didn't question it, he just knew he didn't want another child born of the pain he suffered from every day. He couldn't allow that to happen. He would befriend them first. He found them on the new social media site called MySpace, mainly used to find clients, or more specifically, for their clients to find them. Some even would take his picture to post on their more public online social profiles. None of them suspected the real reason why he was wanting to be their friend. His second killing was in 2001, he used his hands, she was too high on meth to fight back, it was easy, and he felt nothing.

"You want a refill on that drink?" was the sarcastic interruption from the bartender. Thomas had let time pass without noticing, in his own thoughts from long ago.

"Yes, please," another rarity in the bar, manners from the patrons. The bartender loosened up a bit and took Thomas's glass. He could tell this young man was working out some big problems and took his normal bartender judgment down a bit.

Killing came easy for Lanh. His memories coming back as he was now remembering in his birth name. He never considered it as murder, he only saw it as doing what was necessary. He was fueled by what was right, doing things, taking punitive action against people that did wrong things. His father was the first, poisoned. He only felt better when he knew his father was dead. He let his father's body sit on the couch until it began to decompose and smell. Then he burned it in the desert and buried it where no one would find the ashes. Lanh felt nothing then, and Thomas felt nothing now, except satisfaction.

When some nosy neighbor found out he was living on his own and called social services, Lanh was placed in foster care and then adopted. Usually a miracle for a kid like Lanh, but he only saw it as a problem. A middle-aged couple in Albuquerque adopted him after the death of their own son. Lanh brought only one thing, his box of memories. He had kept it hidden from his father, although his father never cared, surely not enough to look in his closet.

Carrie and Clyde Johnson welcomed him. Initially looking out for Lanh, they gave him a better life. They also wanted to give him a new, better name. The news had Lanh's real father's name everywhere, he had disappeared and the police were looking for him. He had been identified on every news channel as one of the drug lords that ran the Southwest. Having only uncovered this criminal history after they, Carrie and Clyde had adopted Lanh, they were motivated to change his name, out of fear, and out of embarrassment, for their benefit, and his too. There weren't many Vietnamese, beyond the Phở restaurants, living in Albuquerque and the Nguyen surname was a known name of the missing drug dealer. His new mom, Carrie, had told him that they wanted Lanh to pick his own new first name. Lanh picked Casey. He was already known by this name, as he too had wanted to escape the racial profiling, and what others called him to his face, "Gook", made popular again by then Presidential Candidate John McCain in a campaign speech, "I hate the gooks. I will hate them as long as I live". This only made it impossible for Lanh to go anywhere with the looks and the matching Vietnamese name, Lanh Nguyen.

What Lanh, now Casey didn't know is that his new mom, Carrie, was cleaning up a week ago, straightening the always messy room of a teenage boy, and found his box of memories, in the back of his closet, under dirty clothes she was collecting to wash. She had gone through Lanh's memory box, without permission. She cried as she found the sad memories of an abused child. She found an old document, one which showed his father's heritage, what was known about it. A document written in only Vietnamese, labeled "giấy khai sinh". Carrie learned by researching online that it was Lanh's father's birth certificate. Lanh's father's name was Duong Nguyen. His grandmother's name was Phuong Nguyen. His grandfather's name, never married to his grandmother Phuong, and the father, of Lanh's missing drug lord father, the only thing written in English on the document that Carrie could read or pronounce, Everest Mantra, US Army.

The bar lighting had gone from dim to dark as less patrons sat at the tables near Thomas. He remembered the power he possessed, from seeing what was wrong and then doing something about it. Taking action to do what he knew to be right. His new father, Clyde Johnson visiting Central Avenue, taking advantage of the services that his real father helped create. A drug culture of addicted young females, needing money, and doing what it took to survive. He killed every one of them that Clyde visited, including the pregnant one. He saw them as doing wrong and he was doing what he needed to do so they would stop. Casey also saw it as Clyde raping them with his money. He buried them where no one would find them.

The final step was his exit plan to leave New Mexico. Being seventeen years of age now, and nearing his eighteenth birthday, he had to take the final steps before turning eighteen years old to leave New Mexico. On what he knew would be his final walk, crossing highway 345, initially following the Rinconada Canyon Trail, he looked around to see only the quiet desert and ventured off the trail. Now sitting at sunset in the shadow of ancient petroglyphs, he had decided what needed to be done. He would kill one final prostitute, knowing he would not have to bury this one, he would frame the "John" who was there, and lay the groundwork for his freedom, and to confuse any future investigation. His plan worked perfectly. He was then a hero at seventeen, in the eyes of the police, he was the teen who killed a killer. His name was kept out of the news and he was easily cleared of any wrongdoing, and his records were made private as he was underage, not yet eighteen, just as he had planned. He made sure to expunge the records himself, the digital age started in 2006, any reference was erased by Casey's hack into the Albuquerque police database. He also deleted all the records of the John he killed, specifically the DNA records. He knew the murderer's body was to be cremated, as he saw the signed death certificate in the police database he hacked. Any trace of evidence would be physically and digitally gone. Clyde and Carrie supported him through the ordeal, as he faked his emotions.

Clyde and Carrie did not know they were the final step in his exit plan. He rewired their home's newly installed HVAC to catch fire and ignite the gas main he had turned on just a few hours before. They both burned to death as he watched from across the street, being held by the friendly neighbor who he awakened just a few minutes ago. The fire trucks showed up, called way late to save the house or the two people inside. The same neighbor that called 911 was now wrapping him up in a blanket as she thought he looked cold. Seeing the flames and the multiple explosions from the many open gas valves, he didn't feel anything other than satisfaction on accomplishing his goal. What he felt was right. Clyde deserved it, Carrie would just have been a loose end. It was Casey's eighteenth birthday.

Casey felt nothing then, and Thomas felt nothing now, except the same satisfaction. Thomas took a final sip of his drink, wiped the glass of any fingerprints out of habit, left the pre-paid credit card, and slipped out of the bar into the now darkening city. As he walked to his car, the timed city street lamps came on and Thomas realized that he had lost track of time.

52

For the desires of the flesh are against the Spirit, and the desires of the Spirit are against the flesh, for these are opposed to each other, to keep you from doing the things you want to do.
  - Galatians 5:17

Mark needed to die. The campaign needed it, the nation wanted it. This presented a perfect problem for a solution Thomas was capable of executing. In the weeks prior, without any specific need, similar to his hack of all the staff mobile phones, the installation of malware in the crime lab was easy. By presenting it as the standard browser cookie warning, for people to accept by clicking the OK button or cancel, people never read these and almost always clicked the OK button. Both buttons, regardless of whether they chose and clicked either OK or Cancel, it would install the malware anyway. This was something he could now leverage to help Joe Callahan and give Jack Rucker what he wanted. The malware monitored the packet flow to and from the secure database and educated Thomas on what and how things were done technically with the network. Who did what (the user), when they did it (real-time or batch), and the protocols he needed to disrupt to do what he wanted, hidden to others as they didn't know to suspect it. Thanks to the exploits of justice from Julian Assange, founder of Wikileaks in 2006. He was inspired as a teenager to learn even more about technology and more important undetectable hacks, called "zero days". He was now using a zero-day exploit, not one others knew about, yet he did. He had used it before, but this time, its use would clear up his sordid past, and frame Mark for the unsolved murders in New Mexico. It would give Stuart and Jack what they wanted, a murder conviction based on the hard facts, showing the "new judicial system" was working.

Earlier that day, he found it. Or more specific, Norman found it. Norman was the name he gave to his malware code that Thomas deployed. His malware code had evolved over the years, each time for a new purpose, but he kept the name. He liked it. He could always count on Norman. The malware identified the records of Mark Solier, then he waited for the database to be updated with his own DNA, the building blocks of life, unique to each person. As he waited for the process to complete the upload, Thomas was proud of his knowledge of DNA and genetic code. Learning about the details a few years ago at Yale. How the two strands in a DNA molecule are held together with bonds between the ACGT, specifically the four types of bases found in a DNA molecule: adenine (A), cytosine (C), guanine (G), and thymine (T). He didn't know how'd he'd use the information then, but he now knew why he learned it. Changing it before it hit the FBI's DNA database, CODIS; changing it from Mark's DNA to his own.

Mark's official DNA would no longer be Mark's, Mark would become Casey. A different kind of identity fraud. The long sought after suspected serial killer of the Central Avenue prostitutes. The bodies who were later found buried in the desert near the Petroglyph National Monument in West Mesa, New Mexico. Thomas had achieved his goal of getting justice for the injustice.

53

I hate vain thoughts; but thy law do I love.
  – Psalms 119:113

The anxiety of detective work comes from the faith that every crime origin is known by at least one person, the person who did it. The job, the pursuit of this faith towards solving it, is what keeps detectives going and also awake at night.

Five detectives, not known to each other, but linked by un-solved murders that occurred in their jurisdiction, all having limited clues, and all short of the ultimate clue, the dead body. These murders had nothing in common, other than the DNA left by the killer, yet to be identified. The location was within ninety miles of each other, and the timeline over a period of four years. They started suddenly, in 2001, and ended abruptly in the year 2005. No bodies were found during this time, and a few suspects were cleared. In each crime scene, there was nobody, the crime scene provided clues to a struggle and small samples of blood for DNA, some was female, likely that of the victim, presumably murdered, and the other sample was consistent, the same male always left samples of his own DNA as if on purpose. Taunting the police.

The governor at the time, Joe Callahan, had his focus on this, as he had lead and worked in law enforcement. Having worked on these cases, and then funding them through his policy. It was a black eye on him. His campaigns were run and won on the judicial justice served and these open cases were an obvious disgrace towards his campaign promises.

The cases were investigated, yet no bodies were ever found. That all changed in 2009. A series of events exposed the long decayed bodies. The coincidence of the 2008 housing bubble caused construction in Albuquerque to stop, although the desert had been prepped for a new housing development. This grading of the earth, now caused the rains to flood the area, forcing the developer to build a retaining wall to channel the water. This construction effort exposed some of the bones, not found by the workers, but a woman walking a dog. She reported it to the police. An exposed bone, a dog walker, and her willingness to report it led to the discovery of the remains of eleven women and girls, including a fetus.

As the case made headlines, Joe Callahan praised the work of the police force. The case, now cases, of active murders and newly unknown, uncovered, victims was a priority. The lab processed the DNA from their bones and skin, that had been miraculously preserved in the dry climate. It matched the five unsolved cold case investigations suspected to have been murdered. The other six bodies had no investigations open. No one had reported them missing. It was frustrating

282

to the lead crime scene investigator that eleven women could be killed and only five were considered missing. These details were kept private, the investigation was now multiple victims, all with the same killer.

Further research of only recently available satellite imagery of the crime scene, taken between 2003 and 2005 showed tire marks and patches of disturbed soil in the area where the remains were recovered. The satellite imagery also showed by 2006, the area was encroached by construction, which began to disturb the unknown burial site in preparation for housing developments. The killing either stopped, or the killer found another place to bury the bodies. By 2009, the area had eroded which led to the inevitable events that exposed the bones.

Joe Callahan initiated, and the federal government put up a one hundred thousand dollar reward, unheard of in a federal case, and a big reward for anyone in New Mexico. Joe was motivated, people knew he was embarrassed. It was a black eye on his record. He was going to be blamed for sure. Joe Callahan still had a ranch in West Mesa, just west of the town he previously served, Albuquerque. The resting place of these dead women was literally in his backyard. He was presumed guilty of not getting it done.

After the bodies were found, Callahan and those who got him elected to be president, pushed and had a special task force to pursue any suspects. No one was named as a full suspect. The most interesting suspect was Lorenzo Montoya, living less than three miles from the burial site. Lorenzo Montoya was killed by a local teenager after being caught strangling a young girl, the vigilante teenager's supposed girlfriend. The killings stopped after Lorenzo's death, no more missing young women in the area, and there were no changes in the soil or new tire tracks in the satellite photos of the burial site. Lorenzo's DNA was not on file, although in the police report it was documented as collected. Further frustrating the lead detective was that Lorenzo's body had been cremated. They couldn't match him using DNA to the killings but the evidence of location and timing pointed to him. The teen was cleared, and his records sealed, his name kept out of the news. His name would later be expunged as he became an adult. He would change his name and go off to school, Yale to be exact. That was all that was known.

Now, months have passed since the discovery of the bodies in February of 2009, the five original and six new case files were collecting dust with no leads, these detectives waking up from sleep they didn't get, were all notified of a hit in the CODIS DNA database. The killer had been uploaded, their building blocks of life, know as A's, C's, G's & T's for those that cared, converted to digital 1's and 0's, identified the person that killed eleven women and an unborn child, in the New Mexico desert, brutally, in a period of four years.

Independently, yet together, five detectives had the same question, "Mark Solier, I know that name, how?"

Jack Rucker knew first, notified Dale, and then sent someone he trusted, Gary Barker, to arrest Mark for a second time. This time, Gary masked himself, covering his entire face, for his own protection. He went with Tim, armed and also masked.

They were professional, experienced, and ready on the outside. They were scared shitless on the inside. Gary knew Mark could kill him if he wanted to, but only if he knew who he was. Tim would have his gun in hand and off safety the entire time.

Jack then called Joe directly. He'd be happy to hear the news before others. Joe had been given a political problem when he couldn't solve these murders, even worse when the bodies were found. Joe ran New Mexico then, doing good, doing well. This problem would now be solved, and the timing could not have been better. The presidential election was only a few months ago and their agenda was proceeding. Stuart was glad this was happening. Not according to his original plan, but nonetheless, Mark Solier would be tried for murder.

54

But avoid foolish controversies, genealogies, dissen-
sions, and quarrels about the law, for they are unprof-
itable and worthless.
  - Titus 3:9

New Mexico was getting more attention than it wanted. First, the election of its prodigal son Joe Callahan, then the national publicity from the uncovering of a washed-out mass grave, that included an unborn fetus. The public debate about its death penalty law, having fourteen of the fifty states already abolish it, the people of New Mexico wanted to be the fifteenth. This had been in the works since the US Supreme Court reinstated that it was legal for the US government to kill a citizen in 1976. Jack recalling his role then, in 1976, as he was the driving force in the case of Gregg v. Georgia. This case was a national news headline where Jack engaged the United States Supreme Court's previous ruling in 1972 which set precedent that the death penalty was considered unconstitutional. They ruled that the death penalty systems then in place were a violation of the Eighth Amendment's prohibition on cruel and unusual punishment. Jack fought then for the justice of an injustice, in the same way, he fought now, determined and relentless. Since then New Mexico, even under the leadership of Joe Callahan, had executed only one murderer in 2001. That was a case Joe investigated, the murder of a child, that only solidified Joe's cause of eliminating case law, focusing on facts, reducing judicial activism, and solidifying his lifelong partnership with Jack.

Jack's problem now was that New Mexico's leadership would cause a delay in the trial, in the midst of its citizen's debate on whether a human has the right to legally kill another human. Jack was now alone, yet frustrated. As he did when he was orienting his feelings, towards justice, he picked up his pen, then picked up the phone. He asked Angela to call the National Park Service.

The eleven bodies were found on state land, owned by New Mexico. Jack confirmed the GPS coordinates, double-checked a few times, as the case file included multiple satellite photos, to confirm the exact location of the disturbed earth between the years 2001 and 2005. The killings were likely done elsewhere, the nearby Petroglyph National Monument was likely.

Jack had a plan but he needed some help. Angela called the number and transferred it directly to Jack when it started to ring.

"Thank you for calling the National Park Service, please press one to get hours and operation," Jack pressed "o" a few times, knowing it would bypass the phone tree and put him in touch with a person. He knew his question had never been asked, he needed to talk to a person or likely persons.

"Thank you for calling the National Park Service, How Can I help you?" said a real person, yet sounded just like the recorded message.

"Hi, I'm Jack Rucker, the Attorney General of the United States, " the silence got more silent. "I'd like to talk to an entomologist and the director of land management for the Petroglyph National Monument in New Mexico."

"Yes Sir," was the response. Jack recognized the military bearing of the operator and appreciated his luck in getting someone who knew how to get things done. The operator was good, he got the names, phone numbers, emails, and their mobile numbers.

"Thank you, what's your name?" Jack was curious.

"I'm Kurt Thompson." said the voice through the phone.

"Kurt, here is my personal number," As Jack gave him his personal mobile number. "Call me back in a few weeks, you helped me, I can help you. Let's talk." Jack was always interested in adding new team members to his network of people that got things done.

Jack gave the phone numbers to Angela. She had them both on hold in just a few minutes, waiting for Jack to pick up the line. He asked that she conference them together, then picked up the line, his plan needed the help of someone focused on bugs and the other who knew the exact outline of the park.

Now checking the details from the report filed by the FBI on the West Mesa mass grave, he asked Ben Godwin, Ph.D. from the University of New Mexico, "I have a crime scene where we found a nesting of dead American Carrion Beetles, ten feet underground in the West Mesa desert, what can you tell me about this insect?"

Ben knew the topic without being told, West Mesa, the Attorney General spelled it out without spelling it out. This was the case of the murdered women.

"There are six hundred forty-five New Mexico insects found in the Insect Identification database. The American Carrion Beetle is one of them. It is named after what it eats. It eats the decaying flesh in both its larval and adult form. They eat the maggots and other insect larvae feeding on the decaying animals, often leaving only themselves, eating the competition."

Jack had thick skin and a tough stomach, yet this visual caused him pause.

"Would you find them in the dry desert, such as West Mesa?"

"No, not the dry desert. You would find them in a moist habitat and they are active all summer, even more so on hot days. Hiding is their preferred method of defense. There are nests of them we've been studying for more than ten years, located in the Petroglyph National Monument." Nearly magic words to Jack's ears.

"Thank You," Jack said and meant more than ever.

Ben shared one more detail, more of a way to cover himself than to help Jack.
"We are operating under a Federal Grant, so we only have access to the Federal section of the park." This is precisely why Jack had Bryant Evers on the phone. The Petroglyph National Monument was unique among the more than four hundred parks run by the National Park Service. It was a federal-local arrangement. Jack was wanting Bryant Evers to help identify the much-disputed lines between Federal and State ownership.

Bryant was able to share the detailed survey map, in digital form, via email. Jack pulled it up on his secure tablet. Ben had shared the precise locations of the nests he had been studying. They were on Federal lands. These lands, six hundred and forty acres, were transferred from the State of New Mexico to the Federal Government in 2001. The murders started then.

Jack ended the call with confirmation of their titles and asked them to be available if needed to testify. There was silence, the hesitant, reluctant agreement based on their tone. Jack had heard it before. He hoped he wouldn't need them. He had what he needed.

This case would now be federal. New Mexico's feelings on the death penalty wouldn't matter. Crimes on Federal land were federal crimes.

Jack also knew the killing, even accidentally, of an unborn baby had the sentence of the death penalty as an option. He knew this, as he had been part of creating the law, defining the future. The Unborn Victims of Violence Act of 2004 was driven by Jack, Joe, and a few key senators. The law applies only to certain offenses over which the United States government has jurisdiction, including certain crimes committed on Federal property. Murder was on that list. Scott Peterson knows this, as Jack drove the behind-the-scenes justice in 2004 for Laci and Conner's Law, the alternative title given to the amendment of title 18 to protect unborn children from assault and murder. Jack made sure justice was served for them.

55

Have mercy upon me, O LORD; consider my trouble
which I suffer of them that hate me, thou that liftest me
up from the gates of death.
  - Psalms 9:13

T his trial was short, the second for the defendant, the prosecution remained the same, yet unbeknownst to Mark. They were masked, he was not. The trial, different than the first was closed to the public.

The jurors vetted from the first round were chosen by Ralph based on Jack's specific requirement to what is defined as 'death qualification'. A juror who is willing to punish by death is different than all others. Death penalty cases pose serious problems not found in criminal cases. Jack knew this, Dale didn't care. Jack, breathing through his full head mask now, felt confident the work done by Ralph in juror selection for the first trial, would select qualified jurors to make the right decision. The history of death qualification often chose men, in this case, it was no different. The jury consisted of only men. They were deemed qualified to kill another human being through their individual vote. They would be locked down in a room with eleven others, having the same power to kill, making their own choices. Hopefully, after careful consideration of the evidence, void of emotion, they would consider the facts, not the past cases. This was now a capital jury, where during the "voir dire" stage of selection, they were questioned about their views on capital punishment. Jack had required it be done, Ralph had always agreed with Jack, even as Judge Ford questioned it, and Joe Callahan weighed in with caution, wanting to keep it quiet.

The courtroom was constructed and decorated with the standard government materials and architecture. What was not standard was the scene before Jack. He peered through the slits in his mask, what he saw was what he created, yet still on the edge of disbelief. The windows had been shaded, creating a dark combination of sunlight wanting to get through, and inside lighting, casting shadows on the jury, now seated in the jury box, not moving as if paralyzed by an unseen fear. They were all masked in what looked like full-face phantom of the opera costumes and cloaked in old judge's robes, faded black from years of use.

The defense attorney sat, unmasked, the only other one was Judge Ford, his outward defiance, seemingly unafraid to show the face of justice to Mark Solier. They both sat quietly as the prosecution shared its case. Facts presented with very little expression. Mark had committed eleven confirmed murders with his hands, who could know how many unconfirmed he killed with his mind. His DNA was all over the crime scene, on every victim. It was him. The jury processed the information, as they stared at the large flat screens put in front of them. The screens glowed and cast even more shadows in the darkened courtroom. The jurors looked carefully, their eyes focused, their expressions covered by their masks. If they had emotions beyond their duty as death-qualified jurors, their true expressions of shock, sadness, anger, fear, were hidden to all, especially the "Mind Killer", Mark Solier.

A closing statement was made by Dale; for once, short, no theatrics to focus on himself. This time Dale didn't want the attention, any of it, as he hid his identity, and kept to the minimalistic words to make his point. He stood in his place, his chair barely pushed back as he stood for the court. He read from a single sheet of paper, one carefully crafted by Jack just that morning. His arrogant tone even gone from his words.

"The United States justice system was created for the voices of the victims to be heard. It was designed for justice to prevail, no matter the distance between the crime and the verdict. There is no statute of limitation on murder. No injustice should go unpunished. No previous decision made through fault should be considered towards the decision today, there is no precedent that would tell you how to judge the eleven murders we can prove, and the hundreds or thousands we can't. Facts are facts. Truth is truth. Today, justice is a requirement, served for those that can not be here to witness it. This includes the previous jurors, God rest their souls, some were your friends, who sat where you sit now."

The jury was staring at Dale, his head down, bowed as his voice cracked at the end of each sentence he read. Jack knew it had an impact, he could see it in the eyes of every juror, it is all he could see, yet he could feel his lifelong cause, his mission of justice for the injustice being served.

Dale sat down, his chair sliding on the old courtroom floors was the only noise being made. Then silence.

The defense attorney stood. Walked to the center of the court, where the light now was focused. He cleared his throat and read aloud. The defense attorney was well prepared and their detailed closing argument was a character summary of the life of Mark Solier.

"A man who was born in the midst of our countries disgusting war, the year 1968 that saw more tragedy and chaos than any year since. Losing his father, the well-respected Jim Solier, who unexpectedly, and suddenly died in his sleep. His only other family, his Aunt Jessica, died from a random bear attack, yet he persevered, even as a baby. His mother, Alice, raised him to do what was right. He was a rare combination of intelligence and an instinctual like awareness of others at a young age. He graduated high school early, went to college, and could have done anything. He passed on those careers that make you wealthy with only money and pursued what was right. He graduated with two degrees, and then went where? to a job to make money? no, he went to Brazil to help people."

The defense attorney was on point, Jack had respect for him. He was stating the facts. Ralph and Mary recognized the facts they uncovered independently and then together to build the case against Mark Solier.

The defense attorney continued his closing statement.

"He joined a large company, Baxter Enterprises, not for his own purpose, but to help them help others. Breaking the perception, or likely reality, of biotech firms being greedy. He lead the company, taking no stock options as compensation, in creating ethical guardrails, keeping Baxter on track to deliver help, or as what Mark called it publicly, love."

The jurors were all looking at the defense attorney, his words, his tone, were compelling. It also had Mary's attention. As she realized how focused she was on her own attempts to prove her worth as a future lawyer. She recalled her time with the evidence, the pictures, the police report, and her time with Susan Backson.

The silence of the courtroom was interrupted by the continued facts about Mark Solier, the defense attorney was reading, he was painting a picture with details of who Mark was, a simple, God-fearing man.

"Mr. Solier's mission was to help, not just fix things, but solve them. Build communities based on love, not hate."

He sat down, Mary saw the jury bow their heads, in unison, as if choreographed by a professional. The room was quiet, Mark looked as if he was praying, his lips moving, yet no sound coming out.

It was now over. Jack sat quietly and was naturally compelled to bow his head, in relief that it was done. What more was there to say, the facts presented showed he killed these people, and only recently was it found as his data was uploaded into CODIS, triggering the connection to the victims, still a shocking count of eleven young females and an unborn fetus. All killed seemingly randomly, yet the crime scenes of a few had DNA from a single unknown male, not in the database back then. It was known, or theorized, as the technology had not yet been confirmed, that the suspect (killer), the unknown male, had been of Vietnamese heritage, which was now seen as a wrong assumption. Jack's internal emotions caused him to tighten his grip, below the table. Jack considered the victims, he thought of the distraught families not knowing for years what had happened. He clenched his own grip tighter, knowing that for years, YEARS!, justice had not been served. He could feel his anger rising, in his blood, an uninvited response. He disrupted his instinct. He knew anger, was the gateway to hate and served no purpose. The facts were indisputable, justice was now served, for those that wouldn't ever know. Jack released his grip, took a deep breath, raised his head, looked at Mark, and realized his goal. Justice for the injustice.

The Judge not needing to provide a regular summary of the case, post-closing arguments, asked the jury to do their duty. The jury moved quickly to the jury room, nearly running and pushing towards the door marked with an old, yet polished, Jury Room sign. A less ornate sign, hung below in a more modern plastic, declaring "Authorized Personnel ONLY". The shadows darkened the room more as the now late afternoon sun moved below the windows, below the horizon. It was the only reference of time for those involved. The door to the jury room clicked closed and the courtroom was silent, everyone sitting still, not moving, not making eye contact. Hours, or so assumed by most had passed, the jury had not revealed itself with a verdict, nor had asked for guidance. Jack had some concern, as the facts were the facts and the urgency felt even by him was high. The jurors, selected for the qualifications to decide on life or death, were even higher. Behind the jury room door, it was handled following procedures, with little emotion from this selected group of men.

The door opened, the jurors as quickly as they left now took their places. The verdict was read, where the jury found the defendant, Mark Solier guilty on twelve counts of first-degree murder. The courtroom remained silent for what seemed an eternity to every attendee.

Judge Ford broke the silence, ordering the bailiff to secure the defendant, and formally released the courtroom. The jurors were being secured as well, bused to a local, unknown hotel, wearing their masks and riding in blacked-out vans. The Judge couldn't allow another person to die, he would be careful himself.

It was now Mark Solier's turn to die.

56

Whoever sheds the blood of man, by man shall his blood be shed, for God made man in his own image.
 - Genesis 9:6

There is so much precedent in killing humans legally, that it could have been seen as routine. The calls for abolishment, the protests, the celebrity statements, the last-minute attempts at getting a stay of execution. All of it, not normal in our daily routines, yet routine over the last hundred years for those experienced or well versed in the United States use of death as a punishment, and hopefully it's other well-meaning purpose of being a deterrent.

Jack being one of those versed in the details of every legal killing, knew this was not normal. The process wasn't rushed, but it was expedited by the nonexistent normalcy of people wanting to not be part of killing. Everyone normally vocal was silent and apathetic. Jack could see it on their faces, either as they made eye contact over the last few days, or their body posture looking only at their shoes, the floor of justice, trying to reconcile this never before known situation. A man was killing others with his mind, wanting them to die in a random event, where there would be no evidence of a murder or the ability to link them together. His father, his aunt, the three bullies in college, the long incomplete list of Brazilian drug dealers, including the drug lord himself and Charles Backson which Mary was the only one to deduce murder. The first jury and how many other unknown accidents? Seen as independent events, but together, not a coincidence.

The trial, the second one, went fast, the sentencing was clear, the murder of one person was enough for the United States Federal Government to kill, having eleven confirmed murders of young women, and another being an unborn child, put this on the fast track for capital punishment, what the public all commonly called the more direct term of the death penalty.

No step being skipped, the State Collateral review was conducted, and then the bureaucracy eliminated, as multiple jail inmates, housed in the same jail as Mark, unmasked and unprotected started dying of low probability, yet proven medical causes.

Although there are limitations on Habeas Corpus Review of capital sentences, Jack knew these as he helped write them, he knew they didn't apply here. The precedent of rulings in the cases of *Penry v. Lynaugh, Teague v. Lane, In re Troy Anthony Davis, Eddings and Lockett, Chapman v. California, Bell v. Cone, Carey v. Musladin, Herrera v. Collins, and Murray v. Giarratano* did not apply. This was new ground, the law of facts, not the rule of others, those that brought their own bias, well-intended or not.

The Federal Government, using the State of Virginia's primary method of killing the proven guilty, was the more humane lethal injection. Mark, citing his religious beliefs, could not have any non-pure substance in his body, his specific selection of words Jack noted. He chose, by default, the alternative in Virginia, the electric chair was his choice. Jack knew the people wanting him to die would recycle the grotesque nicknames it had been given; Gruesome Gertie, Old Smokey, Old Sparky, and Yellow Mama. Jack knew the chair in Virginia had been named Old Sparky from previous killings, this metaphorical label was used by those who hadn't had to convict a person to die in it, or witness its use. Jack didn't call it that out of respect for the law.

Jack had presented the death options to Dale, who knew little of the history. Jack could tell Dale still didn't care, but no longer out of his laziness but his escalated need for self-preservation. Jack thought Dale would be done as district attorney, and part of Joe's campaign would seal that decision for many prosecutors. Those that only learned and prosecuted on the history of law, cases from the past. Those that were lazy, or focused on only winning, those that were inept or unwilling to work at applying the actual law. What Jack knew, that Dale likely never did, or forgot without knowing it, when the guilty chooses the alternative method of death, they waive their rights to appeal, sealing the decision, the verdict applied to the defendant, now guilty. It also quickened the process, no appeal, no motions limiting protests, and the governor's discretionary God-like power to block the legal killing of a human being. It was as if the defendant said "I did it" and pled guilty.

Most didn't know this part of the law related to alternative methods, and Jack knew it because he helped write it. He also knew they didn't care. He proceeded anyway, providing a succinct history of Virginia's leadership role in killing those proven guilty, beyond a reasonable doubt.

Meeting at the courthouse, to organize the invited and expected attendees to the execution, was Jack's idea, although Dale announced it. Angela organized it. They were early, even with the agenda having plenty of time. Most didn't know what to wear, so they wore the standard court-like costumes, dark suits, simple accessories, even Dale this time. Mary was there, invited by Dale, yet she knew at the request (demand) of Jack.

Jack asked everyone to sit down, he grasped the judge's gavel from its holding place and slammed it down. Mary saw Jack as she had not seen him before. Ralph had expected this, yet, Ralph was stunned, he also was seeing Jack Rucker, this form of Jack Rucker for the first time.

Their attention was complete. He turned on the flat-screen television and began a slide show no one expected or was prepared to digest. They didn't have a choice. Jack began.

"Hangings have been carried out for three hundred years until the first electrocution in 1908. The last execution by hanging occurred on April 9, 1909." Jack shared. Looking around the room to demand everyone's attention.

"The first execution in what is now Virginia, Captain George Kendall, was executed in the Jamestown colony in 1608 for spying." Jack advanced the slide show.

"Virginia allows the execution of juveniles." As Jack recalled the D.C. Sniper case, a case tried under a new law with no precedent, Virginia's terrorism statute, Jack helped prosecute, Malvo for life, Muhammad for death.

Mary winced at this, she was young, she knew a lot of young people.

"Virginia does not kill mentally retarded defendants as it is unconstitutional," the slide show only had the case name, Atkins v. Virginia (2002).

Ralph didn't look up, he was compelled to take notes.

Dale initially was already feeling impatient with Jack's soon-to-be lecture to him on capital punishment, but quickly was shocked at what Jack knew, not using notes and even more shocked at the history of a state he was born in and lived in his whole life.

"Virginia has executed more people in its history than any other state." Jack left out the actual number of one thousand, three hundred and ninety to continue the attention he needed.

"On February 5th, 1951, five inmates were executed, the largest number of executions carried out on a single day in Virginia," Jack's tone echoed. He paused.

"The average number of years a convicted criminal sits on

death row in Virginia is," Jack paused, the silence caused everyone to look from where they were looking, whether Ralph from his notes, Dale from his shoes, Judge Ford from the window, "is, eight years."

Jack quoted from the long-time Virginia prosecutor, Paul Ebert, "The Justice System fails if prosecutors forget their role, we have an adversarial system. We bump heads, and out of that fight comes justice." Ralph decided then, that this would be his last case, he had done his duty, killed enough.

"Mark Solier is being executed less than eight days from the start of his trial. Virginia again making history it will be proud of." Jack again making history himself.

Judge Ford, getting the nod from Jack, provided direction to the next steps in the legal killing of another human being.

57

But I say unto you, Love your enemies, bless them that
curse you, do good to them that hate you, and pray for
them which despitefully use you, and persecute you.
  - Matthew 5:44

The execution was to be done at the Greensville Correctional Facility, in Jarratt, VA. A small town never noticed by the travelers on I-95. The execution chamber was moved there in 1991. When the US Supreme Court reinstated the death penalty in 1976, there have been one thousand five hundred and sixteen killed. There have been one hundred thirteen executions in Virginia, today there would be one more. It was a simple building, concrete more to keep things in than keep things out. Unknown to most of the public, it was infamous amongst those condemned to death. The L building was its formal name, Hellsville, is what it was called by those with a future reservation. The death chamber was constructed away from the eyes of the public, located at the rear of the facility.

Those that would witness the execution were both wanting to

stay calm on the outside, yet beyond stressed on the inside, from what they were going through and what they didn't know they would witness. After the customary, yet still a surprise, extensive pat-down, bordering on a clothed strip search at the courthouse, they loaded in white vans, nondescript, and took different, purposely timed routes to the facility. Jack rode in the front, he didn't know the driver. He did know all the other witnesses. Some of which were required of their position; Dale, Judge Ford, and some of those that deserved to be here more than anyone else, the families of the victims killed many years ago. Ralph was there, although Jack noted he was different than before, he wasn't reading anything and had a blank stare, as he leaned his head on and looked out the van's tinted windows. Jack had invited Mary, she was sitting behind him and had little makeup on. He had excluded others who wanted to come, like Thomas and respected the wishes of those that he knew didn't want to come, like Stuart and Joe, and didn't ask them. Canner was never considered, but Jack knew he'd be at the gates.

Jack, nor Ralph for that matter, had been back physically to the L building since they witnessed the execution of Mir Qazi in 2002. Mentally, they returned often as being responsible for the conviction, and then a witness to the convicted and condemned killer's death was not something that ever left you. They were back now, to witness Mark Solier die today. Jack knew he'd likely be back later this year to see the convicted beltway sniper, who was scheduled to be killed in November of this year, 2009. Jack made sure John Allen Muhammad was convicted of all his killings, convicted of the first in 2003, then Jack extradited him to Maryland for another six, and

306

pending another three states. Jack wanted justice for every victim. He knew he'd get justice today. Entering the facility, there was no noise, no ringing of bells or protesters. It's not that no one cared, it's that they did. Even the most dedicated, anti-capital punishment advocates, those that organized the historical protests against the legal killing of another human, had the connections to get attention, were silent. They were choosing to remain anonymous. Canner was standing there, outside the gate, as the white van, the windows dark tinted to protect those inside, drove past him, into the secure facility. Jack looked out at him, Canner looked back not seeing Jack behind the dark window glass. Canner had aged, his physical recovery not complete. He was alone, his long-time producer Sandi had died of her injuries.

Jack knew the executions went fast. Not just the act of killing, the procedures to do so were simple, a step-by-step guide, void of decisions, emotions, and most times remorse. The popular understanding is that of a remorseful, outspoken, guilt-ridden, scared convict in a desperate struggle for their life. Experienced professionals, knew that was not the case. Jack didn't know what to expect from Mark Solier.

The room was quiet, the smallest common noise, made the loudest impression. As the invite-only diverse group, all with their own reasons to be there sat down, they then sat still. There were twenty in attendance, four rows of chairs, all full, and what has become an expected common practice since the execution of the Oklahoma bomber, Timothy McVeigh set the standard of more than two hundred watching on closed-circuit television. Jack didn't know the final list but knew Virginia had broken another record, those deserving to witness it, the victims of the victims. Most were watching from New Mexico, looking for some type of closure since 2001, when the people they loved went missing when the killings first started. The daily stress of the police investigation going slow, having no leads. Then again since early this year, when the bodies were found, discarded in the desert, decomposed beyond recognition, but confirmed by their DNA. The victims of the victims, one demand they all had was wanting to remain anonymous until Mark Solier was dead.

Among those in the physical witness room, in Building L, now just a few feet from where Mark would die, Jack sat down last. From his prior visits, Jack noticed the fresh addition of a darkened one-way film on the glass that separated those that would live tomorrow and the one that would die today. The stress in the room for first-timers was causing the air to have pressure, not like that in other rooms. The process to get here took its toll on human's mental and emotional states. It was rooted from the chaos of the trials, the accidental, yet coincidental deaths of the first set of jurors, the sudden and mysterious deaths of random others associated with the case, and a few of the unfortunate inmates near the isolated cell of Mark Solier. As he waited, even just a few days, people kept dying around him. It was now his turn, the process was in motion, put forth by those legal minds of the past.

The clock over the door read 8:42 pm. It had been a long day. Mark wasn't walking, but more sliding his feet, dressed in the standard blue prison-issue shirt and jeans, bypassing his right to wear what he wanted. He was wearing the standard and required slippers, only those that walked this walk earned the right to wear. Two guards, one at each arm, hooded to protect themselves, carefully supported Mark as he stepped into the room, it was obvious to its purpose, containing little except the lonely chair, a chair that had killed before, placed carefully in the middle. Everything looked older here, the room itself, the chair, looked old, Mark looked old. Except for the shiny new window film that reflected back into the room and the single-camera pointed at the chair, soon to be the final resting place of Mark Solier. The larger guard, helped Mark sit, using both his hands to carefully guide the prisoner down, careful of keeping his head from hitting the hard wooden back, showing a form of compassion needed in this responsibility, regardless of whether it was deserved.

Mark stared at his own reflection being given off by the one-way film on the window to the witness room. Looking at himself, he was staring into the witness room unbeknownst. Mark didn't know he was also being watched nor by whom, his thoughts were to himself. He stared at himself, yet the witnesses felt like he was piercing their souls. Some looked away, some hid behind others, the front row, reserved for those related to the victims, stared back. The private room, who only the warden approved the attendees, had a reflection off the new window film that could be seen across the chamber. The two covered windows reflections from both the observers and private rooms created a lighting dynamic which made the center of the room glow. The private observer's room was smaller, yet filled with those directly connected to the victims, completely filled, not having enough seats, with immediate family members. The fathers, mothers, brothers, and sisters of those that lost their lives, many years ago, yet a closure without closure for those closest would stay private. Jack didn't even know, Ralph didn't care to know.

The guards stepped back and the prison execution team stepped forward, their uniforms specially designed, void of any identifications secured Mark into the chair, it was now his chair. His last one. He was now secured, beyond what was needed, by his ankles, legs, wrists, and chest. Secured by specially made, unbreakable, durable, non-conductive leather straps.

The execution team, all volunteers, stepped back, in military-like drill team precision, as they had practiced in near silence the few days before. They stepped back into their assigned places. The room, with the centerpiece, the chair being its purpose, felt small, although the room measured by design as twenty feet by thirty feet. Jack knew the death chamber and the observation room where he currently sat were both crowded from his previous attendance to the government's authorized killings. The others in the death chamber included a member of the governor's public safety staff, safely hooded and also cloaked in black robes to hide even the smallest of telltale signs of who he, or she was. The execution team was in their place and the warden was the only one unmasked. The Warden assumed Mark already knew who he was, and as a public figure with an important public responsibility didn't find comfort in hiding. He felt, regardless of crime, those sentenced to die, this day, in the next few minutes, deserved basic respect as a human, regardless of their acts. The room looked like a play, well-rehearsed, everyone had their role, timing of their actions, all moving with a singular purpose, to kill a human to which his peers determined to be righteous. The set of this play was dark, grey walls, flat light, but equal in all corners, the actors dressed in the necessary protection, the warden there to be seen as the lead actor. The only color in the room was the red phone, its only purpose to provide an open, instant communication of an unlikely yet legally possible stay order from the only person that could save his life, Joe Callahan, the President of the United States. Now the phone was pressed to the ear of the smaller guard who helped Mark in, and now he played his role of listening for any sign of life, it was silent.

Mark sat up, looked up, his head toward the camera, yet not his intent. It was a coincidence only. He mumbled something, then repeated it in clarity, as if he was alone, speaking to himself. His words not meant for the audience hidden behind the mirrored glass, not for the guards and execution team cloaked in black headdresses, not for those watching on television, too frightened to be there, and too determined to not look into the "Mind Killer's" eyes and listen to his words.

> "Father, forgive them; for they know not what they do."
> – Luke 23:34

There was silence on top of silence now. No one moved. The air stopped.

Mary watched. She realized that she was the start of this, being focused on her own life, wanting to feel different, be different. She felt all her emotions from the last year, colliding together now, not by her choice. Her manipulation of Deputy Jackson to get the police report, the copies of the now confirmed crime scene, her impatience, selfishness, and lack of any empathy, only to get information when meeting with Ms. Backson, her anxiety of meeting Mark for the interview, the stale air of his office at the overly clean Baxter Enterprises, and the uncomfortable small talk of their first meeting. She felt sorry for Mark. Her thoughts pushed her past how she felt most times, this time, they didn't. She sat quiet in her chair, not moving, yet, with her eyes and her heart, she stared at Mark. She was protected only by the recently installed one-way, reflective film. A simple thin sheet of film, that didn't allow the "Mind Killer" to see her soul. But could he feel it? She didn't know. She didn't know if he could know the confusing regret she was feeling, the foundation of the guilt that would come later, and allow him to take his vengeance on her. She could see clearly from her third-row seat, next to Ralph, next to Jack, as if they were intent on protecting her still.

Jack knew the process had been quickened, what was missing now, something different from the normal killing of a human being, was the absence of his defense lawyer. They had always been there, either committed to his client or looking for publicity. There was also no spiritual advisor, who was dedicated to the very last moment, an unselfish act of compassion to forgive and look past what had been done.

Mary saw the governor, whom she had only seen on television, now in front of her, in the room, obvious to who it was, yet unlike the warden, fully masked, and fully robed. He read aloud, in the voice Mary had heard on television, the death warrant of Mark Solier.

Mark was still as if he was already dead. He sat straight, not moving, strapped down, yet not his toes in the slippers, nor his fingers on the end of the wooden arms, moved, not once. Everyone stared at him, through the glass, through their hearts, and through the televisions connected directly to the death chamber.

The time had come, in a routine void of emotion, prior to the start of the actual proceedings the warden had given the witnesses the details of the process, what to expect, and the timing of how it would happen. Although it was a perfect, well-rehearsed, detailed account of how it would happen, no one was prepared. Not Jack, not Ralph, Mary was now changed, her emotions inside on fire, her outside opaque to others.

"We are ready." Officially spoken by the warden.

These were the final words Mark Solier would hear. These were the official words used to legally kill a human being. It was the verbal signal to start the process. It was not obvious to anyone whether Mark was ready.

The electric chair was historically unpredictable and well documented in its efforts, yet completely predictable in its outcomes. It was designed to kill, with escalated procedural current supplied through devices connected to areas shaven on the body to maximize its effect. Mary recognized the start, triggered by the only words spoken, "We are ready", just as the warden had described earlier in the day. She and the four rows of witnesses, like they were choreographed with Mark's actions, stopped breathing, were squeezing the metal cushioned rails of their previously comfortable chairs in unison, as Mark's hands grasped out of reflex the thick polished wooden chair rails of his last moments of life.

It was as the warden described, it was as she researched and read by many before her that had witnessed the killing of a human using a power most of us didn't understand. The moment from the start to the end was over without anyone keeping time, beyond their own quickened pulse from the adrenaline of excitement and fear. It was interrupted only once, between the slightest of delays between the first pulse of power to kill his brain, and the last push of death to kill his body. The time allowed Mark to scream, scare those in the moment, and likely everyone watching for the rest of their life. Mary recognized his words from her required religious upbringing, as the last words of Jesus as he died on the cross.

"FATHER, INTO YOUR HANDS I COMMEND MY SPIRIT."
– Luke 23:46

58

But false prophets also arose among the people, just as there will be false teachers among you, who will secretly bring in destructive heresies, even denying the Master who bought them, bringing upon themselves swift destruction.

 - 2 Peter 2:1-22

L ori arrived early at the downtown diner. She was new to the city but knew Denver well from her research of maps and online guides. It had been a secret she was moving to Denver post-trial. She knew the Colorado weather in April could be unpredictable, so she dressed warm and brought gloves. She also brought some of her mail with her, those letters she sorted as a mystery, those that were not clear of the origin or of their sender. She almost brought the pile of known addressees, the ones from her friends and family. Her mind didn't want the guilt that sometimes comes with the necessary ignoring of those that love you. She wasn't intentional about her disregard for their attention; she was just busy with other priorities. Priorities they knew, as her involvement in the "Mind Killer" case, wasn't a secret. She still winced at the overused term to describe Mark Solier. And of course, the months prior to the execution, her emotional struggles as the "Mind Killer" was to be put to death, where she felt responsible. Was she? She winced again. Just another reason to bring the unknown origin mail, she didn't want the continued guilt of seeing the hurt of the people she ignored the last year. She turned to the bundle of generic mail. She removed the rubber band holding it all together and set the mail on the table. None of it was addressed to her, not anyone specific, it was just sent long ago to the Callahan campaign office. What felt like an eternity ago, when Jack got her a role in the Callahan campaign, Stuart Wilson had assigned her the unwanted task to open the generic mail. She knew it was then, and hoped now, that the mail had been screened for biological agents. She sighed, her posture slumped and then she noticing an envelope with handwritten script first, opening the envelope with her finger, something she hadn't done in a while, and pulled out the single page to read. The waitress interrupted to take her order and she ordered some coffee, she ordered it special. She wanted to slow the pace of her words and needed to work hard to take the edge off her tone. The young waitress was ready and prepared to write her order down, regardless, as she would rather repeat it than have them get it wrong. As she started, a man's voice finished the order. To her surprise, her man had come to her table abruptly, he scared her, but he was smiling. He had been there already, waiting on her. The waitress frowned and departed, she was busy.

Her first kiss as Lori Philbus felt no different than the past six months falling in love as Mary Morgan. Thomas Williams was a handsome man, one that was going someplace, and a man that had actually been someplace already. He worked now in President Joe Callahan's administration, put there after the conviction and execution of Mark Solier just last month. Thomas shared her love of the future. The future of facts, the future of justice, and hopefully their future together.

She was content, bordering on being happy. Being in Denver, leaving the past, starting a new life.

Thomas was excited, twice fold. One to see her and the other to provide that day's update via the paper he had half-open and folded to a specific page. Lori tried to convince him to let it go and just enjoy the moment. He wouldn't shut up and she didn't hear what he was saying in her attempts to try and focus his current enthusiasm. She was the first to shut up as the words came twice from his mouth, "the priest had died of an accident."

"What!?" Lori was shocked

"The priest that gave the 'Mind Killer' his last rights, the one that did it through the jail cell, wearing that strange mask, the one who didn't want to attend the execution. He drowned as the river overflowed, swept his house, the one on the church property from its foundation. It must have been from the freak thunderstorm in Virginia last night," stated Thomas.

"You know I don't like the 'Mind Killer' reference," she pointed out again.

"He is what he was," but Thomas was still lost in the story of the priest's death.

Thomas, always focused on his goals and seemingly distracted at the same time, noticed her pile of mail, and one opened in her hand. He asked her "What are you reading?" His eagerness for knowledge of any kind was relentless.

Ignoring him, "Let me see the paper," asked Lori.

"Here, I'm going to get a real paper," as Thomas gave up the Denver Post and headed out in search of a seller of the Sunday New York Times, thinking there would be better coverage and nearly forced controversy.

He handed the paper to Lori, kissed her forehead, and he walked out in disgust, both for the lack of connection Lori couldn't make between the execution and the Priests murder (?) and the anger, the now confusing hate Thomas was expressing openly for the "Mind Killer". How could the "Mind Killer" still be killing, when he was already dead. How could he do this from the grave?

Thomas checked the traffic, there was none this early in the day in downtown Denver, the suburbs went to church, downtown slept in.

He avoided some of the construction work as he crossed the street, went into the only open store to hopefully find The New York Times.

Lori read the article, not seeing the connection, as it was a simple article about the flood, not about the priest, it was Thomas that made the connection, not the paper.

In her new life, she went back to her stack of mail she brought with her as the waitress put down the coffee. The handwritten envelope had contained a handwritten letter, as she carefully pulled it out, folded sharply.

No greeting, it started, "My name is Doug Barlow and I think I may be the last member of a secret assassination group that has been in place for nearly forty years, since the Vietnam War, responsible for providing **justice to the injustice** in imperfections of the American legal system." Mary noted the same phrasing she heard many times from Jack Rucker.

It was written legibly, but hastily. She read fast, but with caution as her past again came back.

"We tried to kill Mark Solier, however, our group has been systematically killed by accidents over the last three days, everyone except me." Mary flipped the nearly discarded envelope over and saw the date. Three days after Mark's initial trial, the mistrial when the jurors were all killed, where he was set free. She remembered it like it was yesterday.

Her eyes darted back to where she stopped reading. She found where she left off and kept reading. "It was thought to be an inside job, but since I am the last, I'm writing to tell you it was not. We were under-cover, there was no way for anyone to know, especially the "Mind Killer". There is something else going on, I am scared, and I believe he is the devil."

"This is not my real name, I am leaving the Group today, do not come looking for me, you will not find me, and I will do everything I can to protect myself." Mary forced herself to breathe, she had been holding her breath. She turned the envelope over again, it had been sent from Richmond. She checked the dates again. A group of assassins had planned to kill Mark in or near Richmond, three days after his mistrial. She couldn't imagine who asked them to do it. Who would have, or maybe a better question, who could have? Who had the power and connections to hire this team?

Lori got up to find Thomas. She left her purse, her coffee, the Denver Post, grabbing the envelope, clutching the letter in her hand. On her hurried way to the door, she put the letter back in the envelope and stuffed it in her back pocket. She opened the door and left the coffee shop. She didn't know where he went, then she saw him, across the street, through the large glass windows, in the corner store at the counter.

The clerk was clueless looking so Thomas didn't bother to ask, and to his surprise, found The New York Times, overpaid with cash, and walked away from the counter. He quickly started to scan for the news he knew he would find. The front page nailed the coincidence and reported the priest's death. He was always amazed at the connections needed to know the facts and the ability of the writers to get the story written.

He didn't scan this story, he read it, as he walked onto the sidewalk, he briefly looked up to avoid the construction of the sidewalk restoration.

Lori yelled, and then she screamed.

Thomas was mentally yanked into the immediate present, from his immersion in the story to the sound of the bus, the brakes, the horn, and the scream of Lori.

The bus hit the construction area and smoke billowed from the dust and crumbling of the concrete placed to protect the area.

She crossed the street, rapidly and carefully. There was only silence, the bus was empty and the driver was unconscious, slumped behind the wheel, she saw blood on the windshield as she approached the area. Even in shock, she was able to register that the blood was on the inside of the windshield. She looked frantically for Thomas, as the bus blocked her view.

"I'm OK," Thomas strained as he tried to get up from the concussion of the accident.

"You don't look ok, your arm is bleeding."

"It hurts bad, it's probably broken."

"Sit down, don't move, I'm calling an ambulance."

The bus started to hiss loudly, it caught Lori's attention and she saw smoke and then fire, she looked quickly at the driver and saw the unchanged position, he was unconscious or dead.

"Go help him, I'm fine!" Thomas shouted to snap her out of her current state.

She moved quickly, the front door was badly damaged and the back door was jammed partially open, the bus was leaning from the damage. She couldn't open the door but was able to squeeze in. The bus was empty, she quickly checked the floor, and ran to the front. The hiss grew louder. The blood was bad, real bad, but the driver was breathing. An older man, Latino and overweight, seemed in poor health, even without the fresh injuries, was belted in, and there were large chunks of concrete all around the front with multiple holes in the now shattered windshield. He must have been hit by the debris instead of his head hitting the windshield as Lori first thought.

She heard a clanking noise and she spun to see what it was, she was scared, but she saw Thomas trying to get in the side door, the one she barely got it.

"I'll go in the emergency exit." as he rounded the back of the bus.

She heard sirens and then she was knocked flat. No more hiss.

59

For such persons do not serve our Lord Christ, but their
own appetites, and by smooth talk and flattery they
deceive the hearts of the naive.
  – Romans 16:18

She woke up in the hospital. The sunlight was coming in the window, the overhead lights were just turned on, a bright white that blinded her awakening. She could barely see her identification tag that said Lori Philbus. She didn't initially know who that was.

The room was empty and quiet. She knew she was in a hospital, but that was all she knew. It looked as if it was daylight. Her eyesight was fuzzy and the first other human she saw was someone she couldn't identify. Regardless, she asked the question she needed answered.

"What happened to me?" her voice was hoarse.

"You do not have life-threatening injuries, you have a brain injury. There was an accident that killed one man and you and the other survivor were rescued, he is resting in the next room," said the voice.

"I want to see him," she was barely able to talk.

"I'll let him know," said the person, Lori now recognized the voice as the nurse.

Her eyesight was still blurry, she saw Thomas come in, he had his head bandaged in white and he was moving slowly.

She fell silent, confused about what she was hearing when the accent that came out was in Spanish. She barely made out the words being spoken in broken English. The man, she now recognized as the overweight Latino bus driver, the man that had survived, not her Thomas, said in broken English but distinguishable words, "thank you for saving my life." He then said it in Spanish, "mi familia gracias por salvarme la vida."

Thomas was dead, she could now feel it. Her head hurt, her blurry became blackness as she faded back to a coma, partly from trauma, but mostly from the maximum allowable drug flow, the nurse had just turned up on the IV bag valve. Her last thought was barely one. She could no longer process her own thoughts, time was moving, yet she didn't know how long she'd been there.

"How are you?" Lori heard it, but couldn't process it, the learned response was 'good', but she couldn't reply.

"I'm glad to see you, the doctor told me you were recovering remarkably." She now recognized Jack's slow, purposeful, clear, and powerful voice.

She was trying, but couldn't process her thoughts individually or group them into anything of value. She tried to open her eyes and only felt a hand holding hers. She recognized it, it was Jack. He was there for her, again, when others were not.

Her effort and last bit of energy went to an attempt to recall events, and she only had enough to recognize time. Her mind flooded with individual memories of her mother, needles, bright lights, drugged, yet awake, and many periods of black. She was overcome with fear, realizing now that she had been in the hospital for what felt like months, time she could not know, or even recall, lost. Her life built as Mary, reworked and rebuilt as Lori, now lost.

What Lori didn't know, nor would, was the attention brought to her accident, not just from the violence of it, but the abnormal transfer and ongoing visits to the Navy Med by the now highly publicized, new Attorney General, Jack Rucker. They had worked hard to create a new life for Mary to become Lori, one with the ability to live in obscurity, putting her unwanted and undeserved fame behind her.

"How are you?" Jack asked again but with a purposefully upbeat tone as he knew she was improving from the last few months of her medically induced coma, what was called by the medical community, a barb coma, a temporary state of unconsciousness brought on by a controlled dose of barbiturate drugs. One recommended by her assigned government doctor from the President's own team. She knew he meant it, others asked it as a greeting, she knew Jack asked out of true concern and she wanted to answer.

"I'm better, I feel ready."

Jack knew what Lori/Mary didn't, the room was clean, not in a hospital way, but in a way that only the justice department could ensure, it was clean of listening devices. Jack had moved her to Navy Med hospital, he'd been patient, as Lori healed. He was intent on learning and confirming that this was the end, what did she know, what did she remember, and most important, think, about what happened. Jack knew he selected her and trained her to pay attention to details, never give up, and to be relentless in the pursuit of justice for injustice. He hoped the coma would allow her to forget. He also hoped they wouldn't need to induce her again.

An hour of the conversation between them passed, Jack knew, yet Lori was still lost to time. He had confirmed what he needed, she would be OK, and so would the "cause". It would be OK because Mary thought it was an accident. Thomas's death, a real accident, nothing more.

The cause, his cause was protected still. It had started more than forty years ago by a mission-driven, altruistic Army captain. Jack had come to know the "Colonel" as he was called then by his given Bonesman name. He, like Jack, was a Bonesman committed to change. Jack knew him as a mentor then, he had recruited Jack as Jack had recruited Joe. Jack remembered the event that changed his life when Jack lost his way and the Colonel was like a prophet of justice when no one else cared or noticed. The Colonel would not rest. He formed the Group then, in the tumultuous times of 1968, and when needed, he would ask the Group to bring justice for the injustice. It had. Jack was there then and now was sending the secure messages to the Group to follow through on his commitment, as a Bonesman and as his promise to the man who inspired him, the Colonel.

Lori startled Jack, as he thought she was asleep and asked him directly "What?"

Her eyes open and alive with curiosity, what he recognized in her from the beginning. He realized out of his norm, he had allowed his emotions to emit his thoughts. He had let out the words of the Colonel, "justice for the injustice" and she had heard him.

Jack said, "Nothing, I was just thinking out loud."

Lori saw the lie on his face and the sorrow in his eyes, she didn't know why.

They both sat in silence, Lori closing her eyes, yet not asleep. Jack recalled the information he didn't see coming but was thankful for it. It was the final coincidence in the trial of Mark Solier and his mission, the one his mentor, the Colonel, asked him to lead when he decided to disappear. To take on identifying the worthy cause to bring justice to the injustice. Starting each mission with sending the secure messages.

60

For we know him who said, "Vengeance is mine; I will
repay." And again, "The Lord will judge his people."
  - Hebrews 10:30

Jack left the hospital when he knew Lori was asleep. The planned flow of drugs from the IV helped. It gave him time. He met his security escort outside the hospital room. It was in the already secure VIP wing of the hospital where Jack had arranged for Lori to be treated. Two of his security escorts went with him, the other stayed to keep watch. Even in the secure wing, Jack wanted to make sure she stayed protected and also to avoid anyone visiting her. Jack knew Canner was always out there looking to make trouble.

His car was pulled around even before he went out the back entrance to avoid any curious eyes. He got in the car and asked the driver to pull to the back of the lot, where no cars were parked and where no threats would be. The driver did just that, parking under a group of trees as it started to rain.

Jack sat back and closed the internal barrier window between him and his driver. His primary security escort was in the front seat and the other was in a car watching the perimeter around this off schedule stop in the back of the hospital parking lot. Jack was alone. He started to think. He closed his eyes and started to recall the details of how this got a little out of his control.

Angela had called Jack a few months ago, after the execution, what was the beginning of what was now being finalized. He remembered that she had not contacted him through the messaging service, but directly. Something was important. Angela shared verbally some details of an email she reviewed on Ralph's still open email account, from a detective in New Mexico, one of the detectives who was celebrated for closing the unsolved West Mesa murders. He had found something, something of a coincidence, "His exact words, something of a coincidence," said Angela.

Angela continued with the details of what she had read, "In his case file, he found pictures that made little sense when added to his file from years ago, but when he then looked at the now shared case files he made a discovery."

Angela detailed it more for Jack, she continued reading from the email sent to Ralph, "Comparing all the photos from his case file, and from the other detectives that worked the cases of the original five victims and the new six cases opened after the bodies were found, he found a connection between all of them." Angela couldn't herself understand it, she finished by saying, "It somehow aligned with one of the victim's sisters, and someone called Casey Mantra."

Jack was now recalling the past few months in more detail and his memories were rushing at him. The detailed memory of the exact moment he found out Thomas Williams, Casey Mantra, and Lanh Nguyen were the same person.

Jack remembered his stress and his confusion then, and how he had asked his newly appointed government driver to pull over the car. Riding alone in the back and having little time, he like now, then closed the internal barrier window between him and his driver and primary security escort. He knew something of importance had happened and now was happening. He hung up with Angela, opened his secure mobile tablet, synced up his email, and reviewed the pictures from the case files, they were labeled as Casey Mantra. When Jack was looking at the pictures of Casey, he clearly saw a younger Thomas Williams.

The coincidence was, each victim, who had no known contact with the other victims, had a similar-looking person in each of their photographs. The images were part of each case file, but not consolidated into one. The case files included pictures collected by investigators or given to them by family, and others retrieved from early social networking sites Friendster and MySpace. Jack connected the dots on what was discovered. The sister of one of the victims, who was an FBI agent and who had befriended one of the original case detectives, scanned all the pictures from each of the now eleven cases. She uploaded them all to the FBI's new software, the Facial Analysis, Comparison, and Evaluation (FACE) services from

330

the Biometric Services Section, Criminal Justice Information Services (CJIS) division. Jack was a fast reader and was now reading even faster the email sent by Angela from Ralph's email account. The software had identified the same face, the same person was in each of the victim's pictures, a coincidence that was now a smoking gun.

Jack sat back and remembered the day, years ago, he attended the recruitment ceremonies as a senior Bonesman's duty. He recalled meeting Thomas as a recruit to Yale, then again when he was secretly admitted into the Skull and Bones. Jack was present at the ceremony, unknown to others he was there, ceremoniously masked like the others, yet remembering Thomas was from New Mexico. He now remembered the research done by the Skull and Bones, it came flooding into his brain, without needing to look in the file. Thomas's father had been an unwanted child of the Vietnam war, where soldiers away from home, one of which was Thomas's grandfather, fighting a war nobody wanted, would often spend time with the willing Vietnamese women, trading money for sex. This was overlooked by the US command and by the in-country brass. Military leaders had other problems. Thomas's father was brought to the US in the spring of 1975.

Jack was looking closer at the documents on his mobile tablet, he looked at Thomas's birth certificate, which showed what his real name was, Lanh Nguyen. His first name, Lanh, Jack was reading from the research and notes, was a name that was not given to many children, and it meant to be quick-minded and street smart. So much was flooding his mind, he couldn't organize it.

Jack rolled down the window just slightly for some fresh air. He pulled up the private file server on his mobile tablet, linked to the secure network, and reviewed Thomas's file. He saw the birth certificate of Thomas's father, ordered by file name and date. It was the first file image. It was filed on his father's seventh birthday, 1975 and Jack learned Thomas' father's birthday was April 4th, 1968, the same day Martin Luther King was killed. A day Jack recalled, as that was the same day he spent with Joe Callahan, sharing the importance of saying yes to the Skull and Bones, as he himself, said yes to the Colonel to join the Group.

Scanning other documents, reading some, noting dates on others. He could not find what he was looking for, the name Mantra. A name shared by his most trusted mentor, the Colonel, and now a surprise by the person he initially wanted to trust, and then learned he couldn't, Thomas Williams. Or was it Casey Mantra? Or Lanh Nguyen?

Thomas's adopted parents were dead, they died from a house fire just before Thomas came to Yale. Doing some quick math, calculating years, Jack determined Thomas was just around seventeen years old. The fire marshals' report was in the file, as well as the insurance company. Jack read both. It was an accident, ruled by both the reports, they were short, to the point and independently came to the same conclusion, a fire was started by a faulty HVAC installed just the week before. The FBI in his efforts, from months ago, included everything. The FBI had also found the insurance payout, there were color copies filed under financial info. The one for the house was $300,000 and the life insurance payout was there too, $750,000 from both his adopted parents. Checking the dates, the fire happened on Thomas's (Casey's) eighteenth birthday. The payments were both made to Thomas Williams, in August, totaling more than a million dollars. Jack continued to look, and read every document. It started to rain, it came in the window, yet Jack didn't notice. The wind blew outside. A storm was coming.

Jack came back to the present, sitting in the car, the sun was now coming out, shining in the tinted window. He wasn't in the mood to go back to the office. He was in one of his few remaining private spaces, the back of his government car. He recalled the difficult decision he had to make then and as Lori recovered from her injuries, and the efforts put in place so her memory would be interrupted. The goal was for her to be disrupted from putting together the facts that only Jack knew.

He remembered finding the link that turned the coincidence of Thomas Williams into a fact. Thomas, born as Lanh, was renamed Casey Mantra by his adopted parents. He remembered the moment he knew Thomas would need to be killed. Thomas had lied, he had manipulated the facts to get what he wanted. This was not the type of mission he could delegate to the Group. He would have to do this one himself. He recalled renting the bus, finding a willing driver who needed money. What he didn't plan on was the explosion, Lori being almost killed, or having to aid the bus driver in succumbing to his injuries.

This memory brought his attention back to the present. The past was the past. It would stay secret as he was the only one who knew. He looked out the window, seeing the vacant hospital parking lot. He rolled down the outside window for fresh, rain-soaked air, and the emerging sunlight caused his eyes to shut. He felt the warmth on his face. He sat up in the back of his car. It was over, Thomas was dead. No one would know what he'd done. It was his own personal justice for many injustices committed by the one person who had deceived him. Thomas was smart in all the wrong ways. He rolled up the outside window, it was now dark again in the back seat of his car. He was alone.

Jack lowered the internal barrier window, "Let's go." The car started. He then closed the internal window again.

Leaving the Navy Med hospital, Jack knew Lori was in good hands and he signed the authorization for her doctor to stop the flow of drugs. Her barb coma would end and her rehabilitation process would begin. She'd be released in just a few days.

Jack knew his next step, hopefully, the final one, was to make the call. Years of private conversations, years of secrets, going all the way back to their meeting over the now banned and revolutionary book, *Slaughterhouse-Five* by Kurt Vonnegut. He made the call. He gave his security code and the President of the United States answered. Jack said one thing, in the same voice, the same thing he said months ago, the day he made the call when Thomas Williams died and Lori, he still couldn't get used to her new name, was almost killed by accident, with its highest of meanings to the two friends, some thought of them as missionaries.

"It is done." And the phone clicked off.

Jack realized the feeling was the same he had for the last forty years. The same as the day the Colonel had given him his mission and he took over the cause, the mission to bring justice to the injustice. Avoiding the credit and not needing the recognition, he had answered the same call from others, the same one he just made to the President. Many times, he had heard the confirmation of "It is done." No doubt, if successful, he would hear it again, many times. The time was now, the time was right to rebuild the Group. He had an apprentice, he needed to get it ready for her, to train her to drive what soon he would no longer be able to do. He would go back to the source. The Court of Vehm needed to continue. He'd organize her admittance to Yale Law School and then, because of his past efforts to force a vote in 1991, which overturned the 1832 Skull and Bones men-only rule, she'd be indoctrinated as one of only a few Boneswomen. He'd start the cause again the way it began in 1969.

61

For by grace you have been saved through faith. And
this is not your own doing; it is the gift of God.
  - Ephesians 2:8

She had been in Denver for a year now. She lived in the same apartment and was known by her neighbors. They didn't know her past. For the first time in that year, she was rising early, without an alarm set, not needing a snooze, she was feeling better. Lori pulled out everything she had. She unboxed the documents, organized her emails, did screenshots of all her stored text messages. She grabbed her pen and started to write down everything she could. Her memory had come back from months of being subdued by the drugs prescribed to her by the Navy Med hospital. She stopped taking them a week ago. She couldn't believe how on fire she was. The accident, her missing the funeral of Thomas, but seeing it through the eyes of amateur photographers and home videos, it had devastated her, to not process the emotions as they happened. This had been too much for her to handle, and the support structure from her friends, even the power of the new Attorney General couldn't help her this time.

To recover and self-heal, she did two things after getting out of the hospital, the first was turning to the church for answers. All her childhood and early adult life she was raised to fear hell and damnation. She had always been truth-seeking, often skeptical, and to her parents regret, openly critical. Yet still, the last year of living by herself in Denver as a religious non-denominational, and non-practicing Christian, helped her discover who she wanted to be. The second thing to heal herself was to re-investigate everything. She had to clear her mind of the feeling she had missed something. She had to somehow connect the death of Thomas. (It couldn't have been an accident caused by Mark Solier?) as she was there when Mark died, she knew he was no longer alive to kill others. She was there, a witness to every detail. She couldn't, and wouldn't ever, forget his screaming last words. The "Mind Killer" could have no way been part of violently killing what she had once thought could have been her new future.

Even in distress, she was organized.

How could she have missed it? It was a piece that would have turned it in any direction except the path it actually took. The piece of information came from a source that provided no value, so although notes were taken, they were passed over by everyone. Mark was believed by Alice to be an immaculate conception. Mark's dad, Jim, was in disbelief according to an interview that Mary documented with one of Jim's now retired Navy friends. He had said that Jim had virtually disowned the child, shown contempt, even hatred toward him and Alice for her proclamations about his birth, however, it was against his own religious beliefs to leave his marriage.

Lori looked up from her computer to think, she saw her apartment, once set up to be perfect, was now an output of her new life the last year. It was a mess. Her once organized, dustless memories on her shelf, were now knocked over, or put away somewhere she didn't remember. She had spent an emotional time trying to forget. Trying to forget her former life, her love for Thomas, and their hoped-for future.

She closed her computer and now sat on the floor, going through her past, the once organized files. Reading and rereading everything. Re-sorting everything, into new ways of organization. She didn't want the past to corrupt her need to find out the truth.

She pulled out the pile of letters from the morning that Thomas died. The same day her own injury caused her to spend months recovering from her own mysterious brain injuries. These letters were recovered by someone, from the clothes she was wearing when the bus exploded, from the pile she left in the coffee shop, they were neatly wrapped up, and put back in her apartment. They had been here, since then, gathering dust. What she didn't know then, a second letter, one that would connect what only seemed like a coincidence, was buried in the same Post Office bin she carried to her apartment months ago, sitting quietly waiting for her to come back from her long absence. She picked up the strange-looking envelope from the bin, dust filled the air, as she was intrigued by the odd postage and colorful markings. It was from Brazil. She

338

opened it quickly. It was from the head of the Brazil mission Mark started. She read it again, then again, as her memory skills had been diminished from her injury. She learned how Mark helped these strangers in Brazil. He helped them daily, to build a life and build their community. The mission director pointed out both how they had survived, and thrived over the years, specific to the miracles, his words, that Mark had helped with. She reread it three times and said it out loud in her quiet, dusty apartment. "Miracles" written purposefully in plural. The Brazilian mission director provided details, he noted the elimination over the unaccountable, the untouchable scum of Brazil. The murderers, drug dealers, abusers, all of those that had hatred for what Mark was doing. He was spreading kindness and setting the example for others. The letter also shared the extraordinary beliefs of the natives and elders of the local tribe that Mark had special powers. The deaths of the evildoers were accidental on paper, in the one-page police reports. The mission director had included copies of the reports and Lori reviewed them one by one. A variety of natural disasters, mudslides, lightning strikes, fires, and single, violent, yet unexplained, nor investigated, car accidents. They weren't accidents, none of them. The community elders knew better, they had seen it before. He wrote in a language she couldn't understand.

"Quando um anjo vem, o ímpio e o ódio morrem até que se vão."

She pulled out her phone and carefully typed it into Google translate. Careful to pick Brazilian Portuguese. The translation took her breath away.

"When an angel comes, the wicked and the hatred dies until it is gone."

Lori/Mary repeated the word, hatred, hatred, hatred. How could she have missed it?

Did Thomas's death align with this? Did he have hatred for Mark? She confused herself as she processed both what she knew to be fact, what she had learned to be true, and what made no sense. Could the hatred of another, ever silent, impact you? Lori sat down on the nearest stool, she had put herself into a mental, now physical, state of hysteria. She worked hard now to calm herself, starting with her breathing. Her breathing slowed and her heart raced. She leaned forward to write the only thought she had.

Hatred. Hate echoed in her head. She sat down. It continued. Over and over, she wrote the word hatred on her paper until it was her only thought. Her hand hurt and she looked down, on the page, it was filled with the words hatred and hate. Wicked righteousness was the last thing she wrote.

She found what she was looking for in the pile of mail, dirty from soot and the edges blackened from the bus fire. She carefully picked up what seemed like a letter from long ago, the one she had read in the coffee shop when her new life was just beginning again. It was written in haste from a mysterious Doug Barlow, sharing the details without names of his team, the other four members killed by accidents. She didn't know, nor would she ever know Jeff Knowles, Paul Hammond, Adam Hitchcock, or Juan Martinez. Doug himself on the run, alive as of his letter writing to her, now more than a year ago, yet she didn't know now.

She now thought about the jurors from the first trial.

The juror, Julie Sanders killed sitting in her car, in her driveway, her airbag ignited by her car getting struck by lightning with clear skies.

The pilot, then juror, Dave Swenson getting cut in half by his own plane's propeller.

The dedicated Air Marshal, Jerry Russell, who led the first jury, was buried in a first-ever mudslide. It took them a week and trained cadaver dogs to find his body.

The early morning house fire of juror number seven, burning too hot for the fire department to control, investigated, yet no source or cause was ever found.

Then the accident that killed the Channel 5 producer from a firetruck and the crash of the helicopter on live TV.

She leaned back in her chair, how could this all be connected, how could it be happening, caused by one man, she slipped and mentally called him the "Mind Killer". Was he? How?

Had he hated them?

She looked over her notes from the meeting she had with Mark's professor at his first college. She recalled Dr. Bradferst's exact words, she wrote them down and read them aloud now, "those punk kids got what they deserved." She wrote what he said about how they bullied Mark, he was a target for being younger and different. Dr. Bradferst stepped in a few times as Mark told him the problems. Then the three died when their car hit a deer and went into the river. They all drowned and their bodies were swept nearly five miles downriver due to the high current that time of year. Lori had the article in the file and the police reports. It was an accident, how could it not have been?

She remembered Jessica Bonley, Alice's Sister and Mark's Aunt, killed by a bear. How could he? He had been just a baby.

Had Jessica hated baby Mark?

Mark's father had died and Lori was looking at his death certificate. It was unchanged and stated the cause as unknown even after a lengthy detailed autopsy.

Lori sat back; her back was stiff, but her mind was clear now. She breathed with a different view.

She had a revelation, a conclusion forced upon her not by facts but by the coincidence of all of these separate accidents. Each death was connected to Mark as it was determined he was wanting them to die, as Lori had surmised and as he was then legally tried for murder, convicted, and executed. Her conclusion was now even more wild than a "Mind Killer", as by each victim's hatred of Mark, wanting their own righteousness, they had been killed. Their hatred of Mark brought about their death. She had it wrong. Mark was innocent, the victims were guilty.

Mark was an Angel of God.

62

I have not come to call the righteous, but sinners to repentance.
- Mark 2:17

The road into Ackerford hadn't changed. Mary didn't have possessions, let alone a car. She rented a car from the airport to drive the nearly three hours from her home in Durham, North Carolina to Ackerford, Virginia. She was now able to rent a car at the age of twenty-seven. She hadn't driven a car in a while. It was a straight shot up Route 501. She printed out the map and circled where she'd need to turn off, taking a reminiscent needed detour. She had been away from her hometown for too many years, but maybe not enough as she was having flashbacks from the time she spent here. A few memories from her desire to be a lawyer and her frustration from not being able to financially escape.

Making the turn off of 501, she both recognized the road and also not, as there had been a lot of growth of trees and weeds. She knew the town ran short on money and backroads didn't get the attention they had in the past. She slowed down, then slower for about a mile, there was no traffic. Then she pulled the rental car over at what she could remember being the location on highway 29 of Mr. Backson's accident. The skid mark gone from the road, but not from her memory. She turned the car off. The regular springtime bugs and birds were silent.

She sat in silence, breathing slowly on purpose, seeing the scene different now than she did more than six years ago. She had grown a lot, once trying to hide in Denver, then in the hospital from the bus explosion. She had been surrounded by people that cared for her then and still, mysterious circumstances plagued her mind. Where she sat, no cars passed on this early Sunday morning. She had been asked by the pastor of her childhood church to come back and deliver her sermon to the small church she went to every Sunday as a child and sometimes as a rebellious altruistic teen. As small towns do, the word got out, and she knew many would be in attendance. She started the car, trying to move on still. She pulled away from the scene, the place that changed her life, six years in the past. She glanced one time in the rearview mirror, overwhelmed with the knowledge that it was the place she started to fight for what was right. What she thought was right had changed since then.

She came into town on Highway 29, then made the one turn she recalled by memory, nothing had changed about Ackerford. The trees, houses, and even the light seemed to not have changed. There were no other cars on the road, as the people in this town went to church, they all got there early and she was late.

As she approached the church, she became concerned quickly. Something had happened as cars now lined both sides of the road. Police cars, not with lights on, but both of the town's cars were positioned on the street. Billy was standing there, looking at his phone, he hadn't changed either, even if his phone had. He looked up, nearly dropped his phone, and waved fervently in her direction. He was smiling.

"We have all been waiting, Jack Rucker is here too," Billy told her.

"Hi Billy, what are you waiting for?" She said as her concern diminished from his smile.

"You." He said. "We are waiting for you."

Billy told her to park up front, there was a spot reserved for her. She knew this church but didn't recognize it with so many cars beyond what was normally a full lot anyway. She parked her car, noting increased security, plain-clothed professionals with earpieces. Jack really was here. Callahan won his second term, and Jack was still the Attorney General.

She noticed the sign hanging from the large entryway, "Welcome Pastor Mary Morgan". It was hung above the "Founded in 1969" sign.

People were welcoming her she didn't know, and then she saw someone she trusted, Angela. She was far enough away they couldn't greet, yet they smiled and Mary knew who put this all together. As she always had, Angela was there doing Jack's work.

Jack was patient, yet he wanted to exert his power to see Mary now, knowing she was coming from her new world. He waited. He knew she had left Denver after he had killed Thomas and after he organized her long stay in the hospital for simple injuries. Both of which she hadn't realized his hand in influencing. She changed her name back to Mary Morgan and moved to North Carolina now more than six years ago. She took care of her move on her own, not asking for help, and not needing it either. Jack had his team keep close tabs on her, watching her apply and accept an invitation to the Southeastern Baptist Theological Seminary in Wake Forest North Carolina. Far enough from her hometown, but not so far to feel disconnected. She completed her Master of Divinity and then her Ph.D. in Theological Studies. He knew she suspected something was wrong. It wasn't guilt for killing Mark Solier, but he knew she was wary and was starting to put together the clues, turning them into facts and then conclusions. He also knew if she kept at it, she would figure it all out. He was glad she moved on, yet he wouldn't take his eye off her. He needed to be sure the cause was protected, his new Group needed to stay secret. Now she was here, back in Ackerford, walking through the crowd of people gathered at their hometown church, on a direct path to talk to him.

"Hi Jack," she said while making direct eye contact and extending her hand.

Jack smiled, and he didn't extend his hand, he reached out for a hug, and she came to him. He often thought she could be his daughter he never had, and also knew, she didn't feel the same. The Secret Service agents moved a little closer, even at a church, where everyone knew Jack before he was the Attorney General, there was still an abundance of caution. Mary noticed it too.

"I see you brought some of your new friends," Mary was witty as ever.

"It's no longer my choice," Jack quipped, "why don't we catch up later, you have a lot of people to see and I think we are running late."

Mary gave the Attorney General of the United States a departing brief hug and walked away. They wouldn't catch up, nor talk again. Her trust had been disrupted and she didn't give it twice, to anyone, even if they were the Attorney General. She knew Jack and her were in pursuit of two different kinds of justice.

Mary was surprised at the turnout. It was like yesterday she saw Billy as she then poached the accident photos. She saw Chief Waterson, looking the same, but older. Everyone looked older. She saw the news guy, Stephen Canner, who she didn't believe was religious. He had gone on to New York City and made a name in real investigative reporting. He worked missing persons and cold cases, finding people who didn't want to be found and convicting people who thought they got away with it. She remembered seeing the story that Judge Ford had died, thankfully not from an accident. It was cancer. He fought it for the last two years, but it got him anyway. Dale was there with his family. He had met someone, fell in love, and now they had two adorable, dressed-up girls sitting in the front row. She saw someone she recognized, but couldn't remember her name. She said hello, and Mary flashed back to when she first met Louise. She was the same, just older. She saw Ralph there, he was reading something as always, looking up as if he could feel her looking at him. He waved, smiled, and went back to his never-ending curiosity for knowledge. Susan Backson was there, her two children were next to her on either side. Susan smiled at her and Mary smiled back. Her two children were now teenagers. As others just looked slightly older, seeing the two small Backson children, who had grown so much she barely recognized them, really put a time stamp on how long it had been. She saw her law professor there too, Mr. Stacker. She heard a few years ago he quit the school or was maybe fired. He landed on his feet though, starting an online business that connects tutors with students in need. He waved and she waved back. The upfront section for the handicap was empty. She didn't expect to see Stuart due to his ongoing heart problems, although she wished she could have. She wished she could thank him for never giving up. He played an important role in getting President Callahan elected and re-elected. His message of hope and trust was resonating with a lot of people. She knew it did with her.

She greeted everyone, most people she didn't know but they knew her. She moved towards the front, towards the welcoming long-term pastor, he had his arms out, waving, smiling, and asking people to take their seats. It was the same pastor as when Mary came here as a young girl. He started the church on his own, moving to Ackerford after returning from Vietnam, building it with his own hands, starting in 1969. She knew little about his past, but she knew he was educated at Yale, his framed law diploma hung next to his other diploma from her alma mater, Southeastern Baptist Theological Seminary, on the otherwise bare walls of his private office. He was an Army captain as well, she knew this from the only other thing in his office, a shadow box with a folded flag, a stack of ribbons, the two shiny bars of his Captain rank, and a picture of the youthful man he once was when he served his country. She saw this in his office only once as a kid. He invited her in then when she was ten years old to talk about her attitude. She thought she'd be in trouble, yet he encouraged her to fight for what she thought was right. She had called him once or twice over the years. He was always there to help her not know what was right but to encourage her to do what was right. Now, more than fifteen years later, he had invited her to come back home to share what she had learned since then. He wanted her to take over what he started, his church.

"Mary, welcome. I am glad you came," he looked deep into her eyes. She saw the same man she saw every Sunday as a child. He saw the same inspired soul he saw as a child, now he saw a determined woman.

"Pastor Everest, it is nice to see you too. I am ready," she said with emotion in her voice.

"I know." He hugged her and she felt whole, on the right path, finally.

350

Mary pulled her sermon notes from her pocket, walked to the pulpit, its modern microphone out of place on the solid oak lectern made by the hands of pastor Everest himself. It was the first thing he made when he built the church.

The pastor walked to the front row, sat down with Jack Rucker, leaned over, and said in a whisper no one would hear, "Good to see you again Jack. Thanks for everything."

Jack acknowledged with two simple words, "Yes Sir."

Pastor Mantra looked only forward and under his breath so only Jack would hear, he muttered the Army's long-term agreement of, "Hooah."

Jack had known the Colonel since Yale. They had always been aligned with getting justice. They agreed Thomas needed to go. There had been no secrets until now. Jack saw no reason to share that Thomas was his grandson. This one time, what he didn't know, wouldn't hurt him. Jack wasn't sure the Colonel didn't already know. He had always known everything before Jack did. There was no reason to think he'd put his grandson before justice. It didn't matter either way. It was done. Jack returned his full attention to Mary, he was proud of her.

Mary started by adjusting the microphone and placing her hands on the side of the lectern. She had seen Pastor Mantra do this many times.

"Thank you all for coming. I missed you," the microphone making her voice boom in the old church. There were some tears and applause.

She waited until it got quiet. She gave enough time for silence to bring people's attention to what she was about to share. Ralph looked up, Louise sat up, Dale held his wife's hand. Chief nudged Billy to pay attention, Canner put down his pen and notebook. Mr. Stacker looked proud of her. Jack was staring at her. She knew it was her time to bring justice.

"Please open your bibles to Deuteronomy 19: 11-12."

"Today I want to talk to you directly, to each of you about your propensity to 'hate'."

> But if any man hate his neighbour, and lie in wait for him, and rise up against him, and smite him mortally that he die, and fleeth into one of these cities; then the elders of his city shall send and fetch him thence, and deliver him into the hand of the avenger of blood, that he may die.
> - Deuteronomy 19: 11-12

"There are no emotions that are stronger or have more history than love and hate. The emotions are so bipolar that the definition of one cannot be mistaken for the other. It is often there are circumstances that drive the beginning, enhancement, and climax of these emotions. It is rare that they are instant and impossible that the emotion alone can cause death to others unless of course, you believe nothing is impossible. The Holy Bible talks of love and hate as if they couldn't coexist without the other. The belief that one is good and the other bad is a belief of modern religion. The intention of their existence has evolved and is now much misunderstood. Even those that possess the power don't know that they do, similar to those throughout history. We've had powerful leaders that have manifested either love or hate, sometimes both, and also those that possess it without the knowledge that they do. Thus, the power of these God-given controls are manipulated by man, used often as a means to an end. The power is in the means by which they are used and the true power is by those that do not know they possess it. As man learns from birth, the influence of their beliefs towards love and hate are innate to their environment. A parent, a teacher, a priest can inspire either in the same way that a society-defined criminal can show the defined negative definition of hate through their actions, or those proven by society. Regardless of a person's environment, choices are still made, albeit harder for some than others. Choices that are made by a person's thoughts on action or a lack of action towards others as they wield their own power of love and hate, society will decide whether it is controlled or not. Living a life of thought is often a good thing. Thinking in preparation of doing makes a better world. Love more, hate less. Look around you, you'll see more hate than provides comfort to sleep."

Epilogue

Then the eyes of those who see will not be closed, and the ears of those who hear will give attention.
– Isaiah 32:3

Mary was glad it was done. She had been anxious about sounding too preachy to people that knew her before, as young, naïve, and altruistic. She felt it went well. The simple nod from Jack, the attention from the others, and ultimately what she didn't expect, the acknowledgment from Pastor Everest Mantra. He had always been there for her growing up, and he was there for her now. He said thank you to everyone and whisked her away from the others.

"We have a party planned outside, come with me and we'll get some food." He led the way, she followed.

She had a chance to get food and talk to everyone. She even enjoyed talking to Louise as she now had a different perspective. Dale's wife was incredible, no doubt he needed someone like her. Their kids were perfect copies of them both.

Ralph was sharing information he learned and she listened, but although she cared about Ralph and could never thank him

354

enough or ever repay him for his mentorship, she no longer cared about the law. She appreciated that he didn't bring up the case nor say the name Mark Solier.

She had taken a plate of food but hadn't had the chance to eat any of it. During a break in the need for her attention, she moved towards the children's play area. Setup with games to play, a bouncy castle, and tables full of arts and crafts. She smiled as if it was a picture of how everyone thinks Sunday afternoons look at a southern church.

"Hey lady, come draw with me," said a cute boy of around the age of six, Mary guessed.

"My name is Ms. Morgan, what is your name?"

"My name is Levi. Nice to meet you, Ms. Morgan." Mary was surprised at the formal articulation of such a small boy. No doubt good parents.

"Hi Levi, that is a nice drawing of your family. Who is this?" Mary pointed to the caricature that had a big brown beard.

"That was my Uncle Peter, he was mean to me, then he died. He was crushed by a big rock."

Mary stepped back at the details shared and the story being told. She looked at the picture again, now seeing the cartoon X where their eyes would normally be.

Levi pointed at the second drawing, it also had X's where the eyes should have been. It was a drawing of a woman with red hair.

"This is Aunt Emily, she wasn't nice to her kids. She died too."

Mary could tell these were not make-believe stories, they were so matter-of-fact. Coming out of Levi's mouth with such conviction. She then noticed all the drawings had black X's on their eyes. There were more than ten.

She hesitated, but asked, "How did she die?"

The question was answered from behind. An older woman had approached them while Mary was bent over looking closely at Levi's drawing.

"It was a horrible accident, a small tornado split open a tree and sent so many broken branches through the kitchen window where Emily was standing. She didn't have a chance and died before the ambulance could arrive."

Mary felt embarrassed and caught off guard, in the moment, she had not realized what she was doing, talking with a child she didn't know about death.

"Matthew has had a tragic life. Many people he has known have died of terrible accidents." the elderly woman shared.

"He said his name was Levi, but you called him Matthew?" inquired Mary.

"He goes by the nickname Levi, his friends call him that. His birth name is Matthew."

"Are you related to him?" Mary asked without thinking, then realized she knew the elderly woman, recognizing the long-tenured Sunday school teacher, "Hello Miss Ritter, it is so nice to see you. It's been a long time."

She leaned in now to whisper this to Mary, "You are old enough now to call me Alice."

Mary took a step back. Putting her hand to her heart, to catch her breath and keep it from breaking.

Alice shared more, "I feel like his great-grandmother though, he was left on the church stairs and then adopted when he was just a baby."

Mary couldn't breathe. She had to purposefully force herself to exhale and inhale. Slow breaths, she felt faint.

"He reminds me so much of my Baby Mark at this age."

Mary fell to her knees.

Alice bent down, not phased by Mary's sudden change in posture, then whispered that "His foster parents died just last week, yet I have no plans to tell him that."

Mary folded her hands. She said she was sorry and held back tears. She was trying to breathe.

"How did they die?" she hesitated to ask.

"They both died in a single-car accident on Highway 29, just a few miles from here. It is currently under investigation."

Mary knew Billy wrote up a detailed report and would have taken plenty of pictures.

Author's Note

Thank you for reading.

I have a strong sense of justice in me. I don't really know where it came from, but it has been with me ever since I was a young boy. My earliest memories are of me debating with someone about what should be. I would always then, and even now, get the advice or response of, well, that is how it is. I hate the response. Even now, as an adult, I will often hear the phrase, 'It is what it is'. This is just people not willing to take action to fix what is wrong. I hate this too. If you just finished this book, you know hate can be dangerous, I'll have to be extra careful.

I have never given up, but I have failed more than I have succeeded in my pursuit of justice. The wall to climb is too high, or maybe my methods are ineffective.

The subtle theme of *Accidental Coincidence* is that everyone is trying to do the right thing, at first, but it is the right thing in the way they see it. Altruism can be a powerful tool or a dangerous weapon. Justice is often in the mind of the one trying to deliver it.

I started writing in 2005. I took a fifteen-year break to try and be a good dad and husband. My three kids are doing great and I've been married to my best friend for 30 years this year.

With encouragement from my family, I got back to writing. The world has changed, the story changed with it.

As I researched this book, many things would make me mad, sometimes I would get upset because I couldn't believe something was true. No way, I would say out loud, usually with profanity mixed in. Then as I dug deeper, I would get upset, even sad, then mad again.

The specific example is of the change in 1983 between bright-line rules to the totality of circumstances as a means to arrest someone. Go search it on Wikipedia. Wow!

I often think, 'what can I do?' When I see injustice, when I see what can't be explained, I feel it. Whether it is a miracle or tragedy, I think, 'what can I do?'

I've concluded that my best way forward is to write books. Create characters that try to solve problems in the way you would, the way I would. Each of them is willing to try, even if they fail.

I hope, my true wish, the reason I write these stories, is that you put the book down each night, after reading a chapter or two, and it makes you think. It opens discussions with your friends and family about 'What if this was true?' and ultimately, it inspires you to ask yourself the question, 'What can I do?' Come up with a few ideas and take action.

If you have time to write a review, please know that I will read it. I take all feedback very seriously and every one of them helps the next book. Every review increases the chance that another person might read this book, ask themselves the question, 'What can I do?', and then with even the simplest action (like leaving a review), make the world a better place. At least in that moment.

Thanks again for reading.

Sincerely,
  David

Here are two links to make it easy to leave a review. I used the full link as it is sometimes easier to write the review on your computer instead of your kindle. It can be hard to type on the kindle.

Review *Accidental Coincidence* on Amazon:
http://www.amazon.com/review/create-review?&asin=B08RW6XBSS

Review *Accidental Coincidence* on Goodreads:
https://www.goodreads.com/book/show/56738116-accidental-coincidence

Also, you can join my newsletter to get more information about things I've learned in my research, updates on upcoming books, and easy access to ask me questions or give me feedback.

I call it the Common Sense Book Club:
https://davidarmstrong.me/common-sense/

Accidental Coincidence is the first book in a series of books I have planned with similar, powerful themes, it is called *"Justified"*.

About the Author

David Armstrong is a dad of three kids and a husband to a wonderful wife. He has lived multiple lives in one. Growing up in a small town near Philadelphia, serving in the US Air Force, serving as a combat veteran, then a corporate drone and tech entrepreneur. He is a first-generation American. He has never given up on what should be. He defines himself as a former rebel, now a renegade.

You can connect with me on:

🌐 https://davidarmstrong.me

🐦 https://twitter.com/davidmarmstrong

📘 https://www.facebook.com/armstrongdavid

🔗 https://accidentalcoincidence.com

🔗 https://www.patreon.com/armstrongdavid

Subscribe to my newsletter:

✉ https://davidarmstrong.me/common-sense

Also by David Armstrong

Accidental Coincidence is the first book of a planned five-book series. The series is called **Justified**. The plots are not in order, nor focused on a single character, yet they overlap in the timeline, events and some characters will cameo in each book.

 **[FEAR.THE.PANOPTICON] – July 2021**
https://www.fearthepanopticon.com
We live in a world where everyone can know who you are and what you are doing. Think about your behaviors, you don't know who is watching.

Martin lives two lives, the first is someone trying to change the world, the other is a life of mass information, violating privacy for the sake of justice, public shaming with the goal of behavior change, then taking action to change some people's existence. His intent and the consequences lead him down a different path, he is inspired and decides to make a real difference. A difference that was a lot more public and infinitely more discreet in its methods.

FEAR THE PANOPTICON is part of the five-book series **Justified**.

FREE PREVIEW - [FEAR.THE.PANOPTI-CON]

https://dl.bookfunnel.com/htflq7lj6o

There are NO spoilers in this PREVIEW.

In this [PREVIEW], I will review what I learned about the history and current state of government surveillance. I was shocked at the depth of surveillance. I was even more shocked at the apathetic way we all have come to accept it. I will footnote everything I can so you can learn more. Be careful, the rabbit hole goes deep. This is a sensitive topic for me, and likely for you too. I am a first-generation American and a combat veteran. The pride for my country, our rights, and freedom run deep inside me. I feel them every day. I work hard to 'think' so I can see what I can't feel. I want to share this with you, I hope you find it valuable. I did. - Sincerely, David

Made in the USA
Coppell, TX
06 May 2021